Look for:

Spin It Like That
by Chandra Sparks Taylor
ISBN-13: 978-0-373-83080-0
ISBN-10: 0-373-83080-7

Keysha's Drama
by Earl Sewell
ISBN-13: 978-0-373-83079-4
ISBN-10: 0-373-83079-3

Can't Stop the Shine
by Joyce E. Davis
ISBN-13: 978-0-373-83078-7
ISBN-10: 0-373-83078-5

www.KimaniTRU.com

FRESH. CURRENT. AND TRUE TO YOU.

Dear Reader,

What you're holding is very special. Something fresh, new and true to your unique experience as a young African-American! We are proud to introduce a new fiction imprint—Kimani TRU. You'll find Kimani TRU speaks to the triumphs, problems and concerns of today's black teens with candor, wit and realism. The stories are told from your perspective and in your own voice, and will spotlight young, emerging literary talent.

Kimani TRU will feature stories that are down-to-earth, yet empowering. Feel like an outsider? Afraid you'll never fit in, find your true love or have a boyfriend who accepts you for who you really are? Do you sometimes feel that your life is a disaster and your future is going nowhere? In Kimani TRU novels, discover the emotional issues that young blacks face every day. In one story, a young man struggles to get out of a neighborhood that holds little promise by attending a historically black college. In another, a young woman's life drastically changes when she goes to live with the father she has never known and his middle-class family in the suburbs.

With Kimani TRU, we are committed to providing a strong and unique voice that will appeal to *all* young readers! Our goal is to touch your heart, mind and soul, and give you a literary voice that reflects your creativity and your world.

Spread the word…Kimani TRU. True to you!

Linda Gill
General Manager
Kimani Press

 KIMANI PRESS™

Felicia Pride   Debbie Rigaud   Karen Valentin

HALLWAY DIARIES

HALLWAY DIARIES

ISBN-13: 978-0-373-83084-8
ISBN-10:   0-373-83084-X

© 2007 by Harlequin Books S.A.

The publisher acknowledges the copyright holders of the individual works as follows:

HOW TO BE DOWN
© 2007 by Felicia Pride

DOUBLE ACT
© 2007 by Debbie M. Rigaud

THE SUMMER SHE LEARNED TO DANCE
© 2007 by Karen Valentin

www.KimaniTRU.com

Printed in U.S.A.

CONTENTS

HOW TO BE DOWN

Felicia Pride

ACKNOWLEDGMENT

I'd like to thank God for telling me that I can do this and providing the tools for me to get it done.

Thanks to my mother, who thinks everything I do is great. You've encouraged my dreams from day one. i don't know where I would be without your support. Extra-special thanks to my sister, who listened to me on several occasions and gave me wonderful advice that helped me shape the story. Thanks, sis! Thanks to my little self, Ms. Adams, for motivating me to be an aunt you can be proud of.

To Adrienne Ingrum, I'm so blessed that you see a writer in me. This project wouldn't have existed if it wasn't for you. I am truly grateful.

Thanks to Evette Porter and the entire Harlequin/Kimani TRU team for your hard work and dedication.

To Sayiwe, my best friend and cheerleader from the second grade, who knows how it feels to be called an "Oreo." Thanks to Jose, my Tito, for being so good to me.

To my father, Felix, for believing in me, and to Mr. Gordon for your quiet wisdom.

Special shout-out to my cousin Symone, who provided a little inspiration for a few of the characters. And thanks to Erin for being my friend even though I was "the new girl." Who would have thought we'd stiil be friends so many years later?

Thanks to David D. (the future millionaire) and Dr. Dominique B. for pumping me up and encouraging me. Thanks to Stacia B. for always being supportive. And thank you, Terrance, for nagging me about when you could buy my first book.

Thanks to my entire family in Baltimore. All of you inspire me to pursue my dreams. I hope I make you proud.

CHAPTER 1

"This is the most black folks you've been around in your entire life, isn't it?" That's how my Aunt Lena greeted me at the "Back to Baltimore" cookout my family threw to celebrate our homecoming.

I hadn't seen her in quite some time. Actually, I hadn't seen many of my relatives in quite some time. Aunt Lena's mouth hadn't changed much. Neither had Uncle Cleo's deafening laugh. My father's brother was still built like an ex–football player. He desperately tried to lift me into the air, although I had to remind him that I was fourteen, and no longer five.

On my last summer visit to "The City That Reads," I'd welcomed the spicy smell of crabs and the paddle boat ride around the Inner Harbor. But this was not a short summer visit. It was a permanent life-changing catastrophe. This wasn't the usual family gathering where a few of the Parkers congregated to play cards, gossip, and overeat. This was a full-blown invite to the entire clan to discuss how young Nina won't be able to adapt from the lily-white suburbs of Rainhaven, New Jersey, to the urban streets of Baltimore City.

The contrived celebration was held in the square court-yard at the six-family apartment building that A&I bought. I should mention that behind my parents' backs, never to their faces, I call them collectively by their first names, Annie and Isaiah, which I have further shortened to A&I.

Anyway, the concrete area was miserable in comparison to the half acre of grassy land our house in Rainhaven had been situated upon. There were no trees. No shrubs. Not even blades of grass growing from cracks in the concrete. No wonder it was so hard to breathe.

A&I were thrilled that they could purchase this shabby building, which they'd spent the last year or so renovating, in an "up-and-coming" neighborhood in Baltimore City. They hoped to "invest in the community" and "circulate the black dollar." These are their words. Aunt Lena told me it was a bunch of crap and that A&I needed to get off their high horse. I agreed that they were high on something for uproot-ing us from New Jersey, but I kept that thought to myself.

"Ninaaaa!" My mother sang my name all day to intro-duce me to family who I had never met. She was reconnect-ing me with my roots. Her words, not mine. She was wearing one of her long, multicolored African frocks and her left arm was stacked with silver bangles that clanged loudly every time she raised it. She wanted to reacquaint me with three big-breasted, curly-haired women who I learned were my father's cousins. Actually one had rollers in her hair, one was wearing a curly wig that was on crooked and one had what I believed was a Jheri curl. They were squeezed on one of the uncomfortable wooden benches my mother had borrowed from Aunt Lena.

"Hey, baby," they said in unison.

I smiled brightly but didn't dare to speak. Aunt Lena had told me earlier that I needed to leave the white-girl talk behind in Rainhaven. I wanted to tell her that I'd left more than enough in my hometown—friends, a social life, a budding academic career at the prestigious private school Clearview, a beautiful house on the hill, and a healthy distance from crazy family members. But I knew that such a response would warrant a "See, I told you she thinks she's better than us" retort.

The one with the Jheri curl remembered me when I was pooping in diapers and gave me a hug. She almost cut off my circulation between her large bosom and the gold chains that scratched my skin. She smelled like peaches and hot dogs. The other two seemed to be concentrating on something else, perhaps on when Aunt Raquel was bringing her famous potato salad.

My father, with his khaki shorts, leather slip-on sandals, Bob Marley T-shirt, and neck-length dreadlocks, resembled a preppy Rastafarian. He was combing his beard with his hand, which was beginning to gray, while receiving a lesson in the art of grilling from Uncle Cephus. My uncle was wearing one of those Kiss the Cook aprons. His belly protruded from under it like he was due to deliver twins any day.

The rest of my uncles could be found sitting around a brown fold-up table playing pinochle, which my family referred to as the little-known cousin of spades. They were supposed to be sequestered to a basement because their game playing was considered rowdy and inappropriate for young ears. But the building's bottom floor was a boiler room, so they tried unsuccessfully to tone down the cursing for the ten or so children running around playing tag.

"Oh, sh—I mean, smack," Uncle Dwayne yelled. "I didn't have a single heart and I had maybe two spades. That nig—I mean, that Negro is cheating." He looked futuristic, wearing the Robocop sunglasses that he never left the house without.

The womenfolk, as my father liked to say, were either in two places: in the kitchen, cooking too much food, or eating carbs at a picnic table covered with a red and white checkered cloth.

A&I had chosen to celebrate on what had to be the hottest day in August. The smell of barbecue fought hard to float through the thickness of the heat. It was drastically more humid in Baltimore than it had been in New Jersey when I'd left a good two days earlier. The heat stuck to me like the rubber cement I used in art class to bind plastic. I had those embarrassing sweat rings under my arms, but I didn't spend time trying to hide them. I had bigger problems than worrying about minor, inevitable hygiene issues.

When I looked up from the plate of ribs Uncle Cephus had prepared especially for me—extra dabs of his secret sauce and honey—A&I were standing with a tall, handsome man the color of coffee with lots of cream. He was wearing a silky navy button-down shirt and black slacks suitable for work. Next to him was a young woman who looked like she could be a freshman at Rutgers University. She wasn't big or tall, just the opposite, short and petite. Even from a short distance, she exuded a sophistication that the Clearview girls who dated college guys would pay for. Her hair was a bundle of sepia spiral curls that complemented her grayish complexion. Her ribbed white tank top revealed her petite frame. And her knee-length blue skirt revealed womanly curves. Compared to her, I was dressed like a ten-year-old boy.

I surveyed my outfit: white sweat shorts, which I was told by my uncle Cleo looked like booty shorts; run-down Nike cross-trainers that held on for dear life because they were the most durable for me to practice in; and a bright yellow T-shirt that said "Rainhaven Rams."

I didn't have time to be fashionable in Rainhaven. Between my running group, drama club, the young poets' collective and Honor Society, I barely had time to make sure my school uniform was ironed. And on the weekends, I threw on what was most comfortable for whatever outdoor/extracurricular/volunteer activity I was involved in. And might I add in my defense, Rainhaven wasn't exactly fashion forward, except for my friend Amy and a select few.

A&I brought the attractive pair over. "This is Mr. Lamont and his daughter, Vivica," my mother said. "They just moved into the second-floor apartment. Vivica is also a sophomore at Maplewood. The two of you are in the same college preparatory program."

Between the crab juice on my shirt, the odor from my sweat rings, and the ketchup stain on my shorts, I felt too dirty to make their acquaintance.

"Nice to meet you, Nina." Mr. Lamont extended his hand. I brushed mine on my shorts before shaking it.

"We both thought it would be a great idea for you and Vivica to chat and get to know one another before school on Sunday." My mother clapped her hands together, an action she did often, and her bangles rang.

Vivica was completely indifferent. She concentrated on picking dirt from under her manicured fingernails. Every other one was intricately designed with flowers.

"Okay, I'm going to pick up a few more things for the apartment. I'll see you later, sweetheart." Mr. Lamont sounded like a newscaster, well-spoken and personable. He kissed Vivica on the forehead before heading out the side gate.

A&I patted me on the shoulders and walked toward the card game, swinging hands like teenagers.

I didn't know what to say first. I smoothed the sides of my hair, hoping that the action would provoke an idea. The carrot oil that I had put on earlier to control the stray hairs, fried in the sun. I'm sure I looked like I'd just woken up. I thought about saying something along the lines of "It's pretty cool that we live in the same building." But was it really cool?

Earlier, my cousin Mikey was going around the cookout

singing "Where you from, shawty?" I thought about asking her that.

Vivica and I stood face to face without saying anything to one another. My head fell to the ground. Compared to her bright white Nikes, my cross-trainers should have been thrown in a trash can and lit on fire.

The awkwardness was overwhelming, so I spoke first.

"So do you like Maplewood?"

She was chomping on her bubble gum. She smacked it before answering.

"It's a'ight." She didn't sound anything like she looked. I was expecting some sort of articulate response. But people said the same thing about me. With my natural hair and wannabe-Panther parents, they expected me to enlighten— or offend—them with militant dialect and always looked disappointed when I didn't.

"Are you from Baltimore?"

"Nope." Her fingers sure must have been dirty. She returned to attending to them.

"How long have you lived here?"

She shrugged, and then said, "Four years." She lifted her head and wiggled her nose like a dog sniffing out food. She followed the scent and I followed her.

"Do you like it?" I felt like an officer trying to pry answers out of a suspect.

"Where are the rolls?" she asked after grabbing a hamburger from the food table. I directed her into the kitchen and was glad for the respite from our awkward conversation.

We walked back outside and joined my cousin Sondra,

who was sitting on the cracked steps of the building's side entrance. She was labeled "thefastone" by the family because at five foot six, Sondra was built like a brick house. That's why Aunt Lena made her attend an all-girls school. But we all knew that was pointless. Sondra did what Sondra wanted to do.

She had on a snug hot pink tank top that read "Don't Hate Me Because I'm Cute." A denim skirt was riding up her thighs. She needed to do that thing where you stand up, pull your skirt down, and then cross your legs before taking a seat. Flat sandals squeezed her feet and straps snaked around her legs. Every time I saw her, she taught me something new even though she was three years younger.

I introduced them and neither seemed to care about the other. Sondra lifted her eyes briefly from her cell phone to give Vivica a once-over.

Then she asked me if I had any good ring tones.

"I don't have a cell phone," I responded.

She gasped like I'd told her I didn't have a home. Then she shot me a look of pity.

Her phone rang and it blasted some hip-hop song that I didn't know, but I did hear the words "balling" and "New York." She chair-danced and let the song play for several seconds before actually answering it. Then she launched into a loud conversation about getting her hair braided tomorrow.

I returned my attention to Vivica after giving her some time to take a few bites. "So how do you like your new apartment?" She arched her head backward in annoyance and slowly picked it up again.

Then she shrugged her shoulders. Her nonverbal answer told me more than I needed to know. She wasn't very polite.

"So what's it like to be around all those white folks?" Vivica asked. She bit down hard on her hamburger. Her nails dug into the bread.

Her question came out of nowhere like ringworm, which I'd gotten unexpectedly when I was eight years old.

"It's the same as being around black people, I guess." I knew I was lying to her, but I really wasn't sure how to answer. People, mainly my family, looked to me to be the guru on the ways of white folks, like I was Langston Hughes. Fortunately, Vivica seemed content with my answer.

Most of my family, including A&I, didn't believe that I truly loved Rainhaven. In their eyes, I was either (a) delusional, (b) secretly miserable, or (c) in complete denial. And even though there weren't any Tamikas or LaShondas, I formed meaningful friendships with a Jill and an Amy.

Sondra flipped her phone closed with unnecessary force.

"Why are you getting braids?" I asked her.

"Because I'm tired of this weave and I haven't decided what I want to do with my hair yet."

Darn, I lost again. I always played a game with myself to guess real versus fake hair and always lost. Even the girls at Clearview who wore blond hairpieces tricked me.

Maybe if I'd spent more time worrying about things like hair, fashion, and pop culture, I wouldn't seem like such a square. But I left all of that latest/greatest knowledge to my friend Amy, a Jewish girl from a very rich family, who didn't mind knowing more than me.

"You still got that white boyfriend?" Sondra asked intently.

"You got a white boyfriend?" Vivica fired with scary contempt. Her green eyes penetrated my dark brown ones as if she was trying to read me. I wondered if she wore contacts.

Matt had been my on/off boyfriend since we were seventh graders. Our relationship started out as a default merging. Matt was Adam's best friend, who was my best friend Jill's boyfriend. So we were their official tagalongs: a short black girl with puffy hair and a tall, lanky white guy with braces, shaggy brown hair, and freckles. We never did anything—oh yeah, except the one time he gave me a quick peck on the lips. We were really just two oddballs who became friends due to circumstance. But in the middle of ninth grade, I guess it was puberty that made him turn into a total jerk. We hardly spoke after he dumped me. A tragedy Shakespeare could have written.

A&I liked Matt but always asked about the black boys that went to Clearview. They constantly wondered why their daughter didn't have more friends of color. But what choice did I have, attending a school that was 98 percent white? All my life, if I wasn't the only black girl in class, I was one of two. Black guys were even more under-represented. That's when I would tell A&I that there weren't any "brothers" except for Cole. My best friend Jill tried to hook us up during one of my breakups with Matt. After avoiding her for days, Cole finally confessed that I was too dark for him, despite the fact that he was the same complexion as me.

"Uh, yeah, I had one, but not anymore. We broke up." I answered slowly to gauge Vivica's reaction.

"Why y'all break up?" Sondra asked.

"I mean, we were more like friends than anything. But you know, he started seeing someone else, so…"

"A white girl?" Vivica interrupted.

"Yeah, but—"

"Typical," she spat, as if she was the one who was dumped. "But that's how it should be. I can't stand when I see white chicks with black guys or black chicks with white guys." She punched a fist into her hand to enforce her point.

"Why?" I asked. I thought about Jill. I thought about Matt.

Before Vivica had a chance to defend her prejudice, A&I turned down the Motown soul that was playing throughout the cookout and asked for everyone's attention.

"Thank you all for coming. It's so wonderful to see all of us together. It's been years since we've done this. Now that we're back, we have to do this more often." My mother ran her fingers through her graying dreadlocks and looked at my father to continue.

"When we moved to Rainhaven almost fifteen years ago, we knew that one day we would come back home. It took longer than we originally planned, but timing is everything. We are just so blessed. We were able to purchase this building just blocks away from where both Annie and I were raised. I can't tell you how good that feels." My father placed his hands over his heart in a rather dramatic gesture.

"Yeah, you sure can't," Aunt Lena snickered.

My father handled his sister's comment like he always did—he ignored it. My mother grabbed his hand in an act of solidarity.

"Anyway, now that we are back, we want to be closer to each and every one of you. There's nothing more important than family. And with that, I ask that you raise your glasses and toast to family." I think he meant plastic cups, or for some, beer bottles.

"Who toasts at a cookout?" Aunt Lena frowned. "That's some of that uppity-black-folk crap."

"And with that, let's party," my father yelled to avoid any confrontation. My mother let out a shrill laugh and clapped her hands together, making her bangles the background music for her festive mood. Frankie Beverly and Maze—A&I made sure I knew all the classic soul music—blasted from the waist-high speakers my cousin Mikey brought over. Uncle Cleo and Aunt Lena danced like old people with hip pain. Aunt Lena dropped to the ground, legs wide open, and slowly came up like an intoxicated snake.

"Ma, stop droppin' it like it's hot," Sondra yelled at Aunt Lena. Even though her callous comments could make grown men cry, I loved my aunt. But I was also thankful I didn't have to call her Mom. Sondra got up to reprimand her mother.

After Vivica finished her grape soda, she pulled out a compact mirror and reapplied fuchsia lipstick. Her wavy lips and green eyes were the extroverts of her face, while the rest of her features faded into the background.

"So what's Maplewood like?" I asked.

She made a movement with her mouth like she was about to laugh, but didn't. "I'ma tell you right now, Maplewood ain't nothing like that rich white school you went to." I assumed she'd found out about Clearview through the parent grapevine, with the roots being my mother.

"I know it's more diverse." I really didn't know how to respond. She said it with such judgment.

"Diverse?" She released a wicked laugh. "We ain't got no white people. It's black, all black. You sound like one of those white girls on TV. You need to do somethin' about it."

Like what? Take out my pink magic wand, wave it from side to side, say "Kazaam," and instantly I don't sound like Lindsay Lohan anymore?

"And you can't come lookin' all crazy like you do now. Maplewood's about bringin' the hotness, not bein' a hot mess." She shook her head as she pulled one of her curls with her fingers.

"You one of those black girls with a white-girl mind that thinks she's better than everyone else."

"No, I'm not. I don't think I'm better than anyone."

"We'll see." That's all she said, before finishing a piece of pound cake and leaving without saying goodbye.

I was glad when everyone finally left. The last few days left me tired and injured. I sat for a few minutes on the cracked steps in the dark. I didn't want to move.

CHAPTER 2

I woke up the next morning feeling that I'd rather spend the day under my down comforter. My mind drifted to the days when I used to play ship on A&I's queen-sized bed. It was a stupid game, the point being that I lived on a mattress and couldn't leave because I'd die in the water. At this moment I wished I could make my bed my living quarters for the remainder of my existence in Baltimore.

But I was unprepared to do that. My stomach was rumbling and the smell of cinnamon toast seeped under my bedroom door.

I maneuvered around the cardboard boxes in my room and banged my toe on one that contained books. I finally found the white poodle slippers that Jill had gotten me for my birthday as a joke.

I hadn't taken a shower last night. I was too depressed to clean my body. I walked into the kitchen wearing the same clothes and stains from yesterday.

A&I were engaged in their Sunday ritual: reading the *New York Times* and discussing the world over a meat-free meal.

"Lena hasn't changed one bit," my father said.

"She's still outspoken," my mother agreed. She was wearing an oversized Howard University T-shirt from her alma mater, the same college that A&I wanted me to attend in three years.

"I was just telling your mother that Vivica agreed to show you which bus to take to get to school. You can meet her out front at seven-fifteen tomorrow. I know you were nervous to take the bus alone." My father removed his eyeglasses and looked ten years younger. He was wearing a gray tank top that showed that he still exercised and maroon sweatpants that were dusty from doing work on the remaining apartments.

"So did you and Vivica hit it off yesterday?" my father asked.

"Not really," I revealed as I buttered my toast.

"These things take time," my mother said without looking up from the Style section. "Barry says that Vivica is a very smart and ambitious young lady. Sounds like you two have a lot in common."

I looked around the bright banana-colored kitchen. I was never a fan of yellow. It always reminded me of puke. In three days, my mother managed to unpack all the common living areas, including the living room, which had built-in bookcases to house their hundreds of books. She neatly arranged all of her kitchen utensils and apparatuses, although she was far from a chef. She had a repertoire of ten or so dishes, five of which I actually liked.

"It must be so hard to be a single father in this day and age," my father said. He was telling Vivica's personal business. "Especially when raising a daughter."

"Did her mother pass away?" I felt sorry for her. That would possibly explain the attitude.

"No, her parents are divorced." My father freely provided more information.

"I know, but he seems to have it under control," said my mother. "Vivica seems to be heading in the right direction."

If that direction was going toward Viciousville with a stop at Cruelty, then she was indeed on her way. I didn't feel like eating. I left half of my toast soaking in syrup.

"I miss Rainhaven." I leaned on my elbow and attempted to twist my hair, but it was too matted from last night's sleep.

"Hey, missy, cheer up," my father said as he rubbed my arm.

I thought about crying. A&I hated to see me in tears. If I was one of those opportunistic teenagers, I would have used their guilt to score money and other gifts.

My mother got off her stool and gave me a hug that only mothers know how to give.

"Sweetie, in life sometimes, there's change," she said. "We all have to learn how to embrace it. Just because we moved doesn't mean you have to completely leave your life in Rainhaven behind. You can still visit Jill and you two can talk whenever. I'm sure you'll make new friends at Maplewood in no time."

A&I's unwavering optimism annoyed me.

CHAPTER 3

I didn't shower until three o'clock in the afternoon. After spending forty-five minutes daydreaming in hot water that turned lukewarm, I spent too much time thinking about how I would spend the rest of the day. Boredom hit me hard.

Usually the day before a new school year, Jill and I would play tennis or listen to Amy's outrageous plans for ruling Clearview.

I needed to talk to someone who knew the old me. I grabbed the cordless from A&I's room and dialed Jill's cell phone. Maybe she would have some words of wisdom, some grand insight, or at least she would listen to me whine about my dismal life.

I was nervous she wouldn't answer, but she picked up on the second ring.

"Hey, Jill," I said enthusiastically, "it's Nina."

"Oh, Nina, I was going to call you today, but I wanted to give you time to get settled."

It was good to hear her voice, although it was hard to make out what she was saying above the commotion. It sounded like she was watching the New Jersey Nets play live.

She told me she was at the mall with Amy. Apparently all of Rainhaven was there.

"I didn't want to come but Amy insisted. I had to pick up a sports bra for cheerleading tryouts. How's it going?"

A pang of disappointment hit me. Jill and I were going to try out for the cheerleading squad per Amy's urging. My coordination was deficient and Jill wasn't very athletic, but as captain, Amy guaranteed spots for us.

I never needed a sports bra to hold up my swollen pimples, but Jill on the other hand was a favorite among the guys. She was more everything. More busty. More glamorous. More attractive. She made it all seem effortless. I was a chocolate Hobbit to her five-foot-eight stature.

But never once did she make me feel less.

Jill's the daughter of a black father and white mother. She resembled Mariah Carey with golden blond hair. I always forgot that she was biracial because she never made a big deal about it. She was just Jill.

Her parents are like a black and white version of the Huxtables. Her father is a psychologist and her mother is a lawyer. They were two of the few adults in Rainhaven who my parents associated with.

"It's going," I replied. Where to? I wasn't sure.

"That doesn't sound good," she said. Jill was always perceptive about my moods. Plus it was her shoulder that I'd cried on when my parents told me we were moving.

"What's wrong?" she asked. I heard Amy chatting loudly in the background. Jill laughed. She was occupied.

I wanted to say, "Everything." I held back the tears by biting my lip and closing my eyes tightly. I didn't know why I was ashamed to cry in my room. I was alone.

Instead, I said, "Nothing, just tired."

"Amy wants to say hi." Jill put her on the phone.

"How's your new place?" Amy asked in her high-pitched nasal voice. "Fabulous or what?"

"Or what," I responded. "No more house. We are squished into a three-bedroom apartment."

"An apartment? Wow, that's a bummer, sorry to hear that. But guess what? Andrew went to the movies yesterday with Wendy. Can you believe that?"

Amy was a brunette-turned-dirty-blonde because she was convinced that blondes do have more fun. Her world was filled with boyfriends-of-the-week, cheerleader narratives, and superficial fantasies of being the most popular girl in the United States.

A&I couldn't stand her. When Amy's parents found out that my mother was the same woman who had penned the controversial national bestseller *Fear of a Black Parent,* they forbade her to see me for three months. A&I reluctantly went to the Goldsteins' minimansion, drank very expensive tea, and convinced Amy's parents that the book was not racist.

But Amy and I had been friends since the second grade, when she'd defended me against that troll, Erica, who had kicked me in the stomach. Amy pulled her by her hair to the ground and told me to get a hit in. I did, and it felt good. We'd been friends ever since, despite our differences.

To reflect said differences, we classified ourselves by what we ordered at Starbucks. Amy was a latte, Jill was a hot chocolate, and I was an apple cider. Amy always maintained a separate clique, a mixture of cheerleaders and athletes, but she once told us that we kept her grounded.

"Did you break up with him?" I was only partially interested. I positioned myself stomach down on my bed with my feet intertwined in the air.

"Well, not yet. He is the cutest guy at Clearview and I want to take him to the back-to-school dance and rub it in that slut Wendy's face. Then maybe I'll break up with him."

I always marveled at Amy's reasoning, because it never seemed to make sense to me. But her plans always worked in her favor. She was my sinister alter ego. All the things I would never do, she did.

"Have you met any new people?" she asked.

"A girl just moved into one of my parents' apartments and she goes to my new school."

"Is she ghetto?" Amy asked.

I hated when she used that word. To Amy every person who didn't live in Rainhaven was ghetto. Saturn cars were ghetto (her father's buying her a BMW when she turns sixteen), Target was ghetto because it sold things at discount, and Marsha, one of the few black girls at Clearview, was ghetto because she had a scholarship.

"So have you seen Matt?" I changed the subject.

"No, thank God. It's good that you're away from that scruffy boy. I never knew what you saw in him."

I was hoping she would have some news to report, like he was torn up over my move and couldn't get out of bed because he was too distraught.

"It's so different here, you know?" I said. "I really miss Rainhaven."

"Why did your parents want to move to the ghetto anyway? Too bad you are missing cheerleading tryouts. You should see the tacky freshmen that are trying out. They are pathetic."

Cheerleading was Amy's life. She wanted to become a professional one with some pro sports team. She thought it would increase her chances of marrying a rich athlete.

"Ohmigod, is that Mike? I have to go." She handed Jill the phone.

"Let me go and try to stop Amy from doing something crazy," Jill said. But I wasn't ready to get off the phone and return to my empty life.

"I am so glad you called. Maybe you can visit soon. You know you can stay with me."

"Thanks," I said, although I knew that visiting would be too hard right now. I wouldn't want to leave.

There was some banging downstairs that I didn't notice until I hung up with Jill. My parents were still renovating the last few apartments. I looked at my alarm clock, which was sitting on the radiator that made noises during the night. It was seven-fifteen.

I decided to pull out an outfit for tomorrow since the majority of my belongings still occupied boxes.

The thought of unpacking was too much to bear. I rummaged through the cardboard, which held my entire wardrobe. *Limited* didn't begin to describe my clothing selections. Maybe *deficient* or *void* would be more suitable. Years of private school wreaked havoc on one's options.

This is what I owned:

Three pairs of jeans, one of which was severely ripped at both knees.

Tons of T-shirts, mostly souvenirs from my family trips around the world. They all looked similar: some pale color, with Jamaica, South Africa, Italy, or some other country prominently displayed in the middle.

A few dressy outfits: simple skirts, dresses, and blouses.

Tons of sweatpants and workout clothes. But not the cute kind. The practical kind.

A few sweaters, most of which I'd gotten on sale from J.Crew.

Hardly any shoes. Nike cross-trainers, scuffed Hush Puppies, leather Jesus sandals, and a pair of black formal shoes with a block heel that I wore when I had to dress up.

I looked at the clothes that were in a pile in front of me and I sank down to the floor. I didn't have anything to wear.

CHAPTER 4

Last night I should have been nauseous from all the tossing and turning. It was a frustrating sleep. Before I got a chance to wipe around my eyes and the cracks of my mouth, A&I came into my room with tropical fruit salad that my mother had assembled, pancakes topped with strawberries, and a glass of orange juice.

"Good morning, Queen Nina," my father said. "It's your big day. How do you feel?" he inquired with that proud-dad smile.

"I feel like I don't know what I'm getting into," I said honestly.

"It's natural to feel some uncertainty, everything is so new," my mother said. "New city, new school." She searched for a place to put the food and chose one of the boxes.

"I know, but I don't know how to handle all the newness."

"Don't handle it, just continue to do what you do and be who you are," my father advised.

I hardly touched my plate even though I would have chosen fruit salad as my last meal. My stomach was a bundle of nerves. Its low rumbling told me that food might not be a good idea. What if I got some sort of stomach thing on my first day of school? I didn't even want to think about running out of class, down the hallway, and into the bathroom because my insides were on fire.

It only took ten minutes to shower and throw on a pair of jeans and a T-shirt. I scrutinized myself in the mirror. My shirt was a little too big, my jeans a little too worn, my hair a little too bushy for a ponytail. I needed something to give me a boost, but I didn't know what. I opted for lip gloss that Amy had left at my house one day. It tasted like strawberries and made my lips look like I'd just eaten a plate of greasy chicken.

I tucked a notebook, pens, and my schedule into my denim book bag, which was probably the most fashionable item I was wearing. I distributed kisses to A&I and headed out the door.

It was 7:08.

Okay, perhaps I was a little anxious. But I wanted to make sure I didn't miss Vivica. Although I hated to admit it, I was nervous about taking the bus alone. I'd never taken public transportation before. Call it sheltered or call it what it was, Rainhaven was the quintessential small town in Suburbia, U.S.A. There were no buses. No subways. You were expected to be able to afford a car. My parents had had three of them, sold one, and now refused to use one of the remaining two to take me to school. I was to get the full urban experience.

The heat crawled down to a more comfortable temperature, but I was still hot in my jeans. I looked around at the city I visited during the summer and always enjoyed. I'd hang out on Aunt Lena's back porch and Sondra and I would rate the boys as they walked down the alley.

But the city didn't look as vibrant as it did when I'd visited before. The buildings cried out for attention, not like a needy child but like an abuse victim. Pain and misery drifted in the air, along with bus exhaust fumes and the pungent smell of aged garbage. A&I always said that Baltimoreans were built of strength. So in the last few days I'd looked for it in the old man who ran the corner store. I'd looked for it in the way his hand shook when he handled my money. I'd looked for it in his wife as she swept the store's floor. I'd looked for it in the four dudes on the corner with brown paper bags. I'd looked for it in their lean against the store window. I'd looked for it in their dice game. I haven't found it yet.

A mother who wore a skirt and tennis shoes pushed a stroller past me as she held a toddler's hand. Loiterers, this time old men with limps, circulated in front of the corner store. Little kids with book bags bigger than they were, laughed as they walked in the direction of the bus stop. Cars zipped by, happy to leave the neighborhood. I had just arrived.

At 7:18, Vivica emerged from our building. I hadn't thought about what I would say first. Would I thank her for the cruel advice she had given me on Saturday? Would I forget about all the black and white talk and start anew? After locking the door, she turned and paused on the steps. Her look was quizzical. Insecurity swept over me like a typhoon. I began chewing on my fingers like cookies. Before I left the house, my mother had told me to "go to my destiny." What destiny was that? Humiliation? The bus stop? A personal hell called adolescence?

Vivica's pleated skirt bounced as she skipped down the stairs in ballerina flats. Her curls were held back by a purple headband. Her eyelids were also purple, her lips pink. Now she resembled a junior in college. She had gained two years in just two days.

When she reached the bottom of the stairs, she told me I looked like a hot mess without saying a word. We walked silently to the bus stop.

There weren't any other students there yet, just an old lady with several large red, blue, and white plastic bags. She threw bits of bread on the ground and a swarm of pigeons flew over.

"I can't stand her," Vivica said. "She always feedin' those nasty pigeons. Don't nobody want them over here."

Vivica wasn't looking at me. We were just standing there. I started to do the awkward dance of swinging my arms, and considered whistling but thought that might be too much.

"Wait until Sheena sees your hair," said Vivica. "She might just have a heart attack. They ain't have no hairdressers where you from?"

I could wear my natural hair in an array of styles—twists, cornrows, braids—but I usually opted for a ponytail with a big Afro puff at the back of my head. I didn't realize my hair was such a concern to other people.

"And your wardrobe. Didn't I tell you that at Maplewood you need to bring the hotness?" She stopped like she needed a break. She put her hand on her forehead like she was going to faint.

I knew her question was rhetorical, but I tried to answer in defense of myself.

"I used to wear a uniform to school."

"Whateva" was her response. "You're black on the outside, but everything about you is white. How you talk, how you dress, how you act."

Tears were congregating in the corner of my eyes. I looked away as I tried to disband them.

Other students started to gather. The girls were massive and flaunted their womanly goods. The guys had full beards and mustaches. They admired the womanly goods. Vivica was right, these kids were dressed. It would have been a fashion show if the block had a runway. The girls improvised and strutted down the sidewalk anyway.

My stomach started to flip like a gymnast and I instantly grew uncomfortable. Was it because I was around so many black kids? That was crazy, I tried to convince myself. But I knew deep down inside that was the reason.

"Vivica," yelled a girl who resembled a black Paris Hilton. Blond. Tall. Thin. She glided across the busy intersection, not concerned about cars coming her way. She made them stop and wait.

"What up, chick?" Paris Hilton asked as she approached us. She shoved a guy out of her way and then turned around and said, "What?" He put his arms up, and she said, "I thought so." Then she kept walking.

Paris gave Vivica half a hug so that she wouldn't mess up her outfit. She was dressed for an awards show, with a short, tight, mini–black number that should have been accessorized with martinis. Instead, Ms. Hilton used a jean jacket as a cover-up and carried a large brown designer purse. Gucci or Fendi? I wasn't sure which one. No book bag. Her heels were spiked enough to be weapons. A long chain with a diamond cross hung from her neck and she had matching stud earrings.

"Ain't nuthin', Sheena," Vivica answered.

Sheena pulled off her big oval-shaped sunglasses that hid her narrow eyes and looked me up and down.

"What the hell?" she asked.

Vivica giggled and introduced me as the daughter of the people who owned her new building.

"Honey child, your hair. What is goin' on?" She circled me slowly to examine my mane. As she was trying to understand my nappy roots, I was trying to figure out what exactly was black about her. A few shades lighter and she could had gotten arrested with Nicole Richie.

She patted my Afro like Amy's mother used to do. Ms. Goldstein always preceded the petting with "In the sixties my Afro-American, I mean African-American friend Tashi used to wear her hair just like this."

Sheena said very plainly, "Only two types of black girls don't have perms: Angela Davises or Oreos. Which one are you?"

"Can't you tell?" Vivica chimed in. "She's definitely a white girl trapped in a black girl's body." She answered for me.

"I just want to take you to the salon and give you a Bone Strait relaxer. But I don't even know if that would take." Vivica and Sheena laughed at their inside joke.

"Where are you from? Africa?" Sheena's laugh sounded like a car revving up. But in a higher pitch.

"I'm from New Jersey." My voice faltered. Could one person survive all this ridicule? I thought about walking away, but to what? To stand alone with the pigeon lady?

"Oh, yeah? My cousins live in Harlem. You be goin' up there?" Sheena asked as if answering yes would validate me as a real black girl.

I had only been to Harlem once, to attend a benefit at the Schomburg Center that my mother was involved in for her book. But I didn't think Sheena wanted to hear about that.

"Yes, I've been but haven't spent much time there. I would like to go back and explore the area. There's a lot of history there." From the screwed looks on their faces, I knew I'd said too much.

"I don't know about all that. All I know is that my babydaddy, Juelz Santana, live up there. You ever seen any of the Dipset when you in Harlem?"

The puzzled look on my face said it all. Sheena looked at Vivica and telepathically asked, "What's wrong with this girl, is she some sort of alien?"

"Where's Nessa?" Sheena switched subjects.

"You know that girl's always late," Vivica answered. "I talked to her last night she said she was comin', though."

"Jeffrey's lookin' right," Sheena announced loudly. We all set our eyes on a thinly built masterpiece the color of sand in Mexico. Curly hair framed a finely chiseled face in which every feature agreed with the other. He was hot.

"Girl, I know, I saw him one Sunday this summer at Druid Hill Park rollin' in somebody's Navigator," Vivica said. "That made him look even finer than he already is."

Jeffrey was much more attractive than Cole. He had on pearl-white tennis shoes that matched his bright smile. You could tell he kept up his visits to the dentist. He was slapping hands and waving at females like a politician running for office.

"Looks like he's bringing his fine self over to speak to me," Vivica said. She adjusted her curls and pushed out her chest.

"Hello, ladies." In his baggy shorts and oversized white T-shirt, Jeffrey looked like a rapper, but he sounded like a college student. His West Indian accent lingered after he finished talking.

Then he did something that almost sent me to the nurse's office for fainting. He looked right at me, grinned like it was Christmas morning, and said, "Sak passé."

Instantly I replied, "N'ap boule." It was what I always said in response to Mr. Bouray's Haitian greeting.

Jeffrey smiled at me and I smiled at him. We smiled at each other.

He continued to converse in Creole, but I had to interrupt him and inform him that I wasn't Haitian and couldn't speak the language.

"Really? I saw the Port-au-Prince T-shirt and just assumed you were representing. How did you know how to respond to my greeting? From Wyclef?" I laughed. It was a joke that I actually got.

"My father's best friend is Haitian and he taught me. Actually, this is one of his T-shirts that his company makes. The proceeds go to people in need in Haiti."

"That's very cool," Jeffrey said. For a few moments, it was just us, and I forgot that I was a hot mess Oreo.

Vivica and Sheena tried to break through our force field with their intense stares.

He turned toward them and asked about their summers so they wouldn't feel left out.

Vivica stepped in front of Sheena and me like she was Diana Ross and we were The Supremes.

"My summer was crazy. I was at the park every Sunday. I saw you one time in someone's rimmed-up Navigator. Who was you rollin' wit?"

He looked bored. "That was my cousin." He shifted his attention back to me.

"Are you new? I've never seen you before."

"I'm from New Jersey." After I said it, I could hear that I sounded tremendously different than my three school-mates.

"Oh, what part?" he asked.

What should I have said? Rainhaven? Which I knew he'd never heard of? Or should it be a more notorious place, like Newark or Camden?

Before I answered, Vivica bulldozed her way into the conversation.

"You know, my cousin cuts hair in the shop off the

Alameda. You should come and get a shape-up. I could get you a hookup."

"That's okay. I cut my own hair." I felt a little bad for Vivica. It was obvious she was trying too hard. But then again, so was I.

"I have family in Jersey," Jeffrey said. "It's a cool place. Well, welcome to Maplewood. I'll see y'all around."

I smiled, although I wanted to say, "Not before I see you." But I figured that would sound silly. His pleasantries and mesmerizing smile gave me hope for the rest of my first day at Maplewood.

"That boy is too fine for his own good," Sheena said. "He just don't know." She emphasized *know*.

"What doesn't he know?" I asked. They ignored me.

"Why didn't y'all hook up again?" Sheena asked Vivica.

"He wasn't ready for me. Plus it's obvious he don't like light-skinned chicks. He's always goin' after some dark-skinned girl." Vivica directed her comment at me. "You was grinnin' hard in his face. You want a little chocolate, don't you? You probably used to skinny white boys with long hair." Vivica chuckled.

I thought about my skinny Matt with the long hair.

"I remember when Jeffrey first moved around the way. He was all weird and foreign, but he cool now. He grew up nicely." Sheena licked her lips.

Moments later, a middle-aged Latino man who was lugging a big trash bag behind him said, *"Qué pasa, mami?"* to Vivica. He had a thick mustache and his pants were covered with dirt.

"I ain't Spanish, I'm black," Vivica snapped with a venomous tone. She stuck her finger in his face and almost poked his eye out. Her demeanor flipped like a coin. I was officially scared of her. Didn't her father tell my mother something about Vivica being a nice, ambitious young lady? Parents lie too much about their kids.

He muttered an apology as he threw his hands up. Then he grabbed his bag and hurried on his way.

"I hate that mess," she spat. "People always wanna talk Spanish to me. I ain't Spanish. I don't even look Spanish."

"What's wrong with being Latino?" Sheena asked. "They got some fine men. I mean, you are pretty light."

"Whateva," Vivica said. She flicked her fingernails.

"You could be J.Lo's little sister," Sheena added jokingly.

"People act like they never seen a light-skinned black person before," Vivica said defensively.

The bus finally pulled up to the curb. There was a big rush to the door and I got pushed around. Sheena and Vivica took the calm route and waited patiently.

Before I got to the door, I pulled out the monthly bus pass that A&I had bought for me. When I stepped up, I inserted it into the machine.

"Wrong way," the bus driver, who had a Santa Claus beard but a Scrooge smile, barked. I turned it around, and my card was rejected again. "Other way," he snarled. I could feel the impatient breathing of the kids behind me on my neck. The people already seated on the bus looked at me with mild annoyance.

In a huff, Vivica stepped up and asked, "What, you never

rode the bus before?" She took the card from me, showed me the little diagram on the machine, and positioned the card accordingly. Then she stamped *idiot* on my forehead.

The entire bus was full. Well, let me correct that. There was half a seat available next to a very large man who was wearing a neon green shirt and pants as bright as the sun. I thought about squeezing into the small space, but when I moved toward the seat and smiled, he looked at the empty spot, maneuvered a little, and covered the remaining area with his leg.

I turned around and saw Vivica and Sheena standing while holding on to some metal bars. I grabbed a spot next to them while the bus was picking up more riders.

"You never rode a bus in that white town you from?" Luckily, people couldn't hear Vivica's question because the dude next to her had on explosively loud headphones that swallowed his ears.

What was her deal? She didn't know anything about me but had already pegged me as someone she didn't like. Maybe I'll be lucky today, make some friends, and not have to depend on Vivica and her clique for company.

It was hard to keep my balance. The bus had to be speeding. The guy next to me, the height of a basketball player, knocked his elbow into my head. But I was too nervous to say "ouch."

I watched Vivica and Sheena. They were like pros maneuvering all the bumps, lane changes, and abrupt stops. I personally felt nauseous.

The ride to school felt endless. Every stop, we picked up

more kids who were the same color as me but nonetheless made me uncomfortable. They were all much bigger, stronger, and more aggressive than I was.

Some were rowdy. Some were outrageously dressed. Some were pretty. Some were athletic. Some were audacious. None, though, were nerdy like me.

I caught a glimpse of Jeffrey at the front of the bus. His profile put me at ease. It was like a sliver of sunshine in a dark tunnel.

CHAPTER 5

"I'm hyped," Sheena announced as we finally unloaded. "Did you get that brochure about that new college prep program?" she asked Vivica as we walked toward the school.

"Yeah, I applied," Vivica whispered in a tone so low, I could hardly hear her.

"It looked like a complete waste of time," Sheena added without acknowledging Vivica's answer. "I mean, why go to college and pay all that money when I can make money right when I graduate by doing hair?"

Vivica paused and then lied, "Yeah, I know."

The bus stopped in front of Maplewood, and the building didn't look anything like it had when I'd visited early in the summer. A&I had wanted to assure themselves that it wasn't a backward move to take me out of a prestigious private school and enroll me in a public one. Then, the school looked fairly harmless. Now it looked menacing. Three large pillars guarded the doors like a trio of Goliaths.

There was a party going on in the parking lot that I didn't want to be invited to. Shiny cars were mobile boom boxes, blasting music from their trunks. Several Clearview rules were being broken: 1) No loud music, 2) No loitering, 3) No littering, 4) No inappropriate clothing. Even our uniforms had to be worn in a specific way.

Inside, Maplewood was like the neglected stepchild of Clearview. I'd eaten candy off the floors of Clearview. They were that clean. Maplewood wasn't a dump, but it looked like it had received one of those cleanings you do quickly, without expending genuine effort to get rid of the dirt. My mother always told me that I cleaned only for appearance, never really to make it sparkle.

Clearview was bright. Maplewood was dark. Clearview's lockers were miniclosets, where I kept my gym uniforms, tennis shoes, books, and an extra pair of jeans and a tee. These lockers were thin gray metal slivers that couldn't fit books horizontally. The hallways of Clearview were filled with plaques and pictures of celebrities, past presidents, actors, and CEOs who'd visited the school. Maplewood's hallways were noticeably vacant except for the twelve hundred students clogging the corridors.

Sheena was one of those popular girls who didn't mind knowing everyone because in the end she always thought she was superior. She was ultimately put on earth to make everyone a little more fabulous but not as fabulous as herself. That is, as long as you didn't piss her off. She walked the hallways like her parents paid for them. I wasn't sure what preceded what, her brassy personality or her strikingly gaudy appearance.

Vivica was more like Sheena's personal assistant, tagging along behind, answering Sheena's questions when asked but not adding much else. And well, I guess that made me the intern who didn't speak at all. As we walked the halls, kids were parked in the middle, reenacting fight scenes, and shooting the breeze.

After strolling around the entire school to see who she could see, Sheena called us heifers, told us she'd see us at lunch, and then departed.

As Vivica and I went to homeroom, I asked her, "Why didn't you tell Sheena you were in the college prep program?"

"I don't like to put my business on blast," she said. How was telling a good friend the truth about your classes broadcasting your business?

We reached room 215, which was about the size of my bedroom in Clearview. The desks seemed small for high school students. Especially for students who looked like adults.

Vivica selected a seat in the fourth row and I plopped down next to her.

Two guys walked in dressed for a basketball game, with headbands, sleeveless jerseys, and matching shorts. They were chatting loudly about whose Air Jordans were newer.

Another girl walked in with a head wrap and several arm bangles that clanked when she walked. She smiled at the class and said, "Peace, everyone." Her greeting was ignored. Another kid yelled out, "Right back at you, Sister Souljah." She shook her head in disgust. Something told me that wasn't her name.

Ms. Jimu, our homeroom and fourth period English teacher, walked in. She was black! The only black people who'd worked at Clearview were Ms. Sheila, one of Principal Monroe's executive assistants, a stern, heavyset woman who'd worn panty hose three shades lighter than her legs and Mr. Charles, the head of maintenance. Amy used to joke that they were having a torrid love affair, despite the fact that I told her they were mother and son.

Ms. Jimu looked like she could have been my mother's daughter. Maybe she was just one of those old women who had a young face because she used good skin cream. She wore a stylish pin-striped pantsuit and her hair was pulled back in a bun appropriate for a teacher.

She greeted us warmly and began taking attendance. She asked the twelve of us to tell her one thing that we had done over the summer and the last book we'd read.

"Angela Anderson," Ms. Jimu called.

"Here," a girl sang. Seated, she looked taller than me standing. Most of her height came from her hair. It was intricately designed, with curls, ponytails, and knots stacked on top of each other. It looked heavy. I wondered if her neck hurt.

She said she'd spent her summer taking singing lessons. She even sang the title of the last book she'd read, an unauthorized biography of Whitney Houston.

"Ericka Brown."

"Here," said Ericka. "This summer I helped my mother at her day care center. The last book I read was *The Coldest Winter Ever* by Sister Souljah."

"Oh, that book was off the hook," Angela said. Vivica agreed.

While Ms. Jimu continued calling roll, I jotted down the name of the book so that I could find out who Sister Souljah really was.

"Vivica Lamont."

"Here," Vivica said softly.

"Nothin'," was her answer to what she'd done this summer. A&I had told me that she'd completed an Upward Move program that allowed her to intern at a local advertising agency. That could have been her answer.

"Last book I read was one for class last year. I don't remember the title."

"Okay, perhaps you'll remember sometime throughout this year," Ms. Jimu remarked.

"Jay Mason," she called.

"Yeah, that's me," one of the basketball dudes said in a deep voice.

"Uh, I didn't do much this summer but work at Foot Locker. That wasn't too exciting. But I did get a crazy discount and bought mad sneakers. Um, last book I read was 50 Cent's autobiography."

Ms. Jimu looked disappointed. She moved from her post behind her desk and stood in front of it. She pulled off her brown-rimmed glasses and did that bite-the-tip teacher thing with one of the arms.

It wasn't long before she called, "Nina Parker."

"Present." A low rumble from the class.

I hesitated before continuing. I looked down at my hands

and covered my left with my right and then reversed them. I kept this up to keep me calm.

"This summer I visited Italy with my parents for the first time."

"Italy," Jay Mason repeated. "Damn, I didn't even go over West all summer and she said she went to another country. What, you rich? Can I be down?"

The class laughed at Jay. Or were they laughing at me?

"Okay, class, that's enough." Ms. Jimu looked down at the attendance so she would get my name right and then said, "Nina, tell us a little about your trip."

At that moment, I decided to downplay one of the best vacations I'd ever been on.

"We really didn't do much. Just visited a few museums and other tourist sites. That's all." My voice was cracking. My accent was strong. My confidence was diminished.

"Museums?" Jay asked. "That's what you did on vacation? Shoot, I'd be chillin' eating some pasta somewhere." He was officially the class clown in my book.

I think Ms. Jimu could sense that I was uncomfortable, so she switched to the next topic about the last book I had read. Technically, it was *Horrible Girls That Are Rich*, a quick tale in the vein of the movie *Mean Girls*. Amy had recommended it, and I understood why. It was superficial, not too complex, but entertaining. Instead, I said the one that I'd read before that, *Chronicle of a Death Foretold*, by Gabriel García Márquez. Ms. Richardson, my last English teacher, who stuttered but still loved to read aloud in class, introduced me to his work and I was on a mission to read any and everything by him.

"Oh, I'm impressed," said Ms. Jimu. "What did you think about it?"

I looked around at the class and all their faces shouted, "No! End the discussion here. Give a short answer!"

"I liked it." When she didn't ask me anything else, relief flushed away the class's indignation.

There were only a couple of students called after me. Ms. Jimu took a long breath when she finished and said, "Well, it sounds like many of you need to do more reading. But don't worry about that. We will be doing plenty of that in English this year."

A collective moan.

"Now, has anyone heard of Malawi?" Ms. Jimu asked next.

Without thinking, I raised my hand. She called on me to tell the class what I knew.

"It's a small East African country near Tanzania and Zambia."

When the words fell out of my mouth, my accent was so strong that even I heard it. The class burst out into laughter. Even Sister Souljah was grinning.

Vivica pursed her lips and pouted at me and shook her head, right before she turned away from me.

"That's right, very good," Ms. Jimu congratulated me.

"That's where I'm from." She went on to tell us that she had arrived in the United States when she was ten years old and had lived in various cities on the East Coast. She had two master's degrees: one in English and one in education. She taught because it was the best way to give back.

Vivica whispered, "And the best way to be broke." But I admired Ms. Jimu's conviction. She reminded me of A&I.

Our teacher went on to describe the college preparatory program as a cutting-edge curriculum that was one of a kind in Baltimore. We were expected to graduate at the top of our class, with numerous college acceptances, and well prepared to tackle university life.

When the bell rang, Vivica warned, "You better watch tryin' to be the star of the class. That ain't a way to make friends. You want people to makes jokes about you for bein' a nerd?"

"But aren't we all nerds? Isn't that why we're in the college prep program?"

"I ain't no nerd. I already regret that I'm not in the regular classes with my peoples." She fought back.

"But you had to pass advanced placement tests to get in here, so I know you're smart."

"Whateva," she said as she rushed to walk ahead of me to her next class.

Although she wasn't the nicest girl, I was disappointed that we didn't have second period together. Mainly because it was better to know someone, anyone, than to know no one, even if said someone was unfriendly. I walked to gym and she went to her career exploration class.

CHAPTER 6

MS. JOHNSON fulfilled the female gym teacher stereotype. She was short, built like an adolescent boy, and it was obvious that she chose barbells over makeup.

The class was huge, probably thirty-five girls. Suddenly I was alone.

"Ladies, let's get some things clear." A few girls rolled their eyes and picked at their fake nails the same way Vivica did. Some didn't even bother to get changed. One girl sat on the side in her skin-tight jeans and tank top with a neck full of expensive jewelry. She told Ms. Johnson she'd take a zero before she took her chains off.

"Gym is a serious class," our teacher continued. "It's not a class that you will breeze through. It will not be an easy A, as some of you think." I guess this is what Napoleon would have been like if he'd been black and female.

"Young women your age do not exercise the way they should. But this class will change that.

"You will work!" Her voice became scary.

"You will push yourself!" she yelled. She walked past me and a smell of onions and smoke invaded my nostrils. It was a nauseating combination.

"You will sweat!" she roared.

"In fact, your grade will depend on it." The class sucked their teeth. That gave Ms. Johnson a weird satisfaction.

She told us to head outside and get prepared to run a mile. I was excited, because running always cleared my head, and my group in Rainhaven ran triple that amount in one session. But it was far from no sweat.

It was about eighty-nine degrees outside. While most girls walked and talked the entire time, neatly divided into cliques, I ran, because I had no one to talk to.

I should mention now that I inherited overactive sweat glands from my father. After the mile, sweat occupied every crevice of my body, even the hard-to-reach places. My hair was monstrous after escaping the rubber band that tried to hold it hostage.

I figured that Maplewood would have clean showers and fresh towels like Clearview. Wrong again.

Maplewood had one stall that smelled of polluted mop water. The dirt on the tiles seemed comfortable and didn't look like it was leaving anytime soon. Ms. Johnson laughed when I asked for a washcloth. No shower. No deodorant. And no comb, brush, or oil to smooth the edges of my hair.

If I had looked crazy when I'd arrived at school, now I looked plain ridiculous.

I arrived at English class before Vivica and picked a seat

in the back of the classroom in the outermost corner. I was still sweaty, and my deodorant had slowed down tremendously. Vivica took a seat next to the girl with the midget on her head.

Ms. Jimu arrived as the same students from homeroom trickled in.

"Okay, today we're going to go over the class syllabus. We're going to discuss what's expected of you as well as what we're going to cover during the school year."

She passed out the syllabi while the class groaned.

I was surprised to see that we'd be learning about so many writers of color. I'd attended private school all my life, and at the most, we had studied a little Toni Morrison and Langston Hughes.

Ms. Jimu's syllabus included writers like Gwendolyn Brooks, Zora Neale Hurston, James Baldwin, Nikki Giovanni, and Ralph Ellison. All names I recognized from A&I's efforts to supplement Clearview's black-writer reading list deficiency.

After she went over the syllabus and no one had questions, she said, "Okay, I want to tell you about a new extracurricular activity that I'm spearheading. I finally received the approval to start a poetry club and slam-performing group. The group will perform several times throughout the year as well as compete against other schools, and hopefully compete nationally. I'm looking for poets, lyricists, MCs, and spoken-word artists. I want a well-rounded group. On Wednesday I am having a meeting where you can find out more information. I hope to see many of you there."

I glanced at Vivica and she had an excited expression on her face. She did a dance in her seat.

I was a little excited, too. This was something I could get involved in and maybe carve a little space for myself at Maplewood. I'd been in a poetry club at Clearview, although there had been only four of us. Carl Smith liked to write poetry about *Star Trek,* Jenny Tupelo wrote depressing sonnets, and Leslie Mint thought she was the second coming of Emily Dickinson. I had a black and white composition book filled with poems, and thought about which box I had stashed it in so I could pull it out when I got home.

By the time lunch came, I was ready for a break. The cafeteria was complete mayhem. Any bottled-up energy that Maplewood students had held on to during the morning classes was released and recharged here. There were about three hundred too many students in the cafeteria, I didn't care that it looked like a ministadium. I was sure some fire codes were being broken.

Before reaching the line, I could smell the pizza and French fries on today's menu. Vivica had secured a table and thankfully Sheena waved me over. Vivica looked angrily at her friend. Another girl was seated with them. She had on a cap twisted to the side with two long braids extending beneath it. Large gold hoop earrings weighed down her ears and I could see her bright pink lip gloss from across the room.

"Hi, ladies," I said in the most cheery tone I could muster. Sheena offered her usual "What up, chick?" and Vivica just gave me a blank stare.

"Hi, I'm Nessa," she said to introduce herself.

"I'm Nina. Nice to meet you." I meant that. She seemed normal.

She extended a fist and I extended my hand. She banged my hand with her fist.

"I was giving you a pound." She threw her head back in laughter and her braids flew up and knocked her cheeks. She had on a white tank top with graffiti artwork that spelled her name. Her jeans were stylishly ripped, unlike mine, which were just the product of wear and tear. She had on colorful high-top tennis shoes.

"I'm feeling the wild Afro puff," she said. "If you get another one you could be like The Lady of Rage."

"Thanks," I said. Even though I didn't know who that was, it was the best compliment I had gotten all day.

"But you ever thought about getting dreads?" Nessa asked. "They're hot right now. Lil Weezy, Lil John. I mean, Busta cut his off, but he was rocking them for a minute. And of course, the queen of hip-hop, Lauryn Hill, had hers."

"Nessa is a serious hip-hop chick," Sheena explained. "She spins on her head and all that crazy mess. Personally, I only like the fine rappers. If you ain't fine, I don't need to listen to you."

"Well, welcome to the hood at Maplewood." Nessa smiled and put her arm around me.

While we walked to the lunch line, Sheena asked why my hair was bushier than this morning.

"Why you look so crazy?"

I told the Big Three how I had run a mile in gym and thought that I'd be able to take a shower but was wrong.

Thus, I was left sweaty, and my hair always got curlier any-time it received more moisture.

They went on to tell me how being a star in gym was "wack" because it wasn't a real class. Other students walked past me and stared at the greasy Brillo pad on top of my head.

"That's a hot mess," Sheena said.

"My hair?" I asked.

"No, the entire situation is a hot mess." That's when I learned that the term could describe anything.

"Who were you tryin' to impress by gettin' all sweaty?" Vivica asked. "Ain't no dudes in that class."

"I didn't want to get a zero." I knew my explanation was weak.

"Please, when's the last time you heard about someone failin' gym?" Vivica asked.

The line to purchase food curved around the front of the cafeteria. It took ten of the thirty minutes reserved for eating just to purchase food.

We returned to the table with three identical orange plastic trays that carried a carton of milk, a small packet of fries, and a greasy slice of pizza cut into a rectangle.

Sheena took the pepperoni off her pizza and gave it to Nessa. She gave her fries to Vivica and pulled out a water to substitute for the milk she wasn't going to drink.

As I stared at her, she explained, "I'm on a diet. These lunches are all fat." She and Amy could have been sisters. They were both very high maintenance.

"Oh, Nessa, tomorrow's the interest meeting for the spoken-word joint," Vivica said with excitement in her voice. "You know we up in there. Ms. Jimu says she's lookin' for MCs and spoken-word artists."

"Oh hell yeah. I was working on some stuff in class this morning. Check this out."

And right after swallowing a bite of pizza, Nessa rapped:

Sometimes I wonder
If living is for me
'Cause apples don't fall
Far from the tree
And my father ain't
What he supposed to be
I wish there were more
Dads in the sea
That I could choose
'Cause I hate to lose
But I ain't won yet
In the land of bul-lets
Some grab tecs
'Cause death they already met
I wanna give life a chance
But you'll never see me
Prance like Cinderella
I'm a helluva chick that
Even your strongest
Can't mess wit

"Oh, that was hot." Vivica praised her friend in a singsong voice.

"Yeah, when you blow up, I'm goin be your stylist," Sheena added.

"It ain't nothing." Nessa blushed a little. "Just something quick I did. It needs some work but I definitely want to expand it."

"That was good," I added. "It was like lyrics."

"Duh, it was hip-hop." Vivica defended her friend.

"Oh, I just never thought of rap as poetry." The moment I said that, I knew I should have grabbed my foot and put it in my mouth instead of letting Vivica do it for me.

"Where are you from?" Vivica rolled her neck with extreme force. "Poetry is rap and rap is poetry." Vivica said. "What, you think you could do better?" She was challenging me. But little did she know, she had already won.

"V, it's cool," Nessa said to defuse the situation. "Many people don't think rap is poetry. They just need a little education, that's all."

"I really liked your poem, Nessa. I didn't mean to offend anyone. I just hadn't heard poetry like that before. In the poetry club I was in at my old school, we didn't do anything nearly as creative as that." I made a mental note to evaluate everything I wanted to say before actually releasing the words.

Nessa patted my shoulder—finally I'd said the right thing. Over our last few bites of pizza, she and I talked briefly about my poetry club and I told her about my attempts at writing. She told me to bring my book because she'd love to see them.

For the first time that day since seeing Jeffrey, I had a genuine smile on my face.

CHAPTER 7

After lunch, I sat in history class confused. Vivica had a serious chip on her shoulder that was more the size of a chunk. Even though we were almost in all the same classes, she didn't want to sit next to me. I liked Nessa. And Sheena, well, she was Sheena.

Sister Souljah took a seat beside me, and before the teacher arrived, she initiated conversation.

"You have an accent," she said.

At first I didn't feel like being bothered, but the fact that she said *accent* and not something racial piqued my curiosity.

"So what's the plight of black people living in Italy?" she asked.

Huh? What kind of question was that? A&I were obsessed with race, but that was because they were old and from a generation where race decided where they were going to sit, eat, and live. I hadn't heard so much talk about race among young people as I had today. But then again,

I guess the kids in Rainhaven didn't have to concern them-selves with the subject too often.

"Um, I'm not sure." I thought that was a safe answer.

"What do you mean? Didn't you connect with black people when you went there?" Her facial expression went sour.

"Not really. I mean, my family and I just went on vaca—"

"Oh, you one of those black people who think you better than everyone else."

"Excuse me?" I asked innocently.

"I should have known. You rock an Afro but ain't got a clue." Sister Souljah got up, picked up her book bag, and changed seats. The entire time, I stared at her in shock. I spent the rest of class trying to figure out what just hap-pened, only to come up with nothing but a headache.

By the time last period arrived, I was defeated. The ringing of the bell felt like an escape to freedom. As I walked out of my classroom toward my locker, Vivica ended up next to me.

"I told you Maplewood ain't no joke," she said noncha-lantly. "You can't just come through and think because white people like you that we'd like you."

"Why don't you like me when you don't know me?" I asked her outright. It didn't make sense.

"'Cause I know about you. You don't know what you want to be. You only want to be black when it's conven-ient for you. You can't flip-flop back and forth. If you want to be a white girl, go be a white girl, but stop frontin' like you black. Either you're down or you're not."

How could I possibly be a white girl with skin the color

of tar? I walked away briskly, just in time to catch the tears with the back of my hand.

As I was walking out the door, Sheena caught me. I shielded my eyes to avoid any potential inquiries. She invited me to hang out with the Big Three after school. But all I wanted to do was go home, so I didn't care if I had to ride by myself.

The bus filled up quickly with some of the same fashionable black kids from the morning. I was able to grab a window seat toward the back, so I could glance through the glass when the tears decided to flow.

I felt like fried manure. I tried to replay the day in my mind, but it was nerve-racking. Depressing. Pathetic. Someone sat next to me but I didn't waste the energy to turn.

"Hey you," a familiar voice said.

I turned my head lazily to see Jeffrey's smile. It reminded me of a rainbow.

I had no choice but to smile back. He put his book bag on his lap.

"How was your first day?"

I didn't have the energy to lie.

"Horrible," I blurted out.

"Why?"

"I don't fit in. I'm too different. I'm...I'm too white," I concluded.

"Well, you got a bomb tan, if you are a white girl." He laughed.

I flashed a fake grin.

"See, it's not that bad." He pinched my cheek. No one's

done that since I was a kid. Nonetheless, his touch sent shock waves through my body. Very electric.

"When I first arrived to this country as a seven-year-old, I couldn't even speak the language. Kids made fun of the way I looked, talked, dressed. They were really mean. Called me all types of names and told me to go back to my country. It was like everything about me was funny to them. I would go home crying and angry at my parents for moving us here."

"How did you finally adjust?" I wanted to know the special secret.

He pondered my question for a few seconds before answering. I had to catch myself because I was staring through him, trying to see his heart.

"It took time. But I learned how to be down. It didn't happen overnight. I also learned to like myself since no one else did." He smiled a rainbow again. "But it was also something my mother told me that put everything in perspective. She said people usually make fun of you to make themselves feel better. They usually have low self-esteem and want to direct feelings of inadequacy towards something else. I was just an easy target." Another guy stopped in front of Jeffrey and they gave each other pounds. "I see you," Jeffrey said to the guy as he grabbed the hand of a lovely-looking girl.

"I'm not saying don't try to fit in," he continued. "You're going to have to do a certain amount of that, but don't change completely just to make friends. You may realize that the people you're trying to change for aren't really your friends."

"That's great advice. You're pretty wise."

He blushed. I made him blush.

"Nah, I just went through what you're going through. That's all."

He was modest. I liked modest.

"You seem real cool."

I blushed. He made me blush.

Was this a crush?

CHAPTER 8

when I got home, I was relieved that A&I were in one of the apartments doing renovations. I took the opportunity to sneak into my room and think in solitude.

In a soft fury of tears, I retrieved a pair of scissors and my old Clearview uniforms from a box. I began cutting the clothes. It was a makeshift ritual to air my frustration and accept the fact that I was starting my life all over again.

Green and white shreds of fabric collected on the hardwood floor, along with memories of tennis lessons with Jill, bat mitzvahs ceremonies and *Gilmore Girls* marathons. I dropped to the floor.

I picked up one of the fabric scraps and my mind drifted to my old life. I thought about how less than two weeks ago, I was glued to the brick stairs that led up to our big house on the hill. It was strategic. The three movers could barely pass me. I didn't budge. The big one with the scary mustache, who showed off his underwear whenever he bent over, mumbled things as he stepped over me. The skinny one with stringy, girl-like hair gave me fake smiles anytime he passed. The short one with the elephant ears never once looked at me. But I didn't care. These men played a significant role in the ultimate conspiracy: moving me miles away from my friends and forcing me to re-create a life in Baltimore, Maryland.

I remembered doomsday like it was yesterday, although it was more than a year ago. A&I sat me down for a "family meeting." We arranged ourselves in the library on the multicolored floor pillows. My mother sat Indian-style, an ability that her weekly yoga classes afforded her. My father took off his glasses and squeezed that place at the top of his nose between his eyes. I knew what that meant.

The conversation was short. Was it really a conversation? They talked. Explained. Apologized. Convinced. Arranged. I sat quietly until the end of their presentation and softly said, "I don't want to move." My response changed nothing.

I peeked in a box and saw my old poetry book and pulled it out. About three quarters of it was filled with my novice poetic attempts. I found a blank page and wrote "How to Be Down" at the top of it. Part of me felt it was silly to create a list of ways to be cool, but part of me was scared not to fit in. So I was willing to undergo the necessary metamorphosis.

How to Be Down:
Talk cooler (use more slang)
Hide being smart (don't try to answer questions even
    if you know the answers)
Get a perm

Get a better wardrobe
Don't read books (or at least don't put it on blast)
Don't think you're better than others
Learn to work a bus card: upside down facing me
Read *The Coldest Winter Ever* by Sister Souljah
Watch what you say
Learn how to rap
Stay on Sheena's good side

I studied the list. It was predictable and ridiculous. Yet it was my strategy and my lifesaver.

I flipped through the rest of my book to some of my old poems. Most of them were silly musings about puppy love—what I had experienced the first two months of dating Matt—but they were catchy and humorous. I put the notebook in my backpack so I wouldn't forget it.

I decided to e-mail Jill. E-mail was always the best way when you wanted to say something that you didn't have the nerve to say on the phone or in person. I pulled out the laptop A&I had bought me for my freshman year at Clearview.

After I logged on and filtered through the junk mail—a collection of indecipherable symbols, disgusting requests to look at the body parts of strangers, and e-mails asking me to check my bank account—I composed the following:

To: jillnojack@fmail.com
   Subject: Question
   Hey Jill—
So the first day of school was a disaster. Actually, I'm not

sure if *disaster* can really capture the catastrophic collection of events. I'll have to fill in the horrible details when we talk over the telephone. There's really too much to type.

I had a question for you. It's a stupid question, but a question nonetheless. The girls here don't think I'm "black enough." Has anyone ever told you that you need to be more black, or more white, for that matter?

I mean, if you don't want to answer you don't have to, but I just needed some perspective.

How was cheerleading tryouts?

Nina

"So, honey, are you feeling a little better?" my mother asked during dinner. My parents knew my first day was not what they had expected it to be. Although I wasn't quite sure what they'd expected under the circumstances. I swallowed a spoonful of corn while I formulated an answer.

"I need to blacken up." I was curious to see their reactions, because to my artistic/activist/independent-thinking parents, blackness couldn't fit in a neat box.

A&I had identical looks on their faces. A mix between horror, remembrance, and anguish. You would have thought I said that I needed to get jumped into the black culture through a violent initiation rite, like some gangs require.

The label A&I hated more than "Afro-American," which people at Rainhaven still used on occasion, was "sellout". I never really got what "sellout" meant, but I guess today added a little more to my understanding.

A&I had been called sellouts more times than they could count. I think it was because they lived in an all-white town and sent their daughter to all-white private schools yet worked hard to maintain a connection to African-American culture. My father made a living painting portraits of black people. My mother made an even healthier living writing about black people.

My mother put her fork down and gently wiped her mouth. She took a deep breath before answering. "Honey, where did you get that from?"

I didn't want to tell on my new friends. But was friendship an accurate assessment of my relationship with the Big Three? Were they really my friends? I remained silent.

My mother continued, "Now, you know we have taught you that being black means many things. It isn't about how you sound, how you look, how you wear your hair, or what type of music you like."

Her speech sounded rehearsed. She'd been practicing it.

"I know, Ma, but I'm worried that I won't fit in at Maplewood."

"Why wouldn't you?" my father chimed in. "You're smart, funny, and a ball to be around. Who wouldn't want to be your friend?"

Typical Dad answer. It'll have to do for now. But A&I would have to think of something more substantial if I came home tomorrow afternoon in tears again.

CHAPTER 9

I arrived three minutes early to meet Vivica. There was no need to rush to my "destiny." It was 7:25 and she still hadn't come out. I didn't want to miss the 7:29 bus, so I made the lonely walk by myself. It took me forty-four steps.

In the short distance to the bus, I realized that Baltimore was trying to prove its worth. It was like a beautiful woman with a black eye. It was trying to prove that it was the little big city that could. It was more dangerous than it should be. It was trying to prove that it deserved attention. It was loud for no reason. It was trying to prove that it had something to say. So I listened.

When I arrived at the stop for the number forty-two bus, I immediately spotted Sheena because of her blond hair. Nessa wore a red cap and Vivica was standing next to her, but she turned her head and our eyes met. I thought about waiting by myself, but I walked in their direction. Being alone was not something I was used to.

On my way, Jeffrey stopped me.

"Hey, miss," he said. His button-down shirt, crisp khakis, and soft leather shoes made him look like a Gap employee. He couldn't be boxed in.

"Oh, hi, how's it going?" I asked. My mother twisted my hair last night since the bushy ponytail was an overall loser in yesterday's hair game. I played with one of my twists. Did I look cute doing it?

"Chillin'." He lowered his voice a little to respect my privacy. "Feeling better?"

Before I answered, the Big Three joined us to chaperone our conversation.

"What up?" Vivica asked.

"Coolin'," Jeffrey answered before excusing himself. He lightly smacked my arm and told me he'd see me later.

"Hallelujah, you did somethin' with that bush on your head." Sheena greeted me with two fake air kisses like she was French.

"You know, Nina, not only am I going to be one of the meanest hairdressers in B'more, I'm also goin' to be the slickest stylist. You should let me help you—" she paused "—do somethin' with your look."

I thought I did better this morning. In reality, it was just a variation of yesterday's outfit, except my T-shirt fit a little better. And I'd put on newer jeans.

"Why you got on a shirt that says 'Italy'? You want to be white?" Vivica asked.

I looked at the green T-shirt with red and white lettering and didn't equate it with race.

"No, I just grabbed this one, I didn't think about it like that." My answer seemed sufficient, because she didn't continue.

"Nessa, I wondered if you'd look at my poetry book and give me some feedback?" I asked.

She took the lollipop out of her purple mouth, took the notebook, and said she'd return it to me at lunch.

During homeroom, Ms. Jimu passed out study materials for our first round of testing. Our program required regular evaluation of our progress. She explained that if we failed two of the tests, we would be dismissed from the program. We had to take our first test in two weeks.

"Oh, that's messed up," Jay whined. "I don't know if I can deal with all the pressure." The class laughed, as they always did when he opened his mouth.

After class, Ms. Jimu asked me how I liked Baltimore City so far.

"It's okay," I said. I could actually see from the softness of her face that she was fairly young. It wasn't just good skin cream.

"I know it can be hard to move to a new city and have to restart your life. But I wanted to let you know that I'm here if you ever need to talk." Teachers actually cared about you besides what you scored on tests? That was a new one.

I avoided Vivica for the first part of the day. Or maybe she avoided me.

That was until English, when Ms. Jimu had us free write

about a hardship in our life. She then paired us up to discuss each other's writing. I was Vivica's partner.

Before we began, Vivica said, "I saw you all up in Jeffrey's face again. You know he don't like white girls."

"I thought you said he doesn't like light-skinned girls," I countered. Wow, I didn't know I had a little fire in me.

When Ms. Jimu didn't see us actively reading each other's work, she came over and made us. Vivica reluctantly exchanged papers with me.

Vivica's read:

Absent from the beginning
Not long after I exited the womb
Not present at the end when my home becomes a
   tomb
A seed was planted but never fertilized
All in the meanwhile a piece of me dies
Unaddressed pain and anger leads to an early demise
Ears clogged with lies
A heart filled with juvenile cries
Creating faults to explain your indifference
Searching for answers to the nonspecific
Contemplating a way out through means horrific
Visions of a figure with a face just like mine
That I can't even begin to recognize
Flashbacks attack my brain unable to breathe
My eyes can't conceive what my mind tries not
   to believe
A woman leaves doesn't look back

A man on his knees, yelling, every other word please
A child too young to understand slips into a sleep
Dreams of an older woman that she longs to meet
Back to a reality of pain
Playing against sadness in a chess game
Checkmate, I won this session
Only to play this game and never learn the real
  lesson
Not a burden, but a blessing.

Mine read:

A black girl trapped in a white girl's body? Not sure what that means...but it's mean. I wonder if Jill was ever accused of being one. Especially since she's the daughter of a black father and a white mother. I never really thought about how black I am. It was obvious to me that yes, I was indeed black. I'm not blind. But inside I've always felt like Me. Nina Parker.

Now that I think about it, A&I must feel the same way. I'm not black enough. Isn't that why they put me in an all-black high school? Isn't that why they want me to attend Howard University? Isn't that why they want me to know poets from the Black Arts movement and read slave narratives?

I miss my friends. I miss Rainhaven. I miss Jill. I miss Amy. I miss Matt. I miss our house. I miss the certainty in my life. Now I don't know what's going to happen. Will I make friends? Will I be accepted me for who I am?

This feels like a punishment. For being black? For being white? For being Me?

We sat silently before offering any thoughts. Had I known I'd be exchanging papers with Vivica, I wouldn't have been so honest. Now I'm vulnerable. So was she.

"That was intense," I said after a few minutes. "You wrote that in fifteen minutes?"

She nodded. But I really wanted to ask her if she was okay. I wanted to ask her when her mother left. I wanted to ask her how it made her feel. I wanted to ask her if that's why she acts the way she does. But above everything else, I wanted to know why she takes her frustration out on me.

"Did you have any black friends at Clearview?" Vivica asked. Her tone wasn't judgmental but curious instead. I was glad she switched the subject.

"Well, no. I mean, kind of. Jill, my best friend, is biracial. But she wasn't like, black. I mean, I don't know, that sounds funny. How can I say it? She was just Jill. Neither black or white."

"It must be horrible to be both black and white," Vivica said.

"I don't know. Jill never complained about it. She never felt funny or anything. If she did, she never told me. Sometimes she would tell stories about when she was younger, people would look at her father weirdly when they were out because she's so much lighter than him. One time a white police officer pulled him over with Jill in the car. The officer thought he kidnapped her. Jill just laughed it off, like she does most things, but I thought that was pretty crazy."

"I hate people sometimes. They can be so racist."

I agreed. We didn't say anything else, but in the silence we said plenty.

During lunch, Nessa returned my poetry book and said that my writing was interesting but lacked feeling.

"I can't feel your energy in any of them," she told me. That made sense. Flipping through the notebook, none of them were stellar. I'd have to work on them if I wanted to be serious about being a part of the poetry performance team.

Poetry saved Nessa's life, she said. "I know people say that a lot, how poetry or hip-hop was their ticket to a better life. But if I wasn't writing, I think I'd have gone crazy by now. Writing keeps me sane." I felt Nessa. Now I just needed to feel myself.

"So when you gonna let me give you a makeover?" Sheena asked after we all finished the lasagna that tasted like plastic. "I can see you now, straight hair, new clothes, lookin' tight."

"She's goin' to need more than new clothes," Vivica added. "She needs a lesson in being black." Just like that,

she was back to her usual self. Our connection disinte-
grated in the thick energy of the cafeteria.

"She's already black. She just needs more flava, that's
all." Nessa winked at me.

The remainder of our lunch conversation centered
around the interest meeting, and thankfully, not me.

CHAPTER 10

There must have been forty kids in the room for the interest meeting. Sheena tagged along to give moral support. About half of the students from my program were there, including Jay and Sister Souljah, who, as she announced to the room, "came to represent for our African ancestors."

After everyone settled down, Ms. Jimu thanked us for coming and explained her intentions for the club. "Poetry is a powerful form of expression. These days, it takes on many forms, from rap to spoken word. This club will be a place for you to share your poetry, gain feedback, listen to your classmates' work, and express yourself. We will meet weekly. But we are also forming a poetry team that will compete with other schools and lead our performances. Starting next week we will hold tryouts. There will be three rounds of judging. I, along with Ms. Tony, an eleventh-grade English teacher, and Mr. McAllister, a creative writing teacher, will be the judges, although we will consider the response of the audience to determine the eight members of the squad."

I think Nessa's, Vivica's, and my eyebrows raised at the same time. Only eight members? This was going to be a competitive monster.

Ms. Tony and Mr. McAllister looked like the type of teachers who were overachievers. Went above and beyond the call of duty. They stood with Ms. Jimu and added a few comments about how they couldn't wait to hear our work.

"Are there any questions?" Ms. Jimu asked.

There were tons of questions. I had a few, too, but didn't ask them. Should I try out and risk making a fool of myself? What should my first poem be about? Was I even good enough to write poetry?

Before I left with the Big Three, Ms. Jimu told me she was happy to see me at the meeting and that she looked forward to hearing my poetry. More pressure.

A&I were ecstatic to hear that I was trying out for the poetry club. So much so that they pulled out poetry collections from Nikki Giovanni and Gwendolyn Brooks. I remember A&I reading some of the poems before, but now their work resonated with me. I liked the way the two "women warrior poets"—my mother's words—played with language, explored complex themes with vigor, and said what needed to be said. I wanted that type of strength. I tried to write with motivation, but nothing inspiring came to me.

That night I checked my e-mail, and hoped that Jill had replied with some insight about the black-white girl phenomenon. Was it actually widespread? I didn't know. There was nothing there from her. I was desperate, so I decided to give her a ring.

"Hey, Jill," I said.

"Oh, hi, Nina! How are things in Baltimore? How was your first day of school?"

"Miserable."

"Why? What happened?"

"Did you get my e-mail?" I didn't want to come out and ask if she thought I was a white girl with a permanent tan.

"No, I didn't get a chance to check it. These cheerleading tryouts are kicking my butt. I don't see how Amy does it. I wish you were here so we could suffer together." She apologized for chewing in my ear. She was eating dinner.

I sighed.

"What did you say in the e-mail?"

"Uh, you'll see. It's just so different here. I'm not sure if I'll fit in."

"Well, making friends takes time. Have you met anybody yet?" Jill was always so level-headed.

I told her about the Big Three. I told her how they didn't think I had enough "flava." But I didn't say what they meant by that. I told her how Jeffrey made me smile and how I was going to try out for the poetry club. Then finally I asked a question that I'd never had a reason to ask before. "How do you feel to be black and white?"

She released one of her famous laughs, a marriage of uncertainty and genuine amusement.

"Well, it's like having the best of both worlds, I suppose.

I mean, I couldn't imagine being anything else. Naturally, people tend to have more of a problem with it than I do. It bothers some people that I am not one or the other. But that is their issue, not mine."

I really missed Jill.

CHAPTER II

At lunch the next day after admitting that I didn't know who the rapper Juelz Santana was—Sheena's pretend babydaddy—a full-blown conversation about hip-hop ensued. I learned from my cousin Sondra that I was the only black teenager who didn't religiously watch *106 & Park*. It was an offense equal to a federal crime.

"What do you know about hip-hop?" Nessa asked, ready to pull out a lesson plan and begin teaching me.

"Do you know who's hot right now?" Sheena asked. She did an impromptu dance that looked like she was going into labor.

I wanted to say MC Hammer, thinking a little humor might lighten up the serious tone of our lunchtime discussion.

Rainhaven had three radio stations, none of which played hip-hop. But I didn't live in space, which is the only place that hasn't been introduced to hip-hop music, so I did know some songs. But A&I thought cable television was the work of the devil, aka corporate brainwashing, so hip-hop didn't flow in the Parker household.

I was stumped like a contestant on *Jeopardy!* I didn't pay attention to who sang or rapped what song. I finally blurted out, "50 Cent." He was one of Amy's favorite artists. "He's so ghetto and gangsta," she would say, purposefully dropping the "er."

"Yeah, who else?" Vivica asked. "You probably don't even listen to hip-hop. You probably listen to heavy metal or some crap like that." She mocked me.

"I don't listen to heavy metal," I said as a futile way to defend myself. I did like rock and roll. Did that automatically make my black card null and void? Jill and I would spend hours listening to her music collection. She was a connoisseur and she had everything: rap, rock, reggae, folk, jazz, classical. If only she was here to bail me out. We didn't separate the music by black and white; we used *great* and *horrible* as classifiers. Was the British group Coldplay really rock and roll? And what about John Mayer? I liked Norah Jones and Christina Aguilera. I shook my backside to Beyoncé in the comfort of Jill's room. I liked some hip-hop, mainly songs that didn't glorify violence or disrespect women. But those groups seemed to be few and far between.

"Common. He's good." Jill used to play him sometimes.

"Common is not hot," Vivica said dismissively. "That ain't the hip-hop we talkin' about."

"Common's hip-hop," Nessa said in my defense. "Jay-Z

once rhymed about wanting to rap like Common, but instead he dumbs down his lyrics to appeal to a bigger audience. I wish he wouldn't downgrade his brilliance."

CHAPTER 12

I made it through my first week. Barely. The remainder of the week, Vivica continued making comments about my lack of blackness. Sheena almost got into a fight with a girl who allegedly called her a skank. And Nessa and I bonded over discussions of rappers who are poets. The fleeting rays of light were provided by Jeffrey's smile and glimmers of sincerity in his eyes. Although all my limbs were still intact, parts of my self-confidence, self-esteem, and self-worth had been crushed.

My weekend was less eventful, and I liked it that way. I helped A&I paint the fourth-floor apartment. I studied for the first evaluation test and slept. My mother asked me why I didn't study with Vivica. I didn't have an answer for her. I called Jill and laughed with Amy. I thought about the Big Three and then told myself not to think about them. I studied more and slept more.

I also worked on a new poem. Nessa's feedback was pretty valuable. But I didn't know how to put more feeling into my work. I started many drafts only to ball them up and throw them across my bedroom. Then I remembered how emotive Vivica's poem was. And seeing how much her mother's decision to leave affected her, I found a renewed respect and love for my own mother. So that's where I started the poem.

I also added to "How to Be Down":

Keep your feelings to yourself
Make people feel you (how?)
Don't put your business on blast
Don't let anyone disrespect you
Know the hottest rappers

CHAPTER 13

when I arrived at school the morning of the first poetry competition, Sheena and Nessa pushed me into the girls' bathroom. For a moment, I thought they were going to attack me.

"Here, put this on." Sheena threw me a black T-shirt that read "Got Dough?"

I did as I was told and turned my back to change. The shirt was snug on my little body. If I had boobs of some size, I would have appeared busty.

Sheena threw a metallic belt around my hips and told me to exchange my penny-sized silver hoops for a pair of large, orange-sized ones. Today her hair was in a short bob but was still blond. I think it was a wig.

They took a step back, looked at me, and nodded their heads in approval. My reflection in the mirror was stronger than I remembered it. My eyes smiled at the subtle changes.

Sheena looked down at my beat-up cross-trainers and frowned.

"Those shoes throw everything off. What size you wear?"

When I replied that I wore a seven, she grabbed a pair of silver ballet flats out of her designer bag. I put them on and complained about them being tight, but Sheena said that's the price of being cute.

"You carry an extra pair of shoes in your pocket-book?" I asked.

"Yeah, I have to walk four blocks to the bus stop, and when no one's looking I switch out of my heels into those." She pointed to my feet.

"That looks better," Nessa said. Although she wore jeans every day, Nessa had a unique style and I valued her opinion.

"Much better, let's be out," Sheena declared.

At lunch, in an act of kindness, while Vivica and I were alone at the table, I asked her how she thought she did on our first test for the college prep program that we had taken that morning.

"It wasn't too bad," I said to start the conversation. "I studied hard, though."

"I guess." She didn't look up from the *Vibe Vixen* magazine she was reading.

"Did you study for it?"

"Nope." Still no eye contact.

"Did you think it was hard?"

"I didn't finish," she announced, like it was no big deal.

"Did you run out of time?" I was concerned.

"Nope." I felt like an officer trying to pry information from a suspect.

Sheena and Nessa joined us with sick-looking hot dogs on their trays. That was the end of that conversation.

"So today starts round one of the judging for the poetry contest. Y'all nervous?" Nessa asked, although it was obvious that she was something. *Hyper* could describe her continued hand claps, her jittery movements, and her opened journal. She jumped up, pulled up her baggy jeans, and fixed her T-shirt that in big, orange block letters shouted her MC name, Nessasary.

"I'm a little nervous, but I worked on a new poem all weekend, considering your feedback of my book," I said. "That was real helpful."

"I'm glad," Nessa responded. "Everyone has a voice, you know. It's just about finding it."

"I ain't nervous," Vivica said, cutting me off. "I'm goin' to rock it."

"I just hope there goin' be some cuties there," Sheena declared as she arranged her bob.

"Are you going to perform the poem about your mother?" I asked Vivica.

Her face wrinkled in anger. We didn't talk for the remainder of the afternoon.

CHAPTER 14

"welcome, everyone, to the first round of judging for our performance team. I just want to remind you that anyone can be a part of the poetry club. Our weekly meetings are open to everyone and they will begin next month. Today we are judging for the eight-member team who will perform for Maplewood and compete with other schools." Ms. Jimu smiled, which made her look like a schoolgirl. Or maybe it was the knee-length plaid skirt and black Mary Jane shoes she was wearing.

Someone yelled out, "A'ight!" It sounded like Jay. The auditorium was half full, so about 150 or so students came out to watch the competition. I looked around at all the black faces and tried to see myself in them so that I wouldn't be so nervous. And although I didn't see my face, I felt connected, not so isolated. I began to blend.

First up, Sister Souljah recited a poem filled with garbled pro-black rhetoric. She threw around a lot of "kings," "queens," "devils," and "revolutions." The crowd didn't seem to enjoy it. I clapped hard because it took guts to get onstage in front of everyone.

Another girl, who resembled a beaver in designer clothes (I'm not trying to be mean, she really did look like one), performed an ode to Tupac.

Jay did a funny but clever rap about waking up one day as a female. Apparently life wasn't that easy as a girl. His cleverness and command of language made me understand more why he was in the college prep program.

Another girl with maroon braids performed an angry ditty about her child's father. Afterward, she was so worked up that Ms. Jimu had to escort her offstage.

Vivica got up and we all wished her good luck. After having to have the microphone adjusted because she was so short, she dedicated her poem to all the "players and wannabe pimps in the audience."

Let me introduce you to my little friend…

Have you ever met her?
By your actions, I would guess no
She usually shows when you least expect
A strong woman, silly excuses, she don't accept
Some call her the opposition ready to settle the score
I call her my friend, handlin' the dirty work of my
    troubled amour
Smooth and silent the way you say you like your women
Make no mistake she will have your mind spinnin'
A modern-day superhero
Never losin', fighting evil

She will dish out what you have comin' to you
And then some, believe me
I don't have to key your car
Burn your clothes
Or flatten your tires
My girl handles it all
Havin' you wished you would've apologized
I leave everything to her
And move on with my life
There is nothing you can do
Just a word of advice
She don't play, so don't try to seduce or charm her,
Ask one of your boys
You can't mess with my girl Karma

Vivica's body moved with her words. She came alive on-stage. Actually, she became likable. The response from the audience was an animated collection of hoots and hollers. She even elicited a few "Amens" from girls and snickers from the dudes.

Nessa performed an extended version of the poem she had recited the first day of school. The stage was like a second home to her. Her performance was so natural. Effortless. Her hand movements, facial expressions, and mannerisms were perfectly timed. The audience remained under her spell until she dropped the microphone. Then we just erupted. She made me wish I could rhyme.

A few performers later, it was my turn. Nessa had given me some pointers at lunch, but now I felt inadequate. She said, "Do me," as I squeezed by. Sheena said, "Break a leg, chick," and Vivica told me not to fall.

Onstage, it was hard to see. The audience looked like one big, black blob. That helped. So I began slowly. My voice trembled:

A giver like Theresa
A fighter like Muhammad
You have perserved with a tenacity that
Is hard to grasp even by the most accomplished

A simple woman with a complex mission
Take care of my child regardless the situation
This is my life's dedication, I'll have no reservations

Stronger than any army, your drive is amazing
Initiating a positive change in me, my vision, my mission
The woman I want to be and the patience I strive to achieve

Even when you were afraid you assured me that it will be okay
Never letting me see a face
Without a smile
Because I am your child
and you shielded me from anything negative
Your calm words were a natural sedative

So attentive, when I was sick
when I was well
When I fell
scraped my knees
when I had bad dreams
when I entered my teens

It was you I turned to when I was blue
Thought I knew it all, but had no clue
And you stayed true no matter what
No longer in diapers but still cleaning after my butt

You accept me for who I am
You are a God-send and
My savior
Loving me
All the way down
To my most insignificant layer

With you as my light and guidance
I don't have to go through life blind and silent
A beautiful person I have become
Because you gave me life and love
You are my sun

I closed my eyes when I finished and awaited a response.
Nothing but a few claps from Sheen and Nessa, who
seemed afraid to do any more than that. And oh yeah, Ms.
Jimu and the other teachers clapped, but they did for

everyone. I can't even say the reaction was lukewarm. It was unbelievably cold, like a February day in New Jersey. I slowly returned to my seat. Not even a new shirt and hoop earrings could rescue me.

I sat through the rest of the performances stunned and hurt.

"Well, first I want to say thank you for coming and sharing your wonderful poems," Ms. Jimu said. "You are all so talented. I see this is going to be a difficult decision-making process. Next week is round two of the judging. I can't wait to hear your new poems."

I was confused about the crowd's response, so I asked the Big Three for feedback.

"I mean, your poem was good and all, but it was a little boring," Sheena said while scrolling through her cell phone. "You didn't bring the hotness."

"It was corny," Vivica said with a twinkle of triumph in her eyes.

"Is that why you didn't do the poem about your mother?" I asked her. She shot me a murderous look before rolling her green eyes.

"It was soft," she exclaimed.

"Ms. Jimu looked liked she enjoyed it, but you got to consider your audience. They want to feel your energy. It was a decent poem, but I couldn't feel you in it." Nessa rubbed my shoulder to let me know she wasn't being mean.

I guess you have to be careful what you ask for. I asked for feedback, and I got it.

We walked to the bus and I realized I'd left my self-confidence in the auditorium.

* * *

A&I inquired about my first test and the poetry competition over vegetable quesadillas. They made me read the poem. Of course they thought it was brilliant.

"That was beautiful." My mother gave me a long hug and rubbed my back. I could smell her lavender oil.

"I know your classmates liked it," my father said while scooping sour cream onto his plate.

"Actually, Father, they hated it." I wanted them to stop babying me. Maybe that's why I'm soft now.

"I don't believe that," my mother said defensively. Since the poem was about mothers, she thought everyone should like it.

"They thought it was soft."

"Soft?" A&I asked together.

"Yes."

"What do you mean?" my father asked.

I was shocked at how much my explanation upset him.

"That's what's wrong with us as a people now. Everyone wants to perpetrate a hard exterior, like that's going to get us anywhere."

"Honey, did you like your poem?" he asked.

"Yes."

"Did you do your best performing it?" I stopped eating to think about his question. My father looked at me with serious eyes, his dreads pulled into a loose ponytail.

"I was nervous at first, but it felt nice. I know I need some work, but with more practice, I could be better."

"Well then, that's what counts. Don't pander to your

classmates just because they can't appreciate the depth of your character." Bitterness saturated his words.

I lay in bed thinking about my father's advice. I also thought back to Jeffrey's words of wisdom and Jill's thoughts. I was going about this all wrong. But I couldn't sleep. I clicked on the lamp on my nightstand and added "bring the hotness at all times" and "don't come off soft" to "How to Be Down." Then I fell asleep.

CHAPTER 15

on the bus ride to school, Jeffrey grabbed a spot standing next to me. Vivica squeezed past us with an attitude so funky I could smell it. But the scent of Jeffrey's cologne—a coupling of maleness and strength—overpowered Vivica's obnoxious odor. She took a very obvious position behind him, I'm sure to eavesdrop on our conversation.

"I meant to tell you how much I liked your poem on Tuesday. It was really good."

"You were there?" I didn't remember seeing him.

"Yeah, I came in during the middle but had to leave early. I thought it was a sweet tribute to your mother." He brushed the side of his face, where fine hairs were growing.

"Thanks, but no one else seemed to like it." The frigid response floated back to my mind.

"You can't worry about what everyone thinks. That will make you crazy."

I offered a silent nod. He said some good things, but most of them seemed hard to actually put into action.

* * *

Ms. Jimu returned our tests and I was relieved to see that I got a 94 percent. I missed two questions. I looked over to Vivica and she smiled when she saw her score. I was happy for her.

Jay let out a big "Dammmnnnn." Ms. Jimu told him to remember where he was. Angela, who no longer had a small animal on her head but long, Cinderella tresses, announced her B to the entire class.

"Overall, this section did very well on the test," Ms. Jimu said. "A few of you did not get a score high enough to pass. I just want to remind you that if you do not pass two tests, you will be asked to leave the program. Because this was the first test, we are offering a makeup. However, this will be the only test that you will have the opportunity to redo in hopes of a better grade. Remember, we have two tests remaining this quarter. Are there any questions?"

"Nina," Ms. Jimu said as I was walking out of the class.

"I wanted to congratulate you. You received the highest grade in the class." She had a pen behind her ear.

"Thanks," I said.

"Did you study much?" she asked.

That's when I realized that school came easy to me. I studied, but more as a formality. I guess everyone had their talent and mine was school.

"And it was great to see you at the competition. You seem to be settling in to Maplewood pretty well." That was really a comment to get me talking about my feelings. I didn't fall for it.

"Yes, I think so," I answered.

"Good. See you tomorrow."

That night while A&I and I were playing Scrabble on the living room floor, my mother said nonchalantly, "Barry called today. Apparently, Vivica didn't do too well on that first evaluation test for your program. He wants to make sure she'll be successful and pass the makeup."

I silently studied my letters. I also wondered why she was telling me.

"I told Barry how well you did and he asked if you could go over there this weekend to help her."

My eyes enlarged. I remembered Vivica smiling at her grade. Maybe she was frontin' so people wouldn't know what grade she really got.

"And I told him of course you would." She gave me a light shove.

My father spelled *late* using three of his five remaining letters.

"Mommy, the last thing Vivica wants is for me to tutor her. She already believes that I think I'm better and smarter than she is."

"Nina, you don't want to help her?" The guilt trip ensued.

Next to my mother's word, *rain*, I spelled *no*. But I knew it was only a game.

CHAPTER 16

This morning was the first time I got a seat on the bus. That may be because I was running a few minutes late after my alarm clock failed to buzz me awake. In less than seventeen minutes, I showered, dressed, washed my face, threw oil on my hair, slapped lotion on my body, toasted bread, wished A&I a good day, and ran down several flights of stairs.

I was sitting next to a woman dressed like a leopard from head to toe, reading the *Baltimore Sun*. So far, there had been seven murders in Baltimore in September, which wasn't over yet. While I read the woman's paper with her, Jeffrey snuck up on me.

"Hey, Ms. Nina," he said while standing directly in front of me. He had on a gray suit and shiny black dress shoes.

"You look nice." That was all I said. Although I wanted to scream, "Fine! Handsome! Cute! Dashing! Dapper!"

"Special occasion?" I asked.

"I have to give a marketing presentation today in class." That's right, he had told me he was in the business program.

"Good luck." I purposefully looked back at the newspaper so that I wouldn't try to touch him.

"Hey, they have this open-mike poetry event at Gabrielle's this Sunday and I wanted to see if you wanted to check it out." That's what Jeffrey said while leaning in front of me. Was he asking me on a date?

"Huh?" I needed him to repeat himself just in case I was in the middle of a fantasy.

He bent over and was now close enough to touch my lips with his. I wished I had thrown on Amy's gloss. I could almost taste his cologne. He repeated himself and the words actually sounded like poetry.

"Sure, it sounds like fun." I found it hard to breathe. There was the rainbow again. I needed air.

After I got off the bus, I gave him my phone number so that we could make arrangements. My hands were shaking as I wrote down the ten digits. I hoped he didn't notice.

The rest of the morning was a blur, because all I could see was Jeffrey and I, together, alone, on a date. It was a montage of images, really. Jeffrey and I holding hands walking down some nameless beach. Jeffrey and I kissing in a tree. Jeffrey and I at the movies. Jeffrey and I strolling in the mall. Jeffrey and I.

My euphoric feelings spilled over toward Vivica even though she tried to embarrass me by telling everyone during our class discussion about slavery that I knew all about white people. I definitely didn't mention the tutoring thing.

"So why you rockin' that Kool-Aid grin?" Sheena asked

at lunch. Usually her nosiness annoyed me, but today, I was more than happy to put myself on blast.

"Jeffrey asked me if I wanted to go to a poetry event with him this weekend."

"What?" Vivica spit out drops of her milk. She didn't rush to get a napkin. I handed her one with a smile.

"Oh, which one?" Nessa asked.

"He said it was at Gabrielle's," I responded.

"Oh, that's a dope one. I've been a few times but never performed there. You might be able to pick up some tricks for round two."

"Forget performance tricks, are you sayin' that Jeffrey's fine self asked you on a date?" Sheena turned her body toward me and I realized that under the wallpapering of makeup, she was really pretty. Her eyes were graceful and her face radiated innocence.

"I mean, I wouldn't call it a date. We are just going to hear poetry." Modesty took over.

"Well, call it what you want. All I know is that you can't go lookin' like that."

For the past few days, Sheena and Nessa had been taking me into the girls' bathroom to get upgraded. I'd trade my boring T-shirts for one of their more stylish ones. One morning, Sheena unraveled some of my twists to give me what she called the "curly 'fro." It was definitely a change in the right direction.

All of a sudden my nerves clenched like fists. What would I wear? What would I do to my hair?

"Can you give me a makeover?" I finally asked Sheena frantically.

"It's about damn time." She was victorious.

We decided to go shopping for an outfit and go to the hair salon that weekend. After sitting through the entire Jeffrey discussion silent, Vivica said she couldn't make it because she was busy.

CHAPTER 17

On Friday, Sheena, Nessa, and I embarked upon our mission. Our first stop was the Baltimore Shopping Plaza, which Sheena said was the place for designer threads both real and imitation. At four o'clock in the afternoon, it was crowded like the few days before Christmas, when people scrambled to get those remaining presents. I thought for a moment that maybe the mall was giving away free clothes. It was that packed.

As we walked, it seemed like every other girl was dressed like Sheena, in heels, jeans that stopped at the calf, and a coordinating tight blouse. Maybe fitting in wouldn't be all that hard.

We walked into Fashionista, the premier store for the fashion crazy. At least, that's what the sign said. A couple of teenagers were folding shirts. It was obvious by their faces that they'd rather be doing something else.

"Hi," a young salesguy said. His jeans looked like they were suffocating him. I wanted to ask him if he was in pain.

"Well, aren't you a fabulous trio. Let me guess, sisters?" Before we had a chance to answer, Tight Jeans continued.

"My name is Oscar." He emphasized the last syllable so that it lingered for three seconds too long.

"Welcome to Fashionista. I will be your personal fashion consultant for the day. Are you three lovely ladies looking for something in particular?" Oscar winked one of his blue eyes and tilted his head. He rubbed the back of his platinum blond hair, which was three shades lighter than Sheena's. Nessa turned to me and smirked. Oscar was black.

"I love your style, honey," Sheena said. "Very unique." Sheena slapped hands with him. "You can definitely help us. We're lookin' for some clothes for this chick here."

Oscar stepped back and looked at me like he was trying to interpret a painting gone wrong. He raised his fist to his chin and began his assessment.

"I see you like the messy, just-out-of-bed look. You know, that is making a comeback."

Sheena and Nessa covered their mouths to keep from laughing.

"It hasn't quite made it back yet," Oscar added without judgment. "But, girlfriend, Fashionista has plenty of clothes that reflect the latest trends. You're in good hands. This is going to be fun, fun, fun!"

Again he emphasized the last fun, it must have been his thing.

Suddenly things got very crazy. Oscar, Sheena, and Nessa turned into high-powered, well-dressed machines. They pulled shirts, skirts, and jeans off the racks. They ran back and forth between me, the dressing rooms, and the store. They held up outfits to me like I was a mannequin. Not once did they ask my opinion. But I went with it, because quite frankly, I didn't know how to get home, and I really did need something *hot* to wear on my date with Jeffrey.

Some of the price tags made my stomach jump. A hundred and ten dollars for jeans? Seventy-five dollars for a shirt? People always assumed that A&I spoiled me. The only two things that they splurged on were education, which was no longer the case now that I was going to a public school, and travel, which they viewed as education. They didn't believe in becoming "slaves to capitalism." Even at Christmas, it was about the handmade gifts: poetry, socks, or paintings. Luckily, A&I's guilt was worth two hundred dollars today.

I'd gotten my share of handmade goods from my mother, and some of the Fashionista clothes just didn't look that well made.

"Nina, no one looks at stitching or how well it's made. If it's cute, it's cute. Here, take these." That was Sheena's response. She handed me a pair of jeans. "You need a pair of Apple Bottoms. They are made for us, you know, to fit our hips and our butts," she said as she shook hers.

I guess Sheena hadn't noticed that I was built like a fine piece of cardboard.

"Okay, sporty, time for the next round of fun, fun, fun!" Oscar said. "Try on each outfit that we've carefully selected and come out to show us. Don't forget your Tyra strut!"

"Oh, I can't wait to see you in the outfits I picked out,"

Sheena said. The new fabulous trio—Oscar, Sheena, and Nessa—pulled up chairs and waited for me to transform.

Inside the dressing room, I was overwhelmed by the number of clothes. Most looked like things that Sheena wore. But I had to stay focused. I thought about Jeffrey saying "Damn, girl, bring your fine self over here." So I slipped off Nina and pulled on a tight denim miniskirt with an even tighter baby tee.

I walked out to applause like I was on one of those extreme makeover shows. I could hear the announcer say, "Here comes Nina, she's gone from pitiful pauper to dashing diva!"

"Wow, Ms. Thang. Look at how you've instantly changed!" Oscar said.

"That's more like it," added Sheena. "That should be your outfit for your date."

"Cute, cute, cute!" Nessa agreed.

I looked in the mirror and didn't smile. I didn't frown, either. Definitely not me, but I was getting used to doing things that were out of character.

"What do you think?" Oscar asked.

"It's in fashion," I replied, trying to mask my disappointment. What the hell did I know about what was fashionable?

With Sheena's and Nessa's style and Oscar's professional help—although he was probably only a year or two older than me, so I wasn't sure of his consultant credentials—I walked away from the store with a pair of stretch, low-rider boot-cut jeans, two baby tees, and a denim pencil skirt. Sheena said we caught a serious sale.

I was tired like I'd just run three miles with my cross country group, but the journey continued. Next stop: DSW shoe warehouse.

"I go crazy in here," Sheena told me. But I didn't think she could be any wilder than her frenetic behavior in Fashionista.

I was wrong.

Sheena was a madwoman! Mad, I tell you! She was grabbing shoes, carting boxes upon boxes, and fighting over discounts in the clearance section. A few times, she pushed Nessa and me out of the way. I had to nicely step in between Sheena and a stocky, linebacker-shaped girl to defuse a fight over yellow sandals. The shoes were pretty hideous, so I wasn't sure why Sheena wanted to fight over them. Power shoe shopping was exhausting, but I can't lie, I had a ball. I left the store with a new pair of black BCBG boots and Nine West flats. The moment I got home I was throwing out the Jesus sandals.

We headed to our last destination: the Fly Stop hair salon. This place was as foreign to me as Disney World, a place that A&I believed celebrated the worst of capitalism. Yeah, they could be that uptight.

The only impression I had of a hair salon—wait, scratch that—I didn't have any impressions of beauty shops. My mother had taken care of my hair since I was a child. She taught me how to twist it, condition it, and manage a healthy head without ever having to pay someone else.

The Fly Stop was bustling on Saturday afternoon. The minute we walked in, all eyes zoomed in on my Afro. I took it out of the ponytail during the shopping madness. The salon smelled like some of the chemicals my father used to renovate apartments. Amy would probably have described the décor as "cheap chic." There was a long, comfy sofa in the corner that I was sure wasn't real leather. A glass table covered with magazines in front of the sofa had gold painted legs. Chandeliers hanging from the ceiling looked like they were made of fancy plastic. Cheap chic.

We walked over to the counter and the receptionist looked up at me like I had just escaped from the zoo.

"What's up, Tasha?" said Sheena. "This is my girl, Nina. She's here to see Maxine."

Nessa took a seat while rapping along to her iPod. She pulled out her red single-subject notebook that was covered with cartoon-character stickers and started composing rhymes.

"What is Maxine going to do with that?" Tasha asked with an attitude.

"She's gonna perm it!" Sheena responded with just as much attitude. "Now can you get on your J-O-B and tell her she's here." The receptionist rolled her eyes and walked over to a stylist with gold streaks that matched her gold apron. She was pulling big plastic rollers out from a little girl's hair who was playing with a bushy-haired Barbie doll. But who was I to talk about wild-looking hair?

I looked around at the women in different stages of hair metamorphosis. Some had white cream on their heads. Others were seated in high chairs with a hairdresser combing their freshly styled dos. Two women under hair dryers were holding a very loud conversation and strained to hear each other. I was fascinated that I could walk in with hair that was thick and free and walk out with straight, bouncy hair.

Straight. Bouncy. The thought of drastically changing my hair crept up my back and crawled around my neck. I began to itch and squirm. Had I really thought about what I was about to do? I hadn't even discussed it with my mother. A&I would be extremely disappointed. I loved my non-bouncy hair. It was all I knew. And now it could be gone forever? I didn't know how to care for straight hair. It seemed difficult, time-consuming. The heat from the dryers made it hard to breathe.

I...couldn't...do...it.

Before I passed out, I pleaded, "Sheena, maybe they could do something not so permanent to straighten my hair."

"Not ready to get a perm?" Sheena asked, as if she understood.

I shook my head forcefully.

She looked disappointed, but said, "All right, that might be too big of a step for you. Let me see if they got a hot comb in this place." Sheena inquired with Maxine, who shook her head.

She returned to talk with Tasha, the angry receptionist.

"No hot comb? I've seen little girls get their hair straightened up in here before." I could tell Sheena was about to go off. Luckily, before she battled with Tasha, a stylist who didn't have anyone in her chair, stepped forward, lifted a hot comb, and said she could straighten my hair.

It was like she raised a black fist in the air during a sixties protest, I felt the power. *Whew. That was close.* I felt my pressure rising. This was the perfect compromise. A relaxer was *too* permanent.

"Okay, thanks. " Sheena directed me to the stylist. Although I found out later that she was hesitant to let Cynthia do my hair because there was a reason no one was sitting in her chair.

After getting my hair washed and blow-dried, I was completely calm. The shampoo girl massaged my head and I almost fell asleep. I'd come back just to have her wash my hair.

But the show had only begun for the rest of the women in the salon. As Cynthia straightened my hair with that hot apparatus that could double as a deadly weapon, all eyes were stuck to the girl with the half 'fro. I tried to ignore the dozen eyes peering at me.

I opened an issue of *XXL* magazine that Cynthia had given me. I figured I should spend the time wisely and brush up on my hip-hop knowledge.

Here's what I eventually added to "How to Be Down":

Grow a butt or some hips (work on becoming Eye Candy)
Get a weave
Get some bling
Get a hustle

Learn how to do the Chicken Noodle Soup dance
Learn lyrics to all Jay-Z songs
Rappers to know: T.I., Lil Wayne, The Game, Dipset
(this is a group)

Sheena was finished and came over to watch me. Her hair was wrapped around her head and it was held together by hundreds of bobby pins. It looked like it hurt. I still didn't know if it was her hair or not.

"Hold your ear," the stylist told me.

"Damn, girl, I never realized how nappy your hair was," Sheena said. "But she is workin' it out. It's gettin' straight."

Before I knew it, the stylist had swirled my chair around and I was staring at a totally different person in the mirror.

Straight. Bouncy. Beautiful. My hair hung past my shoulders. I had never realized how long it was. I flipped it back and forth like Jill and Amy used to do. The women in the salon who had watched my transformation flooded me with compliments.

"Wow!" Nessa said. "Your hair looks amazing. You look like Lil' Kim on her last album cover." I did look sensational. Where was a photographer when you needed one? I looked like one of the models in *XXL,* just with more clothes on.

"You do look like a different chick," Sheena said. "Damn, I'm good." She gave herself the credit.

I felt different, too. In the words of Lil' Junebug, one of the rappers profiled in *XXL,* "That's what's up."

* * *

We went to grab a bite to eat back at the mall. Nessa and I ate greasy French fries and fattening hamburgers on plastic tables while we sat in uncomfortable plastic chairs. Sheena got a salad and asked me if I knew how to deal with guys.

"Do you know how to even holla at a guy?" Sheena asked.

"What do you mean?" I needed a translator.

"Watch and learn." Sheena got up from the table, looked around the mall with a cheetah's gaze, and attacked the first prey she thought suitable.

Everything about him was oversized. His hat. His shirt. His necklace. His jeans. His boots. He was sinking in his own clothes. She flagged him down and waved him to come to the table. He pointed at himself to clarify that she was indeed talking to him.

"Yeah, you," Sheena responded.

"What's up, ladies?" Supersize said.

"What's up with you?" Sheena asked.

"Nothin', just came to pick up a few things." He lifted his bags as evidence.

"Whatsyourname?" Sheena asked it so quickly it came out as one word.

"Jason," he said, making his voice an octave deeper. Nessa and I tried to conceal our giggles.

"Jason, do you got a girl?"

"Uh, you know, I don't have a wifey, if that's what you mean. I'm just chillin', doin' my thing."

"Where you go to school?"

"Baldwin," he answered, this time making a nasty gesture with his tongue and lips.

"Well, can I get your phone number?" Just like that. She didn't even know him and she asked to call him.

"Oh, mos def," he said as they whipped out their cell phones and she added his number to her pink phone.

"Cool, I'll give you a call sometime this week," she said.

Jason looked like he didn't want to leave, but Sheena dismissed him. It was really quite amazing to watch.

Nessa and I burst into laughter.

As Sheena sat down, she looked for Jason's number and erased it from her phone.

"Why'd you do that?" I asked.

"'Cause I ain't callin' him, I was just showin' you how to holla. I was not feelin' him, those boots he had on were like three years old."

"See, with guys, you got to take control. They like that. They like to be the ones to fall back for a change instead of always havin' to pursue us."

"Take control, got it."

"But honestly, I wouldn't say this if Vivica was here," Sheena said, "I think you and Jeffrey make a cute little couple."

"Is she mad at me or something?" I asked.

"Vivica is just mad moody," Nessa said as she stabbed a fry into a pool of ketchup. I felt relieved that I wasn't the only one who noticed.

"I think she struggles with being light-skinned," Nessa concluded. "She's always talking about it, like it's some illness."

"Like that," Nessa said as she pointed to a black boy and a white girl holding hands. "She'd have a fit if she saw that. I think she has self-esteem issues."

It made sense. And now I felt bad for Vivica.

CHAPTER 18

тhe moment I walked into the house, and not a second later, my mother screamed like she just witnessed a horrific crime. It was one of those high-pitched, disturb your eardrum shrieks.

"What have you done?" she asked hysterically. My father ran from the kitchen to respond to the commotion. He stopped like he was about to run into a crime scene.

"Isaiah, look! Look at what Nina did. Her hair, her beautiful hair is ruined!" My mother was now in tears. She grabbed her dreads to check if they were still there.

"Annie, calm down." My father walked over and hugged me. He smoothed my silky hair, put his palms on my cheeks and kissed my forehead.

"You're beautiful," he whispered.

My mother looked like she was going to fall flat onto the hand-stitched rug behind her. Usually when my mother was angry, she'd get a few forehead lines, which helped me judge the intensity of her mood. This time, there weren't any lines.

Her forehead was just burning red. I could only imagine what that meant. On second thought, I didn't want to.

She stormed into the family room, snatched a picture album, grabbed me by my arm, pulled me down on the couch, and began a rather torturous history of my hair.

"Since you were born," she said between sniffles, "your hair has been kept pristine, unadulterated.

"See, this is you at five years old with the cutest Afro I've ever seen." I looked at my father and he shrugged his shoulders.

"This is you at seven years old with little braids, so sweet." She turned and her eyes burned a hole into me.

"Why? Why would you do this to yourself?"

I wanted to say, "Ma, it's just hair, it's not like I'm telling you I'm pregnant," but I wasn't stupid. Instead, I said, "Mommy, it's not a perm. It's just straightened with a hot comb. I didn't want such a drastic change. I do love my natural hair. I just wanted a different look."

My father started laughing. My mother silenced him with a look.

"All that carrying on, Annie, and it isn't even permed! Our daughter is growing up and finding herself. We have to respect the young woman she is becoming."

My mother wiped her tears with the sleeve of her shirt. "I don't understand why you felt that you had to change your hair. Or get new clothes. It's like you want to be a different person."

She's the one who had transported me from my happy little life in New Jersey to bring me down to the city that

XXL referred to as "the concrete jungle" in their review of the Baltimore-based show *The Wire*.

"I'm just doing what you told me to do, embrace change." That seemed to settle her a little. But I still knew it wasn't a good time to whip out the baby tee that said "Don't You Wish Your Girlfriend Was Hot Like Me." It was a cue to go upstairs and not be seen or heard but wallow in the tragedy that was my new life.

I marched to my bedroom, making sure not to stomp, because that would be asking for trouble. In my room, I dived into my pillows. The day had been a whirlwind like one of those carnival rides and I was beginning to feel sick.

CHAPTER 19

I was scheduled to help Vivica Saturday morning. I tried everything to get out of it, even bribery.

"Mommy, if you don't make me do this, I promise to attend any college you want me to, including Howard." She knew I didn't want to go there. She was helping me unpack the boxes in my room that were making it hard for me to move around.

"While I appreciate your enticing offer, I don't understand why you are so reluctant to help a friend."

"She doesn't like me." A&I couldn't fathom the idea that someone would dislike their perfect creation. They thought they could convert lost souls to believe in the goodness of Nina Parker.

After we finished unpacking my room, my mother told me it was time to go over to Vivica's.

Mr. Lamont answered the door. Every time I saw him he was dressed like he was going to work. I liked that, but I wondered if he ever threw on sweatpants to relax.

"Hi, Nina," he said. "I didn't recognize you at first with the new do. Come in." I walked into the living room, which looked like it could be in anyone's house. The neutral brown carpeting, plain walls, and mandatory sofa made it feel very common. But maybe they were still acquiring things for their new space. The dining room was empty and the kitchen was filled with boxes. The smell of pancakes lingered and made me remember that I hadn't eaten breakfast. Mr. Lamont led me to Vivica's room and thanked me for being a lifesaver.

When Vivica saw my hair, the first thing she did was tilt her head and squint her eyes. I wasn't sure what that meant. Then she said it looked nice. She looked nice just to be lounging around the house. A denim dress, tights, and shoes that didn't look like they'd been broken in yet. I wondered where she was going. I still had on the sweatpants and T-shirt that I'd worked in that morning.

Vivica was definitely one of those girly girls, but her bright pink room confirmed it. The walls, throw rugs, bedding, lamps, furniture, all pink. I felt like I was inside a piece of strawberry bubble gum.

My eyes zoomed in on a copy of *One Hundred Years of Solitude* by Gabriel García Márquez on her antique wooden nightstand, one of the few nonpink objects in the room.

"Are you reading this?" I asked excitedly. "I've wanted to read it."

"Uh…" She paused and thought about her answer. I watched her play out an internal conflict. "Yeah, my father gave it to me."

"Do you like it?"

"Yeah, I do," she said regretfully.

"So you want to get started?" I asked. That's when she closed her bedroom door and walked over to me.

"Look, I don't need tutoring," she said.

"I know, trust me. I'm just here if you have any questions." I didn't want her to feel bad.

"I failed on purpose," she revealed.

"Why?" My mouth was wide open.

"Because everyone thinks the program is for clowns. Plus I don't want my girls to think I'm sellin' out."

"Sheena and Nessa wouldn't stop being your friend because you're in a college preparatory program." I couldn't believe she was hiding her intelligence and purposely sabotaging her opportunities for advancement to fit in. I mean, I wanted friends, but I wasn't about to fail tests to get them.

"I've known them a lot longer than you have," she snapped.

"So you're going to fail out of the program?" I wanted to know if that was her plan.

"Yep." She hopped onto her bed and began swinging her feet. "But my father can't know. So we can just hang out for an hour or so."

"Hang out? Okay." I was skeptical.

Then she said something that I didn't expect.

"Look, I want to apologize for how I've acted towards you. I've been going through a lot lately. But that's no reason to take it out on you." Her diction was perfect. She sounded like another girl.

"You have been unfriendly towards me and I didn't know why. It's reassuring to know that it wasn't me."

"No, not at all." She shoved me slightly. "My mother's been trying to get in contact with me after five years and it's been upsetting to deal with. You know? I'm not ready for that. I'm not ready to talk to her."

"That must be hard," I said.

"It is, but I don't really want to talk about that anymore." She smoothed her ponytail. "You know, I'm not mad or anything about you and Jeffrey. I mean, he and I never hooked up. He has his preferences and I'm not one of them." Her green eyes looked sincere.

Our slate was being cleaned.

"My bad, I didn't ask you if you wanted anything. Are you hungry?" I rubbed my stomach and nodded greedily.

While she was in the kitchen, I tried to imagine what it would be like if my mother left and then after several years tried to come back into my life. I shuddered at the thought and realized how strong Vivica was.

She brought back two pancakes and a glass of orange juice.

"Sheena told me that you got something real cute to wear tomorrow. Are you excited?"

"I'm nervous," I admitted, and we laughed like old friends.

"I can help you," she offered. "I've known Jeffrey for a few years. He likes a certain type of girl."

"Like what?" I asked as I chomped on the best pancakes I'd ever had.

"I'd call them ghetto princesses. Like Sheena, but not so over-the-top." Her index finger tapped her cheek.

"Really?" I was in disbelief.

"His last girlfriend, Tatiana, put the 'fab' in ghetto fabulous. She broke up with him and broke his heart. So he's been looking to fill her role ever since. I know I joke with you about being white, but you may want to tone down your inner white girl just for tomorrow."

My eyebrows curled and I wondered about the best way to do that.

Reading my mind, Vivica said, "I can give you a few pointers. I mean, you have a great start with the hair. It looks much better. And I'm sure your outfit is off the hook."

I took out my black and white composition book and decided to take notes. That's what nerds do. I flipped through the pages looking for an empty one and landed on "How to Be Down."

"What is this?" Vivica asked.

I flipped the page quickly, but she turned it back. She then read "How to Be Down" aloud. She couldn't get through the first few entries without laughing.

I wasn't sure if I should laugh with her, rip my notebook out of her hand and storm out, or silently sulk.

I went for silently sulk.

After a few minutes of listening to her Miss Piggy laugh, Vivica finally said, "No, for real, you've got some true stuff on here. I don't mean to laugh, but it's kind of funny that you are keeping a list on how to be black."

"It's not about being black," I said defensively.

"Don't be angry, Nina. I'm sorry for laughing, I really

am. Look, I want to help you." She sat back down next to me and patted my hand. "I know you're very smart, but sometimes you can say some really boring things. Try to think about what you say before you say it. Ask yourself if what you're about to say will bore Jeffrey." I took meticulous notes. "He's into basketball, hip-hop, and thug life."

"Thug life?" I didn't peg Jeffrey as a thug.

"Yeah. I mean, he's clean-cut but he's definitely a thug. And he's looking for a ride-or-die chick, you know?"

No, I didn't know. But I wrote it down anyway.

"So talk about being down with the streets, act like you know what time it is. Tell him you can help stack dough and that you'd be down for whateva."

"Down for whateva? Are you sure?"

"I'm positive."

Then she demonstrated what she called "hood mannerisms" that I could do on my date. After about an hour, I felt much more versed in toning down my inner white girl and amplifying my ride-or-die chick.

As Vivica walked me to the door, I asked her to keep my list between us.

"Trust me," she said.

And that's what I did. I trusted Vivica.

CHAPTER 20

jeffrey arrived promptly at five-fifteen. From my room, I could hear him say "Hello, sir" when my father opened the door. Then he introduced himself and asked if I was available. He had my father at hello.

I on the other hand, was a wreck. I'd started getting ready at 2 p.m. Matt and I had gone out but not on real dates. We'd go to a museum with his parents, hang out playing cards, or watch some nature show on public television.

Although I knew Jeffrey was cool, deep down inside, I was nervous to be alone with him. What if I said something stupid? Something too white, like Vivica had warned me? Before I put on my pencil skirt, black tights, BCBG boots, and a black and purple baby tee, the outfit that Sheena had coordinated for me, I reviewed "How to Be Down" and yesterday's notes like it was moments before a big test.

Not to mention that I didn't get much sleep because I was too busy protecting my hair by hanging my head off the side of the bed. I didn't know how straight-haired girls did it.

Since Friday, I avoided water like the plague and took baths instead of risking some tragic accident in the shower. But even with so much precaution, I couldn't get my hair to fall like it did when I walked out of the salon two days ago.

After making Jeffrey suffer with A&I for ten minutes, I emerged. And luckily I did, because they were discussing Haitian independence.

My mother flashed me a smile that said she was impressed. My father patted Jeffrey on the shoulder after calling him "son."

"Wow," Jeffrey said. "You look different."

Gabrielle's was a stylish hole in the wall that doubled as a jazz club. Posters of famous black musicians adorned the brick walls, some with signatures. As we walked, the wooden floor reverberated with the sound of the famous feet that had marched on it. An older woman sitting on a flimsy stool took ten dollars from Jeffrey after asking him how his parents were doing.

I had never been in a jazz club before, but I'd always imagined that it would look just like this. Smoke filled the air and gave the club a feeling of cool. Being inside it, I felt cool. I felt my inner white girl being silenced.

Black people of varying ages occupied the twenty or so seats that the club could hold. We grabbed the only available table, close to the front of the small stage.

"Did you relax your hair?" he asked me. I was surprised he knew the right terminology. "I have two sisters," he explained.

"Uh, no, I just straightened it." It felt good to be paid attention to.

"It looks nice," he said.

But then he said, "I liked your natural hair, too, though."

"My bush?" I asked. "Yeah, right." He couldn't possibly.

"No, I thought it was cool." He dropped his head slightly. "I come here a lot with my parents," Jeffrey admitted. "It's like an institution in Baltimore. I think it's been here since the fifties."

"Wow, there's probably a lot of history here," I said. Jeffrey didn't respond. A cue to limit my nerdy comments.

"I've been coming to this poetry series for a few months now. It's pretty good."

"Do you ever perform?" I asked.

A waitress with a beautiful large Afro came around and Jeffrey ordered us two Sprites. For a moment, I missed my hair.

"Oh no, I'm not a writer," he said.

"Right, cause you're too busy handlin' the streets," I gave him one of the looks I'd practiced with Vivica.

"Uh, right. So how are you doing at Maplewood? Do you feel like you're fitting in better?"

"Yeah, definitely. My girls, Sheena, Vivica, and Nessa have been showin' me the ropes. You know. I've been puttin' in a lot of work on the block."

Jeffrey's neck snapped back. I thought he was impressed. "What was your other school like?"

"Just a bunch of white people." I kind of lied and kind of didn't.

"But you had a lot of friends there, right?" he asked.

"Man, those white girls weren't really my friends. But my girls Sheena, Vivica, and Nessa, they get me the way those chicks in Rainhaven never could." I finished my soda in three large gulps. Being nervous made me thirsty.

"I like Maplewood much better 'cause I get a chance to be around my people, know what I'm sayin'." I didn't know what I was saying, but I continued.

"I was brainwashed in Rainhaven. A white girl trapped in a black girl's body. But now I know what's up."

Throughout my troubled monologue, Jeffrey sucked on his straw and listened. Then he started playing with the paper that the straw came with. He was no longer looking at me.

Luckily, a short man with a large cranium jumped on-stage to "get the poetry party started."

We clapped for the first poet, who performed for more than twenty minutes. Next, an older gentleman with short, pointy dreadlocks, got on stage and told a few jokes that I thought were funny, but I didn't laugh. He recited a collection of very intense haikus that addressed urban decay, black empowerment, and self-love. Some of them I didn't fully comprehend, but the ones I did understand were pretty powerful.

Jeffrey didn't clap. He stared at the stage like he was trying to decipher a puzzle.

"That was wack," I uttered with extra cool.

"Really, you thought so?" Jeffrey asked.

"Yeah, it was soft. He needs to bring the hotness." I spit out a Sheena statement.

"I thought you'd appreciate it," he said, confused.

"Naw. I mean, if he was talkin' about, you know, sur-vivin' in the streets or stackin' dough, then maybe I could get wit it."

"What's up with you, Nina? You seem mad different."

"I'm good. I just don't think you really had a chance to get to know me. I'm more down than you think. I'm mean, I'm down for whateva." I gave him the sexy look Vivica and I had practiced in her mirror.

"Really?" Jeffrey asked in disbelief.

"Oh, I'm really real." It was like I was addicted to the cool and couldn't stop.

The next poet impersonated Bush in a poem that ripped through the President's administration. It was witty and engaging.

"What did you think?" Jeffrey asked after the poet was finished.

"Wack." I actually didn't know any other slang words that meant *bad*. Because I knew that *bad* actually meant *good*.

"Wow, okay." Jeffrey kept his thoughts to himself.

I continued acting like a ride-or-die chick without notic-ing how uncomfortable Jeffrey was growing. Until, I asked to see his thug life tattoo. Vivica told me he had one that he loved showing. That was literally the last straw.

"Vivica told me you wanted to date a thug, but I thought she was lying. I thought you were different. Interesting. Unique. And interested in actually getting to know a person instead of judging them or placing stereotypes on them. But now I see that she was right about you." That was the last thing he said to me. He took me home in silence.

CHAPTER 21

I bypassed A&I's questions by declaring that I didn't want to talk about it.

I was hysterical when I called Jill. So much so that she didn't recognize my voice at first.

"Are you okay?" she asked immediately.

"No, I'm not okay. I'm an idiot," I cried into the phone. My tears wetted the mouthpiece.

Between sniffles and uncontrollable chest heaves, I told her how I blew it with Jeffrey. I told her how Vivica had lied to him and lied to me. I told her how stupid I felt for acting like a fool and for allowing myself to be treated like one.

"Oh, Nina." I imagined her grabbing my head and leaning it on her shoulder. "Breathe. I know it seems like you'll never recover from this, but you will. You are one of the most genuine people I know. I've learned so much from you about character, friendship, and trust. You are going through a rough time right now and questioning yourself. But that's really because the people around you are confused and bringing you into their messy lives. This Vivica girl doesn't sound like a person you should associate with. Jeffrey sounds like a good guy, and I'm sure if you apologize to him and explain why you acted the way you did, he'll forgive you in a heartbeat."

"But she played me and I walked right into her trap. I don't understand why she hates me. And now Jeffrey hates me." I didn't bother to blow my nose. I let the mucus drip down onto my new shirt.

"I know it seems like it now, but trust me, it's not the end of the world." Jill's reassuring voice pacified me and helped to end my crying frenzy.

She told me she'd call tomorrow. I wiped my tears to try to see where I went wrong. I wanted Vivica to be my friend instead of seeing her for the troubled person she was. And the person I really wanted to be my friend, Jeffrey, I had isolated with my insecurity. Now I knew how to lose friends.

CHAPTER 22

everyone knew about "How to Be Down." The next day in school it was the running joke that I needed instructions on how to be black. I got three bogus lists from various classmates. I didn't expect Vivica to keep her word, but it still felt like a sharp knife in the back. She, of course, acted like nothing happened and had the bloody nerve to ask me about my date with Jeffrey.

That morning—and every morning—that week, I took the 7:13 bus so that I would cut down on the number of times I had to run into Vivica and Jeffrey.

I spent the day praying for invisibility. My prayers went unanswered.

Ms. Jimu caught me after English class because she suspected something was going on. I didn't go into too much detail because I knew I'd start crying and wasn't sure if I'd be able to stop. I told her everything was fine. Just a little harmless teasing.

"When I first arrived in the United States, people expected me to act a certain way because I was African," Ms. Jimu said. "They—and when I say 'they,' I mean some black and white people—treated me with a cool inferiority. It hurt that people who looked like me could make me feel like I was less of a person." She just stared straight ahead.

"It was really hard to adjust. But I can say that it was an experience that made me a stronger and wiser person. You may emerge from all of this with some scars, but you will be a better person from it."

And she walked off, leaving me to bask in her words.

During lunch, Sister Souljah gave me impromptu black history lessons. Nessa and Sheena asked me why I had deserted them to sit at another table. I directed them to Vivica.

CHAPTER 23

After school on Wednesday I sat on the front steps of my building to get some fresh air and fresh perspective. There was no way I wanted to show my disgraced face at today's competition. Plus I no longer wanted to be on the team. I was confused. And alone. I saw Jeffrey today and he'd ignored me with such vigor that I thought my wish for invisibility had come true. I pulled out my book and looked at "How to Be Down." I contemplated ripping it up, but instead I decided to write a poem to try to make sense of everything. I thought that's what Nikki or Gwendolyn would do.

While I was trying to get the words right, a white lady approached the building but didn't get any closer than about ten feet. She was just staring at it. Her long trench coat and her blue pumps made her look like she had a career. But then I thought she might have been mentally disabled, because she would walk a couple of steps and then retreat. Walk a couple of steps, then retreat. She kept shaking her head and taking deep breaths.

It looked like my cue to take my behind into the house. But maybe she was a prospective tenant wanting to see an apartment.

"May I help you?" I spoke loudly so that she could hear me and I wouldn't have to get any closer to her.

"Uh, maybe you can. I'm looking for the Lamont residence. This is the correct building, right?" She pointed up.

"Yes, are you looking for Mr. Lamont?" I asked.

"Yes. Yes and no. I'm also looking for Vivica, Vivica Lamont." She came closer and looked at me.

It was the green eyes that gave her away. They were the same as Vivica's. Just older and sadder.

"Are you Vivica's mother?" I asked.

She nodded while smoothing the front of her dress, a way to keep her hands busy.

"She's not here right now." I said bitterly. She was at the poetry competition, probably getting a standing ovation, while I was sitting on hard steps that were making my butt hurt.

"Oh, okay. Um, I'll just come back. I didn't think she'd be home. I, uh…it's not necessary to leave a message. I'll just come back. Yes, I'll just come back at another time."

Just like that, Vivica's mother, the woman she hadn't seen in five years, scurried away like a mouse in daylight.

And just like that, anger spoke to me. It told me to run like a track star to the bus stop. It told me to board the first one that came.

It bounced words around in my head like musical notes. Jeffrey Black Not enough Thug White boy White girl

Biracial Insecure Sabotage Real Fake Down Race Racist Inter-
racial Frontin' Betrayal Trust Friendship Green Eyes Vivica

It told me to take out my notebook and scribble them
down. And without my realizing it, a poem came. Anger
aided and abetted my creativity.

It told me to hop off the bus and run into school. It told
me to frown at Vivica when she smiled at me.

It told me to get onstage after Sister Souljah performed.

I was sweating. Panting. I caught my breath and wiped
my face with the sleeve of my Rainhaven T-shirt.

Anger told me to dedicate my poem to one of the realest
fake girls I ever met. It told me to shout-out Vivica.

Then anger dripped from my mouth and cascaded into
a puddle on the stage as I performed:

What's the deal, *mami?*
What's really real?
Your green eyes
That you use to despise
Everything not black enough
Made a fuss about
The way I talk
But hear this
Miss Black or should I call you Ms. White?
'Cause your mommy who's
The color of Bush's house
Stopped by looking
For her Spanish-looking
Daughter with the green eyes

That she uses to despise
Everything not black enough
She gave me, the foolish black-white girl,
A message
To give to you
Let me recite it
Your white mommy
Loves you
When will you start
Loving yourself
Made me feel bad
About being me
Because you hate you
Is this poem
Hard enough
For you
Is it the real
you seek
the real you
claim to be?
'Cause your eyes
They…will…always…be…green

When I finished, relief hit me first. I was no longer angry.
Then, as I looked at the silent crowd, I was unsure how I
felt. I felt nothing. When Vivica ran out of the auditorium,
I watched her. I watched her run and didn't run after her.
Sheena and Nessa got up to follow her and shot me daggers
of disgust as they walked out.

But the audience, the audience roared. They loved it. They loved that I'd dissed the hell out of Vivica. They loved that the poem was hardcore. They felt it. They felt me.

At that moment, I hated myself. I walked slowly offstage and looked up to see Jeffrey staring at me. I looked away because I needed a rainbow and he wasn't smiling.

I became a different person on that stage. I let anger occupy me and navigate me to a place that I shouldn't have gone.

CHAPTER 24

when I got home, I confessed to A&I what I had done. The guilt wrapped tight around my neck and threatened to strangle me.

Their faces screamed disappointment but I deserved it. I actually craved their disapproval.

"It wasn't your place to tell the world about Vivica's background." My mother was furious but she didn't raise her voice. "If she didn't feel comfortable broadcasting it, you should have respected that, even if you felt that she was being a hypocrite." She was right. I knew she was right.

"I just feel like all of sudden I don't know who I am. Have you ever felt like that?" Tears choked my words, making them nearly incomprehensible.

"Nina, you've just been taken away from everything that you know and thrown into everything that you don't know," my mother said as she smoothed my smooth hair. "But you have to remember that throughout it all, you are still Nina. Naturally you're going to grow as a person, but at the core, you'll always be Nina and no one can take that away from you."

"But who am I? I'm black. But I'm not black," I shot back.

"James Baldwin once wrote, 'I don't like people who like me because I'm a Negro.' Do you know what he meant by that, Nina?" my father asked.

My head was now in my hands on the kitchen table.

"He meant that he wanted people to like him for who he is. The person inside. Being black isn't easy. It's especially not easy when you push past stereotypes and embrace individualism." My father motioned for me to come to him. He hugged me the way only a father can.

"We want to apologize to you for trying to pin our insecurities on you," he said. "Because sometimes we aren't accepted by our race, we wanted to protect you from that, by making sure you engaged with black people." My father exhaled.

"You already had a good head on your shoulders," my mother continued. "You weren't consumed by race like us. And we should have prepared you more, without sacrificing who you are." We were all crying for acceptance.

That night I washed my hair, and in the water, I searched for Nina.

CHAPTER 25

the next day at school was triple more miserable than the first one. I saw the Big Three. I saw Jeffrey. I was alone, again.

Even Ms. Jimu looked at me with a mixture of pity and disappointment during homeroom. Sister Souljah congratulated me for exposing a fake sista. Jay told me that he didn't think I had it in me to "bring the ruckus." I wanted to see Vivica's green eyes but she never looked at me.

"You received quite a response to your poem yesterday," Ms. Jimu said after homeroom. I wondered if I was the only kid that she showed concern for. Was I really that pitiful?

"Yeah, I brought the hotness," I said. The sarcasm came easy.

"I wish I could have persuaded you not to do the poem," she said sadly.

"At that moment, the way I was feeling, I don't think anyone could have dissuaded me. But I realize what I did was wrong, and I am going to try to make things better."

"I'm sure you will," Ms. Jimu said. I could tell she believed in me.

It took me a few days to decide how I would apologize to Jeffrey. I ended up composing a letter because I couldn't face him and explain myself at the same time. I gave him the letter after school. He asked me what it was and I couldn't look into his eyes. I stared at the cracked concrete and asked him to please read it. I felt him nod as he walked past.

It said:

Dear Jeffrey,

You were like a breath of fresh air on my first day of school. Just the fact that you talked to me made my day easier. But you didn't just talk to me, you talked with me. I could tell that you were different and you saw in me an individual light and I will always thank you for that. Somehow between that first day of school and when we went out, I got confused about who I was. I tried to be someone else to please everyone but myself. You were right when you told me to just be me and I'd be fine. I wish I would have taken your advice.

I am truly embarrassed by my behavior in the past week. While there is no truth in Vivica's claims (I wasn't looking for a thug), that doesn't excuse my actions. Please believe me when I say that I just wanted to get to know you. And for you to get to know me. It's unfortunate that we didn't get that opportunity. But if you are ever interested in giving me

*a second chance to be your friend, I'd welcome it with
open arms. Also, I hope you can make the final round
of the poetry competition. I hope to redeem myself.
The real me.*

   Sincerely,
   Nina

I stood in front of Vivica's door several minutes before actually knocking.

When I finally did, Mr. Lamont opened the door wearing a blue T-shirt and matching sweats. The clothes made him look different. Younger. His eyes went straight to the ground as he waited for me to speak.

"Is Vivica home?" My voice was heavy with guilt.

He shook his head and let me in without speaking. I told him I was there to try to make things right and apologize.

"That's very mature of you. I appreciate that." He knocked on Vivica's door and talked with her in her room before telling me it was okay to go in.

Vivica was lying on her bed looking at an old photo album. She had on pink children's pajamas and a scarf on her head.

"I would show you a picture of my mother, but you already know what she looks like," Vivica said without looking up. Tissues were strewn across her bed. Her nose was red and puffy.

"Remember when I asked you how your friend Jill felt to be black and white?"

"Yes," I answered softly.

"I wanted to know if she felt like I felt."

I went over to her bed and sat down.

"Do you know why my mother left?"

She didn't wait for me to respond. She didn't want me to.

"Because her family disowned her. I've never met my grandmother, uncles, aunts, no one. They never wanted me to be born. Can you believe that? In the nineties people still felt that way?" She laughed, but not because it was funny.

"How does it feel to be me? Black kids don't want to hang with me because they think I'm not black enough. Black girls think I'm too light-skinned and hate on me. White kids just look at me as another black girl. I spent the majority of my childhood alone." She flipped through the pages of the album, not concentrating on any one image.

"After my mother left and my father and I moved to Baltimore, I made a decision. I was going to be black." She looked up and pointed her finger in the air for emphasis. "I was going to erase the white parts of me like chalk. I was going to be the blackest black girl I could be. And it was working for a while. I finally made some friends. But I always felt incomplete. Then you came, and you didn't try to be anything but yourself. You openly admitted to having white friends and a white boyfriend. I was jealous that you seemed to be comfortable in your skin. You made me realize that I didn't know how to be black because I didn't know how to be myself. And I hated you for it."

I couldn't say anything. I just listened.

"I deserved to be exposed, to be put on blast. I'd become a terrible person who didn't even like to look in the mirror anymore."

"No, you didn't deserve it," I said.

"No, I did. The only problem is now that I can be myself, I have no idea how to."

That's when she pulled out a notebook and flipped to a page that read at the top, "How to Be Myself."

CHAPTER 26

"This is the final judging round to determine who will be on Maplewood's inaugural poetry team. We have fifteen contenders and eight slots, so I don't have to tell you that the competition is steep. I will make the decision after the last poet performs." Ms. Jimu wished everyone luck before leaving the stage.

The auditorium was filled to capacity, like this was a mandatory assembly. Word spread like rumors around the school about the personal battles raging at the competition.

I sat alone, although I would have been welcome to sit with the Big Three. I needed time out. Ever since that day at Vivica's house, she and I had become closer, even though we hadn't spoken much since then. She needed time out as well.

After Jay and Nessa recited poems that guaranteed them spots on the team, Vivica and I were the last to perform. This must have been strategic placement by Ms. Jimu to either avoid drama during the middle of the competition or to keep the audience in suspense to the end.

The last time I was onstage, I was driven by anger. This time, I was driven by purpose. I stepped up to the microphone and could tell that the audience wanted the hotness. So I brought it.

You tryin' to be down?
Peep this
Well you goin' need
10 cups of hotness
Don't mix it
Just keep it
On you at all times
Make sure you know who rhymes
Best not to miss an episode
Of *106 and Park*
Whether you light or dark
Keep yo' appearance tight
But everything else
Bottled inside
If you soft
Try to hide it
And when the teacher asks a question
Remain silent
'Cause that's what's up
And being smart
Ain't
Paint a mug on your face
'Cause fake is real
And real is disrespected

If it ain't reflected
In the streets
Where you from
Oh the streets
You know the mean ones
Of Rainhaven
Jerzee
Where we bus'
Pens
Yeah I've gotten
Good at pretendin'
Only to forget
How to be me
And now I'm
Lost 'cause I tossed
Me aside to be
Down
'Cause that's what's up
But oh wait
Here's the remix
To your single mindedness
Accept me for me
Accent, bushy hair and ripped jeans
And I'll do the same
Let's change the game
And stop worryin' how to be down
And start loving to be ourselves

I didn't concentrate on the applause, although it sounded like an explosion. As I walked back to my seat, Nessa looked like a proud mother and Sheena gave me a go-girl snap. I looked down a few rows and Jeffrey flashed me a rainbow after the storm.

Vivica was already onstage with the microphone in her hand when the audience settled down. Her green eyes were closed as she began:

Sometimes I don't
Recognize my own face
This is how it feels to be invisible me
If race was erased
I'd be invisibly free
From your judgment
Tough luck
Negro girl you can't eat here
But miss you're okay
because of those green eyes
I don't say anything, I pass
but lies, little or big
Eventually become
Rattlesnakes
Cobras
Boas
Disrupting
Choking
Poisoning
Me
Lies
Short or tall

Eventually
Become
Racism
Genocide
self-hatred
Destroying
Killing
Eradicating
What is left of
Me
So you see
I'm conflicted
Too light to be down so I fake it
Too dark to pass so I just kick it
In purgatory
But I'm in control of this story
Tired of perpetrating a slicker version of me
So I'm stripping down to my essence
Like my name was Cinnamon
Releasing the tons of pressure
On my shoulders
Taking bolder steps
Towards me, myself, and I
And in time I'll smile
At how it feels to be me
The biracial prize
With the big, beautiful green eyes

I wasn't the first one to stand when Vivica was done.
Eventually, the entire auditorium was on its feet. Not

because it was hardcore, but because it was honest. Re-freshing. Bold. I was proud to call her my friend.

After she exited the stage, Vivica walked up to me with a tear in her eye. She tried to give me a pound, but I messed it up. Then she gave me a hug. And I got that right. The audience erupted again.

DOUBLE ACT

Debbie Rigaud

In loving memory of my Mummy, Viviane Rigaud
and my Dada, Madone Nicaisse.

ACKNOWLEDGMENT

Thank you to Adrienne Ingrum for this exciting opportunity. It's been great working with you. *Me daw'ase,* Bernard, for your love, support and inspiration. To Golda, my twin spirit. You understand. Shirley, Judy and Jerry—you guys are the best. And sweet thanks to Ana, Isaiah, Julia, Derek, Gregory, Xavier and Zora for teaching me more than they will ever know. Thanks, Pappy, for your musical kinship. Mummum (Lamercie)—your strength, love and humor are legendary. Jessica (Seca), I appreciate you always being my junior reporter. *Merci,* Grace, for being my muse. Thank you, Yvy, a gifted educator, for letting me speak to your students. And thanks to East Orange, New Jersey, for being the perfect setting in my personal life story.

CHAPTER 1

I studied both jump ropes as they turned. The cable ropes slapped the scuffed gym floor one at a time. Their hastening one-two, one-two rhythm kept pace with my heartbeat. Loose hair strands from my tucked ponytail swayed from the draft that the speedy rope motion spurred. The turners led the double ropes into an egg-beating frenzy. I stood alongside them and prepared to hop in when signaled.

Not wanting to break my concentration, I stole a quick glance at the competing jump rope team. I wanted to see how their jumper looked while waiting for the start signal.

My brain quickly processed her stance. The back of her shoulders looked steady and ready. Definitely not as tense as mine felt.

Come on, Mia Chambers, I scolded myself. *You just found out that you aced all your classes with straight As and yet you're letting an informal double-Dutch competition turn you into an insecure pile of blah.*

The shriek of the start whistle knocked me back to reality. I jumped in at the perfect opening, clearing both ropes. I successfully avoided either one of them. Stepping on the ropes would mean sudden death in this competition.

Once takeoff was complete, my body switched to autopilot. Imaginary springs grew underneath my heels. With as involuntary a reflex as breathing, my feet skipped and hopped rhythmically. The whirring cords formed a wall that enclosed me in a capsule. That capsule created its own intense microclimate. I owned that inner space. I felt myself becoming a force of nature with it.

While I jumped, I faced the only turner I trusted—my best friend, Stacie Morrison. After five years of jumping together, we pretty much could read each other's double-Dutch minds. I knew that if I concentrated on her rotating arms as she weaved the two rope ends, my feet would keep the pace. I pretended she was my puppeteer.

"Move up," Stacie shouted to me. "You're too far back."

I inched forward in one hop.

This trial was set up to find out which jumper lasted longer when the ropes were at top speed—me or Kendra Shelton. The team knew Stacie was our best turner at this double-rope sport. Now they were curious to identify the best speed jumper.

It was the day before the last day of school—or as I liked to put it, the eve of my last day as a freshman. Stacie, Kendra, me, and the rest of our neighborhood double-Dutch squad had carefully planned this speed jumping competition. Choosing to meet after school at East Orange City

High School's gym was the best idea. It was tough getting everyone together, but the fact that we were all students at City High made it a little easier.

Our squad was called Rope-a-Dope.

Actually, Stacie and I got the idea for both the name and the squad after watching a documentary about legendary boxer Muhammad Ali on ESPN Classic. Funny how you never know when inspiration will strike. We were struck by it on a rainy day last summer, when she and I had nothing else to do at my house but sit in the den and channel surf. As I absentmindedly clicked the remote from channel to channel, the sight of a cute face on black-and-white film jolted Stacie from her boredom.

"Hold it right there!" she said, swooning. "He is a *dime*."

"For real," I agreed. We were spellbound.

For the next hour and a half, Stacie and I watched Muhammad Ali's life story. When the narrator droned on about the charismatic fighter's inventive boxing technique called the rope-a-dope, I perked up.

"That would be a cool name for a double-Dutch squad," I breathlessly announced.

"Yeah, 'cause we're dope in the ropes," Stacie squealed, offering me her mood-ring-adorned hands to high-five.

In one swift movement, Stacie pulled out her Ideas notebook, turned to a blank page, and scribbled down our new name with a purple-ink pen. "Ropeadope."

"I think we need to throw in a hyphen here and there." I pointed at the pad, doing what comes naturally as the daughter of a Scrabble-champ, wordsmith dad.

Looking at Stacie now, I'm glad we chose that name. Each end of the ropes was wrapped several times around her knuckles like a boxer's hand wrap. The swift rope-turning motion made her upper body rock quickly from side to side, reminding me of Ali's bobbing and weaving movements in the ring.

In the year since Rope-a-Dope had started, our membership had grown from three to eight super-skillful jumpers and turners. Stacie was right. All we had to do was take Kendra on board and girls would flock to our tryouts. Kendra was like a social pied piper.

The whistle sounded again, signaling the turners to increase their turning pace. I followed suit, not feeling tired as I jumped, one foot at a time, over the ropes. From the corner of my eye, I could see that Kendra had successfully made the transition, too.

But I didn't have to sneak a peek to find out if Kendra was keeping up. I could hear the reaction of the small crowd that had formed around her.

Kendra never lacked attention. But just like McDonald's still comes out with self-promoting ads, Kendra worked at staying popular. She was the most outgoing, most outspoken sophomore at East Orange City High. And somehow, like a bunch of moths to a flame, people were drawn to her.

That explained the crowds around Kendra now.

I was just surprised that up to this point in the competition, none of her "friends" had jumped into the rope with her just to wipe her brow. After all, they were known to laugh at her jokes before she even got to the punch line!

Obsequious, my dad would call them.

But maybe they were just afraid to be the brunt of Kendra's notoriously mean jokes. They probably reasoned that it was safer to be a "friend" to her instead.

With the next whistle, the turners upgraded the pace once again. Now the one-two, one-two slaps of the ropes were going so fast, they almost happened in sync. The rope made whirring sounds like a small windstorm. I hardly had enough time to pick my feet up from the floor before having to lift them again.

It was challenging to jump at this super speedy pace. To keep up, I focused on Stacie's arms as she turned in fast motion.

With all of Kendra's fans rooting for her now, I felt like Stacie was my only supporter. Every few seconds, Stacie would nod her head once to encourage me to keep jumping. My calves were starting to cramp. I ignored it. But it was getting tougher to disregard the dull ache at the back of my neck. I had been holding my head low as I jumped. Both my turners were a lot shorter than my five-foot-five-inch height, so I was afraid that my high ponytail would clip the rope as it traveled overhead. That would be a bad way to lose.

Stacie's face suddenly beamed. She began nodding her head excitedly. I didn't catch on why at first.

"You got it, Mia," she told me as she kept turning. "You won!"

I shot a glance over to where Kendra had been jumping and saw the collapsed ropes. I stopped hopping and slapped Stacie's outstretched palm. "Good job turning," I told her and Dana, the other turner.

"Yeah, you got that," Kendra's voice boomed like she was speaking into a microphone. She stuck a lollipop in her mouth. Like a WNBA star at the free-throw line, Kendra then launched the candy wrapper right into the trash. "You got that," she repeated between sucking sounds.

She even made losing look cool.

"My legs ain't built like Daddy-Long-Legs Mia over there," she continued. Her entourage started chuckling from the moment she said "built."

Their laughter echoed in the gym.

"Sounds like something a sore loser would say," Ms. Landrieux, our school guidance counselor, who doubles as our drill team advisor said. She walked into the gym just in time to catch Kendra's comment about my legs.

"Ms. Shelton, are you here to try out for next year's drill team?" she asked Kendra, who huffed in response.

"I don't think so," Kendra shot back, obviously feeling dissed and annoyed by the loss of the social upper hand. Her brief reply was loaded with attitude. Plus her expression made it clear that she thought the drill team was corny.

"Then I'm going to have to ask only those from the drill team to remain." Ms. Landrieux's Caribbean lilt sounded pleasant even as she shooed away the moths who had stopped in to watch us double-Dutch. "If I don't see you tomorrow, have a nice summer vacation, people."

Stacie and I were on the school's drill team, so we stayed

behind as the other teammates started trickling into the gym for our final meeting of the year.

"We'll see y'all at practice tomorrow," Stacie called out to Kendra and the few other Rope-a-Dope members who were with her. It was Stacie's fourth time this hour reminding everyone. She was like Santa—she wrote a list and then checked it twice.

Our final drill team meeting of the year was bittersweet. Stacie and I were given an induction into varsity. That meant that next year, as sophomores, we would be more active members of the team.

The graduating seniors were honored for their work on the squad. Pep rallies and halftime performances at the home football games had been so much more fun because of their amazing energy and cool choreography.

I had learned a lot from them.

I had come to appreciate the drill team as a cheerleading squad with a unique approach to getting the crowd energized. I was glad to learn that they incorporated double Dutch into their halftime performances. That's one reason I was excited to come to East Orange City High.

And as the creative partner of Rope-a-Dope, I invented most of our squad's choreography and made our musical selection. So it was important for Stacie and me to get all the performance experience possible from the drill team.

Our plan was to make Rope-a-Dope a star double-Dutch squad. That meant we had to prep the squad to perform tricky athletic and dance techniques inside the egg-beating ropes the way it's done at competitions. Joining City High's highly regarded drill team was the perfect training ground for our goal to take Rope-a-Dope to the state championships. Once we won at state level, we'd be qualified to enter the premiere double-Dutch championships in Harlem, New York. There, jumpers competed from as far away as Japan! I got excited just thinking about it all.

After the meeting, we hugged the seniors goodbye and wished them good luck. As I headed out the gym with Stacie, Ms. Landrieux walked up to me.

"I need to speak with you about a private matter, Mia," she announced.

I didn't know what to think.

"Meet you outside," I told Stacie. She nodded, but looked at me quizzically as she headed to the double-door exit.

"Congratulations again on your stellar academic performance this year, Ms. Chambers," Ms. Landrieux began once Stacie was out of earshot.

"Thank you," I said cautiously. I didn't know where she was going with this conversation. *Maybe I scored a gift certificate or some prize for getting straight As,* I thought to myself. I couldn't read Ms. Landrieux's expression. She had the same pleasant lilt in her voice and the usual polite expression on her face.

I wondered what might make her snap and spit out something like "Oh nnno, you did-*ent!*"

Ms. L couldn't have been any older than 30—32 at the most, but she dressed as if she were twice her age. If the author Jane Austen had been reincarnated and come back as a black woman from the island of St. Lucia, she would have dressed and acted just like Ms. Landrieux.

"I've called a conference with your parents for tonight," she said. "We're going to discuss how we can make your high school experience a bit more challenging."

"It *is* challenging," I offered in a panic. *I hate being singled out,* I thought to myself. It was bad enough that my upbringing made me stand out. "I'm taking AP classes, and next year my extracurricular activities get more demanding since I'll be on the varsity drill team."

"You're easily excelling in your advanced placement assignments, Mia." Ms. Landrieux gingerly picked up her briefcase and zipped it closed as if to indicate that our discussion was over. "I'm recommending that you be advanced one grade in order to start your junior year this September."

It was amazing how Ms. Landrieux could sound so kind as she was shattering your hopes and dreams. Her words almost floated by me unnoticed. I had to play it back in my head as she flashed me a sweet smile. When she offered me the same "If I don't see you tomorrow, have a nice summer vacation" that she had tossed at Kendra and her crew, I didn't react. I didn't even move from the spot where I stood. The same feet that had been light as feathers as I'd jumped rope not that long ago were suddenly too heavy to lift.

Ms. Landrieux answered her cell phone and dived into a new conversation. She was too preoccupied to notice I wasn't following her out.

CHAPTER 2

ONCE I finally walked out of the gym, I saw Stacie in the hallway waiting for me. She followed her confused expression with the obvious question.

"What was *that* about?"

"She asked to speak to my parents and so they're coming tonight," I tried to make it sound like it was no big deal. But detail-needy Stacie wouldn't leave it at that.

"What do you think she wants to talk to them about?"

"I guess she wants me to take more challenging classes or something, I don't know." Desperate to change the subject, I thought of something to distract Stacie.

"You think Kendra is gonna hold it against me that she lost?"

I held the school's heavy front door, waiting for Stacie to catch up. Talking about my parent conference put her in a pensive mode, which made her walk slower. The sunny outdoors and the energy of all the students hanging out in front of the school eventually snapped her out of it.

"You know Kendra." Stacie skipped down the grand limestone stairs. "She's always got to have a chip on her shoulder—whether you or someone else put it there is beside the point."

That was true.

At the bottom of the stairs, a group of boys were looking through the newly distributed yearbook.

"Aw, yeah, I got the *ballerific* profile goin' on," Faison, a sophomore, said as he checked his picture in the book. His friend Alex gave him a soul-brother handshake to congratulate him.

"Yeah, but too bad your shape-up wasn't as tight as mine," said Alex, making reference to Faison's overgrown afro.

"That's a'ight," Faison countered. "'Cause your girl signed my yearbook like, 'Call me—Alex is going down South this summer.'"

I had to laugh at Faison's falsetto girl voice and fluttering eyelids as he imitated what Alex's fictitious girlfriend would sound and look like.

The group of boys all shouted, "Oooooh!" and cracked up.

Stacie and I were out of earshot, so we didn't hear Alex's comeback. But we caught the explosive reaction it got.

"Touché for Alex," I giggled with Stacie, looking back to catch more hand slapping among the group.

The *thump-thump-thump* of bass from a souped-up car stereo soon drowned out their voices. An SUV drove by, loudly playing the latest True MC song. Stacie and I bobbed our heads to the beat.

True MC was a recent graduate of City High and his

songs were hot on the charts. You couldn't turn on BET or watch *TRL* without catching one of his hip-hop videos. He'd taken our fair city of East Orange, New Jersey, worldwide in a way few had before.

True's good looks and clever lyrics made him a media darling. And through it all, he hadn't forgotten where he hails from.

Months ago when we'd heard that his latest video, for the song "True Life Story," would be shot locally, everyone was excited. Stacie's big brother Joss heard from his friend's cousin that the camera crews would set up on the corner of Douglas and Tubman, near the high-rise buildings Kendra lives in.

On the day of the shoot, Stacie and I searched her closet for the hottest gear we could find.

Once she had pulled together the perfect look, Stacie playfully announced: "I'm gonna be on the camera like…" and she busted an exaggerated dance move that made her look like superstar Beyoncé performing barefoot on hot coals.

I dropped to her carpeted floor, laughing.

"And then I'm gonna be like…" I said, then stood up to demonstrate one crazy spastic movement that had Stacie cracking up so hard her eyes started tearing.

Maybe Stacie and I took too long getting ready for our imagined close-up. By the time we got to the shoot, the crowd that had gathered was so thick police had to redirect traffic. The closest we could get was a block and a half away.

When the video premiered on TV a few weeks later, it

was the biggest thing to happen to East Orange—or even New Jersey—in my memory. The video was filmed with Hollywood flair. Shots of East Orange flashed on-screen as True MC rapped about the place where he'd been born and raised. Our school even got a cameo! But most of the city sites selected were the more blighted areas of the community. Nowhere represented were the fun shopping center, the parks, the friendly retirees who worked as crossing guards on almost every school zone corner, or the city's tree-lined blocks that also sprouted Victorian-style homes, like the street I lived on.

I guessed places like those wouldn't give True the street cred a rapper needed.

Still, we were excited to watch the video premiere. I watched it from the living room in Stacie's crowded home. It was like playing a game of Where's Waldo? When different locations flashed on-screen, someone tried to be the first to recognize it. Shouts of "Oh—there's the Jamaican pattie place!" or "That's over by Lettie's Hair Salon!" erupted while True repeated his hook: "This is my true life—true life story/Things ain't been too right—too right for me."

But the video's biggest sighting of all was the quick close-up shot of Kendra Shelton!

Of all the people in the crowd, cameras zoomed in on *Kendra's* face. We could all see her, plain as day. Her especially feminine facial features stood out more than usual because of her freshly lightened hair and newly waxed eyebrows. But the fixed "I wish she *would*" scowl on her face and the subtle flash of her gold tooth added that trademark street slickness to her look.

Her cameo was all anyone could talk about at school the next day.

People showered her with "Kendra, you were reppin' hard!" and "Kendra, I saw you on MTV!"

After that, more girls wanted to come to our Rope-a-Dope tryouts, just to be cool with Kendra.

How is it that someone like Kendra could be such a crowd favorite? I wondered. She wasn't anything like you'd imagine. She wasn't particularly nice. In my opinion, she was full of herself and she didn't seem to care about anyone's feelings or opinions.

Yet she just arrived on the scene where hundreds of people were crowding and found the perfect spot to stand, and a music video director spotted her. Then and there that director decided that Kendra had the image they wanted beamed out to millions of TV sets across the country, and possibly the globe. How was that for justice?

Something about her caused film editors to include her two-second clip and leave countless minutes of quality footage on the cutting room floor.

I could just imagine the editor and director discussing that decision. The conversation probably played out something like…

DIRECTOR: Stop right there. Yes, *her!* The one with the scowl on her face. She's got the look.

EDITOR: I knew it the moment I saw her.

DIRECTOR: I bet everyone loves to be around her. Heck—*I* wish I knew her!

EDITOR: Somebody should track her down and make her a star.

DIRECTOR: But it must always be known that we discovered her first.

Meanwhile, if they had seen my face in the crowd, the exchange would've gone something like...

DIRECTOR: Stop right there. Yes, *her!* Shouldn't that girl with the wide-eyed look be home rewriting entries on Wikipedia or something?

EDITOR: Yeah, remind me to call her the next time my term paper's due.

[*They both chuckle.*]

"You know, I'm kinda glad the cameras didn't zoom in on our faces that day at the video shoot." Stacie snapped me out of my daydream. She seemed to pick up that I was thinking about that day.

"Oh no?" I asked, curious. "Why not?"

Before she spoke again, she waited until we had walked past a man mowing his lawn with a loud, old-fashioned mower.

"Well, I'd rather people want to hang with me because they genuinely like me," she continued, shrugging. "Not just because my face was on a popular music video."

She kicked a pebble with her lime-green flip-flop. "I see

different kids come up to Kendra at the oddest places, and it all seems so fake," Stacie commented.

I couldn't disagree with that.

I nodded, feeling better and worse at the same time. Better, because Stacie's bright perspective lifted my mood a bit. Worse, because it made me realize how envious my reaction to Kendra's cameo had been. My shame silenced me for a second.

"So, I don't know about you, gurl." Stacie smiled, pretending to frame her face with her hands. "But this face don't have to be on any screen to be considered fly."

I smiled. It was true what kids at school teased us about. A pretty girl, Stacie did look like the poor man's Beyoncé, just as much as I resembled the superstar's buddy Kelly Rowland with my mocha skin and button nose.

"Except on Chris Brown's cell phone screen, talkin' 'bout some *Cawl me!*'" I winked at Stacie. I couldn't miss the opportunity to tease her about the R & B singer she had a huge crush on.

That sparked a fit of giggles that we couldn't put a stop to for two blocks. Just when we thought we'd caught our composure, the sight of a middle-aged man riding a bike with the ashiest bare feet and ankles we'd ever seen got us cracking up again.

By the time we reached the intersection where we parted ways, we were feeling light-headed.

"You sure you're not coming over?" Stacie knew I liked to hang at her lively house just as much as she loved to come over to mine for peace and quiet. There was never a dull moment at the Morrison residence, where Stacie lives with two sisters, two brothers, and a constantly squawking pet parrot. "We still need to go over a few details before tomorrow's Rope-a-Dope meeting."

"I have to help my grandma with something," I lied. The truth was, I wanted to get home early enough to catch my parents before they headed to that conference with Ms. Landrieux. "Call me in a few hours and we can go over it then."

Stacie pulled out her pad and started briefing me anyway. "It's just a few things I wanted to mention." The girl was so organized, she kept a calendar detailing which outfit she'd wear each day for the following two weeks.

"If we want to be ready for the winter tournament, there are some things we need to take care of soon," she began. Stacie talked about the next school year like it was next week.

I barely caught what Stacie was saying. My mind was elsewhere. Usually, we stopped and chatted at this intersection for a few minutes before parting, but today I was having trouble concentrating.

"All right, I'll check you later," I told her when she'd finished.

"See ya." Her voice trailed behind me as I walked in the direction of my street. She was so excited about her plans for the winter tournament that she didn't notice that I was getting more worried by the second.

When I reached my block, I saw my grandma Bibi picking flowers from her mini–rose garden in the front of the house. She was wearing a wide-brimmed sun hat and humming Debussy's "Clair de Lune." She didn't know the name of it, but would always ask, "Can you play that dah-dah, duh-duh-dum?" the minute I sat on the piano bench to practice. But I didn't mind playing it. I loved the piece myself. And plus, I would do anything for my grandma.

"Hey, Bibi," I called to her. I'd been calling my grandma that ever since I could talk. The story is that years ago, I loved to have her read me a particular children's book titled *Bibi,* the Swahili word for grandmother.

"Hey, Sugar." She turned to face me and smiled warmly. "What's new?"

"One more day of school to go." I smiled back, walking up to her. "But tonight Mom and Dad are meeting with my guidance counselor."

Bibi caught the look of my furrowed brow before I leaned in to kiss her cheek. "They want me to skip a grade," I told her.

"Oh, *that* explains why you're home so soon." She laid a few freshly clipped roses into the basket on the ground. "I thought you and Stacie would be hanging out a bit longer."

"Am I pathetic?" I exhaled and started nibbling my thumbnail.

"No, but I'll tell you what I see." She reached out and gently pulled my hand away from my face. The sun rays that poked through the tiny openings in her straw hat became soft beams of light gliding across her face. I waited for what she had to say. Bibi always had a wonderful way of breaking things down. She could find the baby in an Olympic-size bathtub.

"I see a worried girl who's terrified of change." She gave me a knowing look before I headed inside and upstairs to my bedroom.

That's because whenever Mom gets involved in anything, things change, I thought as I belly-flopped onto my bed. My mother considered herself a problem solver. The only problem was, she preferred to shake things up rather than go with the flow. The woman actually feels flutters in her belly when she senses that a change is brewing. It excites her because she believes change brings the opportunity to grow and learn. It's what she calls "Living Life."

Problems frustrate Mom. She prefers to scrap something altogether and start from scratch rather than beat what she considers to be a dead horse. If it hadn't been for my dad's strong love for stability, I suspected we'd be living like a traveling circus sometimes. Especially when you considered the parade of characters Mom had befriended in the past.

"Mia, honey, come play something for my friend," she'd call out to me when we had guests. I'd go to the living room to find another eccentric person sitting at the "listening lounge," as I liked to call the chaise lounge near the piano. I tried hard not to crack up when one wannabe hip listening couple started snapping their fingers and beat boxing to the classical piece I played them.

Aside from getting her "change" fix by redecorating our home every few seasons, Mom loves to get acquaintanted with people from all walks of life—preferably those who speak no English. She then embarks on learning how to communicate with them. All that comes in handy at my mom's high-profile job.

I once witnessed her in action. She took me to her offices in nearby New York City for Take Your Daughter to Work Day when I was in the seventh grade. She was amazing to watch at the board meeting she let me sit in on. There, when she pointed at the large screen projecting her PowerPoint presentation, all eyes were fixed on her.

My mom is statuesque, with arms so long I felt she could almost embrace us from the head of the boardroom table. Her mahogany skin glowed, her dark eyes twinkled, and her teeth sparkled as she spoke.

Dressed in an elegant blue pantsuit with her hair pulled away from her face, Mom captured everyone's attention with her engaging personality. Her words came to life in her listeners' minds.

She was genuine in her appreciation of her foreign clients, who had flown in from Japan that day. At one memorable point, Mom said something in Japanese and the clients were tickled.

I could just see her meeting Ms. Landrieux tonight. I bet she'd pronounce Ms. L's French last name better than even Ms. L herself! Mom would probably ask her a question in French or something and my guidance counselor would be immediately smitten.

And how could she not be? Mom really has a wonderful way with people. The problem is, she fails to see that I do not.

It took me most of my grade school years to find a friend

I felt comfortable hanging out with. And that connection came about not because of who I am, but what I did—and that was jump double Dutch well. My mom didn't seem to get that kids I met at the playground didn't care that I'd been taking piano lessons since age four, or that I'd visited almost every museum in New York City.

Sometimes I thought that I was my parents' social experiment to create some "well-rounded" child in the hood. When they decided to raise me in the same city where my grandma Bibi raised my mom, my parents had hoped to create a future leader in a girl with humble beginnings and worldly talents. But all I'd ever wanted to do was to blend in.

Being able to read college texts at a young age didn't make me a leader. It made me a nerd.

Two hours later, I heard my parents' car pull into our long driveway. I got off the phone with Stacie, said a quick prayer, and met them at the back door through the kitchen.

"We *have* been to the village in St. Lucia where she's from—remember Scott?" My mom was asking my dad, who looked eager to catch the last 12 minutes of *Jeopardy!*

Mom had obviously gotten familiar with Ms. L.

"Hey, Pumpkin." Dad affectionately squeezed my shoulder as he walked by me and into the house.

How could they act so nonchalant at a time like this? My social life—the little there was of it—was hanging by a thread.

"Well?" I asked them, searching their faces. "How did the meeting with Ms. L go?"

"That's Ms. *Landrrur.*" Mom Frenchified her name. "And, Sweetie, why do you look so flustered? You know we always have your best interest in mind."

Dad took a seat at the kitchen counter instead of in his study, so I knew something was up. Mom dropped her oversized bag by the kitchen table and kicked off her pumps.

"It's safe to come on in, Mia." She led me inside through the doorway to the seat next to my dad. "What's got you so worried? Things are great. Your teachers think very highly of you."

"So highly, in fact, that they want to skip you a grade, you genius daughter of mine." Dad playfully poked me in the ribs, trying to make light of the situation.

"But I don't want to do that." I didn't giggle like I usually do when he does that. "I don't think—"

"We know, we know," Mom interrupted. "We agree with you. There's no reason for you to skip a grade at this point."

"Good." I exhaled. "Thank you *so* much."

"That's why we're going to transfer you to a more academically challenging school instead," Mom said softly.

"St. Claire Academy in Millwall Cliffs is an exceptional girls' school," Dad continued.

St. who? Girls' what? My mind was reeling.

"So, that's it?" I glared at my dad and then at my mom. "You just rearrange my life like my opinion doesn't matter?" Their lips parted, but they didn't speak. "You can't do this to me!" I heard myself yell louder than I'd expected.

"Mia." Dad reached out to touch my arm but I sprang out of my chair.

"Nothing you can say will make me feel better right now." I nodded and slowly walked backward toward the door. I felt betrayed. And because I knew how strict my parents were about education, I knew that their decision was final. Just like that. When I felt the tears welling up, I turned around and stormed back to my room.

My parents didn't follow. They gave me the space I needed to let it all sink in.

CHAPTER 3

That next morning, I pretended to be asleep when my parents peeked into my bedroom before heading to work. I was still so mad at them.

An hour later, I couldn't even bring myself to say more than two words to Bibi when she offered to make me breakfast. "No, thanks," I mumbled before walking out the front door.

Who feels this low on the last day of school? I asked myself. I dragged through the eight-block commute to the school building.

When Mr. Gatwick's fenced-in German shepherd greeted me with an intimidating growl and slobbery barking, I didn't flinch or cross the street like I usually did.

My eyes rolled over the grade school's brick structure as I walked by it. The playground next to the building looked so much smaller than I remembered it being when I was a student there. That was where I'd met Stacie five years ago. Stacie and her friend were trying to get a game of double

Dutch going, but they needed a third person. She spotted me leaning on the fence reading a book from the American Girl series.

"You turn double?" she called out to me, inquiring about whether I had the right rhythm to be a strong turner.

"No, I turn well." I cringed inside as soon as I said it. Although grammatically correct, I thought it would've sounded less nerdy to say "turn good," like other girls at my school would.

But Stacie didn't judge me. She just handed me the rope ends, and we've been tight ever since.

I'd had no friends up to that point. As the only child in my family, there was usually a thirty-year age gap between me and the folks I spent time with. I cherished my summertime visits to see my favorite girl cousins in North Carolina. They were the ones who'd schooled me about double Dutch. But when I was back home, my college-professor dad and advertising-exec mom introduced me to intellectual ideas, people, and places. Too bad they didn't prep me with the basics of schoolyard social skills.

Unlike most kids, Stacie overlooked my awkwardness. She just cared that I liked double Dutch. Today, she and I were a double-Dutch duo.

Elementary school girls walked by in a flurry of pigtails and giggles. They obediently formed a cluster next to Mabel, the crossing guard, who had something sassy to say to every kid she helmed across the busy street.

"Now, why did your mama let you leave the house with

breakfast crumbs still sittin' up on the side of your mouth?"
she was asking one child.

By the time I got to my locker at school, Stacie was there
waiting for me. That was when I wished I'd used my walk
to school to think of an easy way to tell her that I wouldn't
be coming back to City High next year.

"Guess what, gurl?" she said before I could say hi. "I
thought of a perfect advisor who could write a recommen-
dation for Rope-a-Dope."

Once Stacie got in one of her excited moods, you could
forget about getting a word in edgewise.

"Ms. L!" she answered before I could pretend like I was
eager to hear who. Stacie looked like she'd just been named
the next contestant on *The Price Is Right*. *What ever happened to the art of building suspense?* I thought.

"That's great." I forced out a weak smile.

Talking about Ms. L made me feel guilty about not using
this as a chance to segue into my news. I started scratching places on the back of my neck that didn't itch. Now
was not the time to tell her. It would spoil her happy moment. Instead, I swung open my locker door and tried to
avoid eye contact.

"If I can get her to write it by the end of today, we'll
make the application deadline and be considered for the
winter competition."

I nodded but didn't look away from what I was doing.
As she spoke, I continued to take down the photos I had
taped to the inside of my locker door. A picture of Stacie
and me jumping during our first halftime performance as

drill team members. A clip of my favorite poem by Gwendolyn Brooks. I peeled the extra tape off the birthday card Bibi had given me when I'd turned fifteen last month. The girl on the front of the card looked just like me. Her tight auburn curls were worn loose, like a weeping willow at the peak of autumn. My illustrated twin had an air of confidence that I wished I had. She looked proudly unique rather than awkwardly different, like I felt. I'd kept the card taped on my locker door for weeks, hoping that one day as I reached for my algebra text, she'd whisper the secret of social success to me.

"Anything wrong, Mia?" Stacie said with mock concern in her voice. "You look like that girl from the tampon commercial after she realized she bought the wrong brand."

"We're gonna miss you next year, Ms. Chambers," called out our history teacher, Mr. Reynolds, as he strolled by. "Good luck in your new school."

The power trip Mr. Reynolds felt when he monitored the hallways obviously affected his judgment. For someone who had spent two class periods lecturing us about privacy laws, he had no qualms about putting my personal business on blast.

"What does he mean by that?" Stacie said.

"Stacie." I shut my locker door and faced her. "I was meaning to tell you. I just found out yesterday." She didn't look convinced. "It's true—today's my last day at City High."

I watched the transformation of her face and spirit go from smiling to disturbed, disappointed, and dismayed. Stacie just looked straight-up dissed.

"Stace, I—"

She put her hand up as if to keep me at a distance—physically and emotionally.

"That's cool. I understand." She took a step back, then walked away. "See you later at practice."

I was the last to arrive at practice. The girls were on the empty side of the park's basketball court. A group of four guys was playing at the other end. I recognized one of them as Stacie's crush, Eric, or E-Dub, as his friends in the junior class called him.

Stacie had obviously noticed Eric was playing. She was making her announcements to the Rope-a-Dope squad with more enthusiasm than usual.

"Ms. L gave us a fantastic reference in just one day. I have it right here." She held the slender envelope up high like a picket sign. Everyone else was plopped on the ground, so they had to crane their necks to see it. "So I'll send off the application tomorrow. Hopefully by this fall—" she paused as I leaned against the fence and joined the meeting "—we'll know whether we've been selected to compete in the winter competition." Stacie eyed me cautiously before continuing. "Of course, some of us won't be at City High in the fall...."

"Oh, yeah," Kendra chimed in. "I heard about you bouncing, Mia."

I cleared my throat. "Yeah, guys. I'm switching schools." That felt odd to hear out loud. "But that won't affect my involvement with Rope-a-Dope." I felt like a busted politician at a congressional hearing.

"You sure double Dutch ain't too ghetto for you?" Kendra stood up and wiped the dust off her shapely brown legs and brushed the back of her shorts. "Don't they have a squash team or something up in Millwall?"

"Squash?" the girls giggled. "Don't you eat that?"

"You're nice in the ropes, but let's face it," Kendra continued. "You didn't completely fit in. To start off with, you kinda talk and act white anyway. I guess that's cuz you're from the *good* part of East Orange."

I guess I was shocked that Kendra had called me out like that. At that moment, I should've spit out a cold comeback. But unfortunately, as I took time to wonder how Kendra could get away with talking to me like that, she got away with doing it.

Kendra looked around for a backup "True" or "Yup" but instead got feeble "Humphs" and downward glances. The other girls obviously felt uncomfortable with where this was going. Kendra soldiered on solo.

"Kendra—" Stacie's tone pleaded with her to quit.

"Nah, let's be real. You'll have a lot more in common with them than us, that's for sure." Kendra crossed her arms, as if to challenge me to say something.

My response was to pick up my bag and walk away silently. I had to make a quick exit, before anyone could see the tears rolling down my face.

CHAPTER 4

"I can't stand by and watch you let this summer slip by." My grandma Bibi was standing in my bedroom doorway, watching me burn yet another one of her old CDs onto my iTunes list.

"But I thought you said that Nina Simone helped you through many heartaches when you were growing up." The jacket photo showed the late jazz singer circa 1958 sitting on a park bench.

It had been three weeks since the "Kendra catastrophe," as I liked to call it. Stacie and I had spoken briefly once, but only on the phone. I couldn't beat Stacie in a grudge match. There was a record nine days that she didn't talk to her own brother—and he lived across the hall from her! Besides, her summer romance with Eric—E-Dub—was heating up. And when you took into account her summer job at the movie theater, there was little time for hanging with me.

I turned to music to keep me company.

"I loves you, Porgyyyy," Nina crooned sadly.

"Oooh." Bibi pointed her palm heavenward and sat on my bed. "Now *that* takes me back. Mm, mm,mm."

I swiveled my chair away from the desk to face her. "Oh really, Bibi? Tell me what this song reminds you of," I teased. From the look on her face, I could tell there was a juicy-story itch begging to be scratched.

She looked at me from the corner of her eye. "I don't know.... You fifteen yet?"

My limbs were like crab legs as I scurried across the room to Bibi without getting out of my rolling chair. "You know I am. I can handle it."

"Well..." She puckered her lips. Bibi was a master at the art of suspense. "All right. But this stays between us."

I nodded and mimed locking my lips with an imaginary key and then tucking it in my vintage New Jersey Nets baby tee.

"Well, back in the days when I couldn't walk one block without someone asking me if I modeled—"

I rolled my eyes.

"Hey—don't be fresh. Where do you think your mother got her looks from?" she asked me. "Sure as heck not from her daddy, bless his soul. Genes are a tricky thing, my darling. Your mom got lucky. Now, as for your uncle Lenny, I apologize to him all the time for choosing a husband with my heart instead of my eyes."

"Bibi!" I coughed out a shocked laugh.

"I didn't appreciate it enough back then, but I was a stunning beauty. My classmates were so jealous they constantly picked on any flaw they could find in me. It was torture." Bibi's eyes looked sad for a moment. "They told me I wasn't even fit to be a model student, much less a fashion model. They talked about my broad nose and my taller-than-average height until I began to feel distorted. By the time I was your age, I didn't feel beautiful at all. I hardly liked to look in the mirror when I got dressed in the mornings. And I avoided being photographed for months. Then I met Delroy."

"And how did he look?" I asked, curious. I wondered how it was that I'd never heard this story before. *Maybe I was too busy daydreaming to pay attention the last time she told this story,* I thought.

"Like a Nubian prince. He was an artist and asked me to pose for one of his pencil drawings."

"Oh, he used that old pickup line, huh?" I teased.

"Exactly what *I* thought—oooh, I taught you well, Ladybug," Bibi gushed, her rings colliding as she clapped in amusement.

"Great—I can't even tease you without you taking it as a compliment," I chuckled. "How on earth did a mirror-dodging girl grow up to be you?"

"It wasn't easy, I'll tell you that. But each self-esteem-boosting moment was like a stair step closer to where I am today. And one of those first defining moments happened because of Delroy."

"Where'd you meet him?"

"At school. He was a year ahead of me at my old high school." Bibi had grown up in Charleston, South Carolina, but moved to East Orange once she married my grandfather Julian. "Every time Delroy and I crossed paths, I'd turn down his offer to do a portrait of me. Around that time I wouldn't even let someone take a picture of me, much less allow some boy to study my features and bring them to life on canvas. But Delroy was politely persistent. He said he had to complete a portrait for his art class assignment and that he couldn't imagine doing his best work on any other face than mine. I thought Delroy must be blind. I couldn't understand what he saw of beauty in me."

"When did you finally give in?"

"It was on the day my church youth group and I had successfully convinced our local radio station manager to play more black artists on the radio. Just think—I joined a group that stood behind an important cause. About seventeen of us stood outside that radio station with protest signs for hours each day after school for fifteen straight days. On that fifteenth day, the station manager came out and spoke to us. An hour after that, Nina Simone's 'I Loves You, Porgy' was played on the radio for the whole community to hear. That happened in large part because of our organized protest. And I was a part of that."

Bibi's glassy eyes were looking in the distance, focusing on the memory, while her chin jutted out with deep, quiet pride.

"I was walking from the station, feeling proud of what I'd helped to achieve, when I ran into Delroy. This time when he offered to sketch me, I surprised him with a yes answer."

"He must've been *ex-ci-ted*," I said.

"Yes, he was. He didn't want to risk me changing my mind, so he was prepared to do it then and there. I sat on a park bench, just like Ms. Simone does on her album cover. Under an hour later, he was done. But he didn't let me see the sketch. He insisted I meet him at his art class a week later so I could see the finished project—painted and completed."

"I wouldn't be able to wait." I shook my head. "I'd be too eager to see it."

"When I walked into that classroom that next week, I was immediately drawn to a painting by the window. It was a portrait of a young woman with an inner spirit so strong, you could see it on her face. She wasn't smiling, but her eyes were. I couldn't take my eyes off her."

"It was you, Bibi?"

"It was *me*. I was still speechless when Delroy came over to ask me how I liked it. I was amazed by his talent, but also at the fact that he had tapped into the positive way I was feeling about myself that day. He captured my inner radiance—the pride I felt from the successful protest—and etched it forever in time right there on that canvas. Delroy and his family moved out of state later that year, but he let me keep the portrait. I treasure it to this day."

I'd seen that gold-framed painting on the wall above Bibi's dresser a million times, but I'd never appreciated the story behind it. I began to understand why Bibi had given me the birthday card I kept in my locker. She was trying to help me tap into my own inner radiance. No doubt lately I'd been walking around like somebody had turned off all my indoor lights.

"Bibi," I said, looking down at my long brown fingers,

"if you can go from feeling that low to becoming the diva you are today, I guess that means there's hope for me yet."

Bibi smiled and softly nudged my chin. "Yes, there is, Ladybug—and don't you forget it."

Twenty seconds had gone by since I'd last rang the bell. It wouldn't have been impolite to go for the second ring. By the time my finger reached the button, my new piano teacher, a woman in her early thirties, answered her door.

"Hello," she greeted me with a close-lipped smile. "You must be Mia."

"Yes, Ms. Simon," I sighed.

"Uh-uh." She tossed a quick glance behind her as she led me through her home's foyer into the room where the piano was waiting. "Call me Nadine."

"Okay, Nadine."

My effort to sound enthusiastic failed. Maybe my lack of socializing this summer was turning me into uncool company. Ever since my talk with Bibi the day before, I couldn't stop thinking about what a portrait of me would look like if it were done now. Lately I'd been feeling so un-sure, I probably wouldn't even know which way to face an artist painting me. The portrait would probably be of the back of my head!

At least I had my music to guide me in the right direc-tion. My mom had been raving about this piano teacher for weeks, and suggested I start seeing her. It had been four months since my last visit to Mr. Alston, the piano teacher I'd had since the sixth grade. When he'd moved across the river to Brooklyn, I'd stopped taking lessons. Besides, our Rope-a-Dope meetings had taken up any spare time I had. Now that those meetings were on hiatus for the summer, it was a good time to get back into my piano.

"How's your mother?" Nadine was asking me. "She's such a dynamic woman."

"She's fine," I managed to offer. By "dynamic" Nadine probably meant "pushy."

My mom had met Nadine at a Broadway show. Last summer, my parents had had orchestra seats to *The Color Purple,* and during intermission, my superfriendly mom went over to compliment the pianist on her fancy finger work. That pianist was Nadine Simon. After the show my mom approached Nadine and found out that she hailed from East Orange and still lives here. Lord knows whether or not the poor woman actually was already moonlighting as a piano teacher or if my mother talked her into doing it.

"This is how I'm sensing you're feeling today," said Nadine as she sat on the shiny black piano bench and gingerly lowered her fingertips to the keys. Her piano started narrating a moody tale, using statements of tender high notes flowing into notes so low I could feel them reverberate in my chest. It was like Nadine was using sound instead of paint to create a portrait of me. And I didn't sound like a happy camper.

"But that's just my opinion," Nadine said when she stopped playing. "I could be way off. Am I?"

There was no use denying it. Those annoyingly premature back-to-school commercials starting to air on TV were making me feel extra nervous, and it was showing. In just a few short weeks I'd be starting school at St. Claire Academy.

"Nope," I said, shaking my head. "You're pretty on point there. Nice guess."

Nadine smiled at me and we both laughed. Her brief aural psychology session actually broke the ice and I felt myself relax in her company.

"Let's chat a bit about your expectations before we get started. Please, have a seat."

I didn't realize I'd been standing next to the piano since I walked in. Once I'd eased into the pin-striped loveseat nearby, I noticed the room's décor for the first time. Unlike the coordinated furniture at my house, no two pieces here matched. The piano bench didn't even go with the piano. Nadine would probably lose at a card game of concentration, but somehow the look as a whole worked in a charming and eclectic sort of way. And I could already tell from Nadine's quirky personality that she felt more comfortable in a mismatched world. She chose personal style over trends. I admired that about her.

By the time my lesson with Nadine was over, my outlook on things was a little rosier. Maybe Nadine was right. Judging from her impression of my mother, Nadine figured it was in my blood to set out on new adventures. "Heading to a new school can turn into the perfect opportunity to discover new things about yourself," Nadine told me.

I still secretly hoped that for once I'd meet people who were cool with any aspect of my personality that I chose to explore.

CHAPTER 5

on the first day of school, I had to wake up an hour and a half earlier than I usually did at City High. Instead of a ten-minute stroll through East Orange, my new commute would involve two New Jersey Transit buses and be seventy-one minutes long.

The distant hum of my parents' car rolling backward out the driveway each morning became my cue to hit the shower. I had to be at the city bus stop at 6:40 at the latest if I wanted to get to St. Claire Academy by the 7:52 bell.

Luckily, I had two commute routes to choose from. I could walk one block to the number 34 bus stop to Bloomfield, and then transfer there for the number 60 bus to Millwall Cliffs. Or, if I was running late, I could walk the eight blocks to the number 60 bus that goes straight to school.

Maybe it was nerves, but I got to the number 34 bus stop a lot earlier than I'd planned. I felt my grandma's eyes watching over me as I left the house. I turned around to see her distant figure standing next to the shrubbery she had carefully pruned into shape. She nodded when I waved.

She was willing me to be strong and face my day confidently.

Once on the bus, I chose a window seat halfway down the aisle. I smoothed my new uniform—blue and gray were the Academy's colors—and stared at the scene outside. About twenty minutes later, I pressed the strip on the wall, alerting the driver of my stop. The transfer was perfectly timed. The number 60 arrived at the next stop just as I did. Even though I had to stand for the first mile or so, passengers began to get off by the load and I found a seat quickly. By the time the bus reached its last stop, which was Millwall Cliff's town center, I was one of the few people left on it.

From there, I walked up a quiet side street past the large, gorgeous homes and up the hill to where St. Claire Academy was perched. That was when I saw the cars lined up in front of the Academy like the school was a luxury car dealer. Girls squealed and rushed to hug friends they hadn't seen since last school year. Soccer moms in minivans waved at their daughters before driving off.

Great. It was barely 7:45 a.m. when I suffered my first episode of culture shock. This sight was a lot different than the scene outside City High. For one, a majority of the students there walked to school, because their parents, who were at work, weren't available to take them.

Perfect, I thought. *If I feel this out of place before I step foot through the school's front doors, I can only imagine how this day's gonna be.* Where was Oprah when you needed her? The media icon had an uncanny way of turning any crowd into a "Kumbaya"-singing sisterhood. I needed some positive vibrations, quick.

On my way to the principal's office, I noticed that the students wore their skirts a lot shorter than my below-the-knee-length skirt. I wore mine as the school handbook required. But apparently I didn't have to take the rules so literally. Some girls wore funky-colored or patterned tights under their skirts, and cool shoes. I was glad we could bend the dress-code a little.

The middle-aged secretary at the front office blinked three times fast when she greeted me. I wasn't sure if her coffee was to blame for that or if it was because she was surprised I wasn't white. Her behavior after that didn't let on either way. She tapped on her computer keyboard to note that I'd arrived for my first day and then printed out my class schedule.

"According to your placement test results, you scored somewhere between our B-level and A-level standards," the secretary said while multitasking. "So we're putting you in a mixed bag."

Oh, uh-uh, I thought when I read that I'd been placed in B-level classes and just a few A-level ones. *How did I go from advanced placement in City High to intermediate level here at St. Claire's?*

"Your homeroom is just down the hall to the left," she said. *Sounds easy enough,* I thought as I headed to the door. "But homeroom is ending any minute so you have to head to your first class in the annex."

Before I could ask her where this "annex" was, the principal swung open her door and strutted out of her office. She silently handed a yellow file to the secretary, who blinked three times fast before she sprang out of her seat to reach for the yellow file.

Not wanting to interrupt their office dance routine, I set off to find the class on my own. The other students making their way through the halls didn't seem to notice me or my confusion. They just chatted breathlessly to each other before the final bell rang.

A-level humanities was my first class. Ms. Veltz was the teacher. Classroom number A-04. *A* for *annex,* I assumed.

For the first time, I noticed the school hallways. The tiled floors were gleaming. The lockers seemed brand-new and the equipment in the lab I peeked into looked high-tech. City High students wouldn't have believed their eyes if they'd stepped into this place. The crumbling plaster and broken bathroom faucets at my old school couldn't hold a candle to St. Claire's pristine building.

The kids joked around and chatted nonstop the same as the kids at my old school. But still everyone here was different. They wore their hair differently, held their book bags a bit unlike City High students did, and even laughed in their own way.

I assumed the annex was the newer part of the building that was connected to the main building by an enclosed footbridge. That footbridge reminded me of the ones built to connect office structures in downtown Newark so corporate employees could walk from work to the car lot without mingling with urban locals.

The annex was even cooler-looking than the main building. The classroom door locks were computerized, and some of the rooms had flat screens on the wall. I saw room number 4, so I walked in and chose a seat halfway down the first row.

As students piled in, some glanced at me and smirked before whispering to each other. I fiddled with my notebook and new Bic pens.

"Your tan is rockin', girlie," I heard a high-pitched talker say.

I thought it would be too obvious if I turned to look at the person she was referring to. Just as long as they didn't compare their tan with my natural one, everything would be fine, I thought.

The teacher walked in without a word, but her presence hushed the gabbing. With one swift movement, she reached for a long piece of chalk and began scribbling on the clean blackboard: "Ms. Dalton, American History."

My heart leapt to my throat. I was in the wrong class. My chair scratched the floor as I stood to leave the classroom.

"Is there a problem?" Ms. Dalton looked squarely at me.

"I—I'm in the wrong class," I stammered, uncomfortable being the focus of attention.

"Okay, before you head out there and get lost again, can anyone help this new student find her class?"

"I got her, Ms. Dalton," a confident voice from the back of the room called out.

"Okay, Allie, she's all yours," said Ms. Dalton. "Good luck on your first day."

I walked out as the bell rang. My escort met me in the hallway with an outstretched paint-stained hand.

"Hey, I'm Allie Snierson, a sophomore," she said before she caught my expression.

"Oh, that?" She referred to the blue on her fingers. "I was just doing some painting this morning. I do my best artwork early in the day."

"That's cool." I tried to sound interested, but I was too concerned about being late for my class. "I'm Mia Chambers. I need to get to room A-04 and I thought this was it."

"Oh, common mistake," said Allie. "That class is downstairs in the basement—each floor has the same room numbers. Confusing, but easy once you get it."

Allie looked like she didn't have a care in the world. With each leisurely step she took, her feet landed with her toes pointed outward. She didn't seem to mind that her fingers were blue or that her nail polish was chipped. She walked slower than a tourist and let her arms swing at her sides. Allie obviously didn't share my memories of speed walking through crowded New York City streets with my mom.

The obsessively obedient girl in me began to get super worried. I didn't want to be late to class and risk making the wrong impression on my humanities teacher.

"Thanks," I told her. "I don't want to keep you from your class, so I think I can make it from here."

"Sure." She must've gotten my hint. "But let me just tell you how to get there." Allie pulled out a mini sketchbook that was tucked in the back of her uniform skirt's waistband. A pen materialized from her long, messy-chic auburn hair, and she began sketching faster than even my mom could walk.

"Just walk down the corridor and make a left when you see this door. Ms. Veltz's class should be on your left. She's the lady with short curly dark hair and thin lips with a mole right above her right eye." Allie sketched everything she said until she'd illustrated a clear picture. "I think she's wearing a long skirt with butterflies or some mess on it today."

She then drew a figure wearing a flowy ankle-length skirt with a nondescript pattern on it. She tore the sheet out of the pad and handed it to me. "For reference," she said, smiling.

I smiled in spite of my on-edge nerves.

"Thanks, Allie." I chuckled and looked into her friendly eyes for the first time. Her slow-down-and-smell-the-roses vibe seemed to have influenced me for at least that brief moment. Then I sped down the stairs to Ms. Veltz's class.

Thanks to Allie's sketch, I was there in less than one minute. I slipped in and quietly grabbed the closest empty seat as Ms. Veltz's back was turned. Ms. Veltz went for the same name-on-blackboard technique Ms. Dalton had used. Maybe it was in this school's teacher's handbook or something.

"For the few of you whom I *hahve* not *hahd* the pleasure of meeting, my name is Ms. Veltz and this is *Humahnities*, glorious *Humahnities*."

Sure, her hair was bent into dark fluffy curls, just like the wig Bibi had worn years ago when she was battling breast cancer and undergoing chemo. Ms. Veltz even had the plump mole over her right eye and a flowy skirt exactly like in Allie's picture. But Allie had failed to mention what to me was the obvious detail—Ms. Veltz's faux British accent. But I guess visuals were to Allie what sound was to me. Like bats, I used sound as my own road map. The *tap-tap* sounds of the double-Dutch ropes helped me decide when to jump in and how fast to jump. I could identify a song after hearing no more than three or four notes. And people's voices sounded like notes on my keyboard.

"To *staht* this brand-new *yeahr,* I've got a teaser for what this *clahss* will be like," Ms. Veltz was saying as she handed out papers for the first person in each row to pass down.

"This, ladies, is a *pawp* quiz," she continued. "I just *wont* a *hahndle* on your under*stahnding* of the *ahts,* literature, and phil*aw*sophy."

I reached for the pile that the girl sitting in front of me blindly held over her head. That was when I realized that this *pawp* quiz was stapled and two pages long.

"Try your best—you *wohn't* be graded," Ms. Veltz added, and left us to it.

I skimmed the pages. The questions about great ancient civilizations—some multiple choice, a few short essay ones—seemed to cover every continent except Africa.

So much for my chance to impress the teacher with my knowledge. That was not to say that those African history books Mom and Dad had gotten me years ago were wasted. I realized now that if it hadn't been for finding out about stuff like those ancient African universities where Greek philosophers learned, I would have been sitting here thinking Africa had been in the Dark Ages while folks everywhere else in the world were getting their learn on. But I guess if nothing else, I could hold my head high because I knew that Black people did have a lot to do with civilizing the ancient world.

An extra perky, extra lean girl was the first to spring out of her desk to hand in her quiz. I was barely finished with the first page when an unmistakable whiff of cucumbermelon lotion (Stacie's favorite) wafted by me as the early bird bounced by on her way to Ms. Veltz's desk.

"Oh great—Emma Bishop," the exasperated girl next to me mumbled to herself, rolling her eyes.

"*Thahnk* you, Emma." Ms. Veltz looked proud. "And do tell your *fahther,* our *deahr* mayor, that I'll be sure to bring my famous *cahsserole* to his next function."

Suddenly it hit me harder than before—I wasn't in Kansas anymore.

At lunchtime, I grabbed an empty table. I created a protective fortress of textbooks and notebooks so it didn't feel like I was sitting alone. If I'd had my stuffed teddy bear, I would have been clutching it for dear life. But this would have to do for now.

"The freshmen don't have their lunch hour until next period, which means you must be a new student here." I looked up from my turkey sandwich to see a blond celeb clone standing over my Fort Knox of books.

"Y-yeah, I'm new—I mean, new to you," I began clumsily. "Mia," I told her.

"Mia." She tried it out. I could tell she'd expected me to have a more ethnic-sounding name. "Mia," she repeated, but this time giving it an unmistakable edge. "I'm Jennifer Octavian—junior class," she announced as if her name were in lights and "junior class" were some blockbuster feature film. "You just moved to town?" she asked.

"No, I'm from East Orange—I transferred from City High."

Bingo. Jennifer's eyes widened with new interest—just when she was going to write me off as boring.

"East Orange City High, as in True MC?" Jennifer was obviously intrigued. She raised a freshly waxed eyebrow. Bibi had taught me how to detect what she called people's "lightning"—the body language that comes before the thunder of the voice. For example, when I snacked on animal crackers around Stacie, the corner of her mouth would quiver before she asked, "Ca-I-avesum?"—Stacie-ese for "Can I have some?" And my dad almost always smoothed his goatee when he was about to debate you on your last point. So I braced for Jennifer's thunder once her eyebrow rose and twitched.

"Well," she began with a twinkle in her eye. "Big change from metal detectors and random locker searches, huh?"

"That's not—" I started.

"Mia, hey!" Allie the artist moseyed up to the table, tray in hand.

"Hi." I was glad to see her. I slid my pile of books over, beckoning her to have a seat.

"Oh, so you two know each other?" Jennifer looked disappointed. Maybe it wasn't badass enough for someone from East Orange. I wasn't sorry to let her down.

Allie and I both shot her a blank look.

"So, Mia—anytime you want to run your 'true life story' by me—" Jennifer held up her fingers to mime air quotes "—I'd love to hear it. See you around."

"Who is she now, Barbara Walters? What did she mean by that?" Allie was confused.

"She thinks the rapper True MC and I have more in common than our mutual hometown." I watched Jennifer join a table of ultra trendy girls. While they leaned in to hear what she had to tell them, they cast occasional glances at me. "I transferred here from East Orange City High," I explained to Allie.

"I haven't proven it yet, but I'm pretty sure Jennifer Octavian is an embedded tabloid reporter working for the *St. Claire Dish* or some kind of gossip rag." Allie picked the onions out of her sandwich. The blue paint from this morning was now completely washed from her hands.

"Well then, she probably just scooped her next cover story. I could picture the headline—" I put one hand in the air for dramatic effect "—East Orange You Glad You're Not Mia?"

Allie dropped the long droopy onion ring she was holding and cracked up. "No, it'll be something like 'Blood Transfer,'" Allie said in that trademark movie-trailer-announcer voice. "New Urban Student Brings Terror to Quiet School."

"Good one!" A belly laugh escaped from me for the first time in days.

"But seriously," Allie said after we got over our laugh

attack. "How are things going so far? Did you find that class okay this morning?"

"Yes—thanks to your diagram. By the way, what are you, some kind of courtroom sketch artist?" Allie smiled despite her mouth full of food. "But yeah, things went okay—aside from this tough pop quiz," I continued.

"I got one of those this morning, too." Allie swatted an invisible fly. "But that's just St. Claire trying to live up to its academic reputation. They can't keep that up. After about two weeks the teachers realize that tons more papers to grade means less personal time for them."

I decided that Allie was just one of those people who find no use in worrying. It was refreshing hanging with someone with her perspective. We made plans to have lunch together again the next day.

By the end of my first day, I couldn't have left the building faster if my name was Marion Jones. But somehow, another girl wearing the gray uniform skirt beat me to the bus stop. I was a half a block away from the stop when I saw her standing in the bus shelter.

St. Claire has another mass transit commuter, other than me? I thought. It was like one of those rare Bigfoot sightings. The next second, the bus pulled up and she boarded. I could've run and made the bus, but I decided against it. *I mean, why run the risk of tripping, falling, and losing a front tooth? Then think of how many dental visits it would take for me to regain my ability to pronounce my last name clearly again. So not worth it.*

It was nice to learn that there was another bus commuter—and especially cool that there was another sistah on campus. Aside from myself, the three or four black students I'd spotted, and Mr. Rick—the hardworking custodian who had flashed a secret smile at me earlier—I hadn't noticed many African-Americans at the academy. Yes, this was a huge difference from City High, where there were three or four white students and teachers—altogether!

The first thing I wanted to do when I got home was call Stacie to tell her about my day. After briefly chatting with my grandma, I dashed up to my room and dialed her cell number.

"Hello?" Stacie responded as if she hadn't checked her caller ID.

"Hi, Stace, it's me."

"Hey, M-I-A." She spelled my name out like she often did—only today, I couldn't help picking up on its double meaning. "How did things go today?"

"Gurrrl, lemme tell you—it is night and day from City High. Aside from the uniform and the all-girls thing, it was like an all-around culture shock."

"Let me guess." Stacie was enjoying this. "They were comparing tans."

"Yes!" I squealed, excited to be speaking to someone who understood without explanation.

"And they were checking against your arm to see how close their complexions got to yours!" Stacie continued.

"*Hell* no!"

It was nice bugging out with Stacie like we used to before things got so complicated. I wanted it to last longer.

"So whatcha doing now? Can I come over?" I asked.

"I'd love that, but Eric and I are supposed to hang out. Rope-a-Dope practice went a little longer than we thought and I'm kinda running late."

"Oh, that happened already?"

"Yeah, gurl, at 3 p.m.—the usual time." I could tell Stacie felt awkward breaking the news. I glanced at my alarm clock, not realizing the time. I'd forgotten to factor in my commute time.

"We took a vote about whether to practice later so you can make it, but most of us can't meet that late," said Stacie apologetically.

Starting this month, the squad planned on meeting once a week to practice for upcoming fall community exhibitions at churches, youth centers, and street festivals. Aside from co-choreographing our routines with Stacie, my job was to book gigs for the squad. Since June, I had already successfully booked four appearances for October and November.

Stacie's responsibility was getting the Rope-a-Dope costume design hooked up. She'd always been a natural at fashion. She was the reason I'd stepped it up in the wardrobe department. I considered Stacie to be my personal stylist.

It was tough downplaying my long legs and arms. I was medium height at five foot five, but my limbs made me look infinitely taller. Stacie showed me how to work around that when shopping for clothes. I was grateful to her.

"No, that's okay," I said. That out-of-place feeling I'd been experiencing all day took hold of me again. "I understand. Thanks for voting on it, though."

"We'll work something out." Stacie tried to sound upbeat. "I'll see if we can meet late at least twice a month. I'll call you later in the week to let you know what the upshot is."

"Sounds good." Now it was my turn to try to sound upbeat. "Tell Eric I said what's up."

After we hung up, I heard my parents' car pull into the driveway. I knew that as soon as they walked through the back door, they'd be calling me downstairs. My dad especially would want to hear all the details about my first day at school. I knew he'd crack up when he heard about my humanities teacher's fake accent. I'd been all ready to act out the whole humanities class scene for Stacie, but we'd had to cut our conversation short.

I was glad Stacie wasn't sulking over the fact that we were now at different schools. But it was weird how *over me* everyone seemed. Eric was now the person Stacie brought home to hang with her siblings, and the squad that I helped to start needed to be convinced to include me in practices at least once a month! Nice to know how unforgettable I was.

"Mia." I heard my mom's voice travel up the stairs to my room. Eager to talk some more about my day, I went down to greet my parents.

CHAPTER 6

The mystery commuter from St. Claire was on the number 60 bus the next morning. But oddly enough, I didn't even notice her until the near-empty bus got close to our Millwall Cliffs stop—and she was sitting right in front of me!

I heard her before I saw her. She was softly humming along to a song she was listening to on her iPod. Her singing voice sounded studio-recording great. Even though she was only lightly humming a few notes at a time, there were layers of emotion in her voice. Had I been an A & R exec from a top record label, I would've signed the girl on the spot.

When we got off the bus, I tapped her on her shoulder.

"You have a beautiful voice," I told her.

"Was I that loud?" she asked, embarrassed to be disturbing the peace.

"No, no—not at all. I only noticed it a few blocks ago because I was sitting right behind you."

"Oh." She looked relieved. "Thanks." She put away

her iPod and eyed my uniform. "You go to St. Claire, too? Freshman?"

"No, I'm a new sophomore—I transferred. I'm Mia Chambers."

"Hey, nice to meet you, Mia—I'm Bonita Johnson, a junior." She smiled timidly.

"You've been here since freshman year?" I asked as we started walking up the long hill together.

"Yeah." She looked at me as if to say, *And I know all about the culture shock you're going through.*

"What school did you transfer from?" Bonita was curious.

"East Orange City High."

"Oh." Her eyes lit up. "My cousin just graduated from there. You must not live too far from me—I'm from the north side of Newark."

"Really?" I was excited to meet someone from my area. "So you've been doing this long commute for going on three years?"

"Yup." Something in Bonita relaxed, because she didn't seem as self-conscious anymore. She had a sweetness about her—I could easily see it in both her personality and her appearance. Bonita struck me as the kind of girl who unsuccessfully tried to downplay her good looks. But with her high cheekbones, defined nose, clear cocoa skin, and shiny jet-black hair, it was too tough to hide the pretty. "And I've been walking through my neighborhood in this uniform with a heavy book bag while everyone else is rocking the hottest gear," she said.

"I'm starting to notice the stares they give me." I nodded.

"The kids on my block think I must be some rich nerd because I go to private school," she admitted. "If only they knew that I'm on a scholarship."

"That whole 'nerd' thing is annoying," I agreed. "Why is it considered uncool to care about your grades?"

"At the academy, it's uncool *not* to care," Bonita explained. "Anyway, I'm tired of frontin'—I'm trying to become the first doctor in my family." She paused to think about her declaration. "The first *professional* in my family," she confessed, almost to herself.

"I hear you." I was impressed that she already knew what she wanted to pursue as a career. Not the case with me. All I knew was that I enjoyed tutoring Stacie and others in math. Maybe being a teacher was my calling.

"Dealing with the stereotypes some folks at the academy have about you is another story," she continued.

"Humph." My grandma's loaded response was all I could muster.

Bonita and I walked in silence for a few minutes.

"Hey, ever hear that nineties rap song by A Tribe Called Quest called 'Bonita Applebum'?" I asked her playfully.

"Yes, I know that song all too well." She smiled. "It's still my dad's favorite—the remix version, that is. He named me after it."

"Your dad sounds like a cool guy," I told her.

Bonita reached up and tucked her chin-length hair behind her ear. She suddenly looked self-conscious again. *Was it something I said?* I thought.

"When's your lunch period today?" I asked once we'd walked through the school's front double doors.

"Fourth period."

"Me, too. I'll be in the cafeteria having lunch with Allie Snierson. You should join us."

"Okay, see you then," Bonita said as she turned to make her way down the hall to her locker. I headed in the opposite direction toward mine.

Bonita and Allie were already seated together by the time I got to the cafeteria. The know-it-all Emma Bishop was also in my A-level algebra class, and her last-minute question had kept everyone a few minutes after the bell. Our stern math teacher thought her answer was worth cutting into lunchtime. I just wanted out of that class so I could privately deep-breathe through my anxiety. I was close to hyperventilating when I realized the teacher was moving faster than I was used to. And things only got worse when the class repeated a math rule I'd never heard of that she'd taught them the year before. What was worse, they sounded like they were reciting some easy nursery rhyme. It felt like everyone except me raised their hands at least once during the fifty-minute class. If I couldn't excel at the subject that was supposed to be my best, there was little hope of academic success at St. Claire Academy. I'd be known as the dumb transfer student from the hood—which probably wouldn't come as a surprise to most people.

"We were beginning to think you got lost again," Allie teased when I took a seat at their round cafeteria table.

"Oh, if there's one thing I could always find, it's the place where the food is," I said, deciding that the best cure for my anxiety was to pretend it didn't exist. Besides, I liked that I felt comfortable enough around Allie and Bonita to crack jokes.

"Well, then, it sounds like you're the right friend for me," Bonita giggled. "There's always room in my heart for a fellow greedy girl. Welcome, my sister."

"It sounds like I need a padlock on my lunch," Allie covered her brown paper bag with both her arms and cowered in faux fear.

"I'll tell you right now—if you packed tuna, don't turn your back on it for not one second." I pretended to act serious. "I'm scary, I tell ya."

We all busted out laughing. This drew unwanted attention from the table where celeb-clone Jennifer Octavian and her friends sat. They stared at us for a beat, then turned to each other in a gaggle of whispers.

"It looks like the tabloid staff's daily meeting is under way." Allie rolled her eyes.

"Tomorrow's headline: Joker's Wild...Because She's From East Orange," I added.

"You guys are so corny." Bonita laughed harder.

"I'll tell you what's corny," Allie wiped her tears of laughter as she spoke. "I'm gonna try out for the winter production this year."

"The school year just started and there's already talk of a winter event?" I asked, incredulous. *Must everything be so intense around here?* I wondered.

"Tryouts are in less than two weeks because rehearsals go through October and November," Bonita explained. "The annual show always has a touchy-feely, self-help slash socially conscious theme in honor of the holiday season."

"It's a big deal," Allie said. "St. Claire is renowned for the productions it puts on. A former student was even scouted by a Broadway producer in the audience one year."

"Yup, I remember that." Bonita nodded and pointed. "That was cool, because usually the guys from the Mount get all the accolades."

"The Mount?" I was confused for the umpteenth time today.

"That's our brother school, Mount Yeager," Bonita said. "They're an all-boys' high school not too far from here."

"Oh," I said simply.

"And this year we'll be staging *Merry Go Round*," Allie was thrilled to announce. But the name didn't ring a bell for either of us. "It's the off-Broadway musical that my amazing art teacher wrote! That's why I just have to be a part of this."

"Are you gonna try out for a major character role?" I was curious. I couldn't picture Allie getting into any other character but the one she was born with.

"Auditions aren't just for actors and singers," she informed me. "I'm trying out for a set designer."

"Oh," I said simply again. Then I thought, *Oh!*

"What about auditions for the band or orchestra or whatever you call it here?"

"That's going down at some point, too," Bonita told me.

This was my chance to get in where I fit in. I didn't want to go out being the mediocre urban student. While I worked on my grades, I'd sign up to audition for the winter musical's mini-orchestra. My academic status might not have been up to par in a private suburban school, but my piano skills were. That I was sure of.

"Okay then, I'll audition to be a pianist," I said proudly.

"Really?" Bonita looked impressed. "You got it like that?"

"Nice." Allie liked where this was going, so she decided to raise the stakes. "What about you, Bonita? Care to join us?"

"I'm not an artist or a musician, so I guess that leaves me out of this." The shy Bonita was creeping back in. "But I'll buy an opening-night ticket to show my support."

"Not good enough," Allie coaxed.

"I think you're being modest," I chimed in. "You have an amazing voice—I heard it this morning."

"Bonita, you sing?" Allie looked at her, then at me.

"No, Allie—this girl *saangs*," I corrected her.

The twinkle in Bonita's eyes told us all we needed to know.

"Okay then," Allie announced, holding up her hand for a high five. "Let's use the next two weeks to sharpen our skills."

"Word." I accepted the challenge and met Allie's palm with mine. We held that position while waiting on Bonita's answer.

"People are gonna think we're playing London Bridge or something if we stay like this," I said.

Bonita raised her hand and touched ours.

"Let's do this." She sounded happier than I thought she'd be.

When the day of the mini-orchestra auditions came, I walked into the crowded auditorium feeling totally prepared. I eyed the attractive piano waiting on the stage and then looked around at the coed crowd, most of them sitting with instruments and sheet music in their hands. I wondered what music they planned to perform.

My piano teacher, Nadine had helped me select the perfect audition number: Alicia Keys's "If I Ain't Got You." Then she agreed to train me for it. She scheduled me in for four lessons during the two weeks before my audition.

"You're ready," Nadine proudly told me on the fourth meeting. Her vote of confidence made me feel ten feet tall.

Too bad that feeling didn't last. When the three members of the casting panel began calling people up to the stage, I was instantly blown away by everyone's incredible talent. Virtuoso violinists, badass bassists, dope drummers. My only solace was that no pianist was called before me. Until Lin hit the stage.

It was like this girl Lin had ten fingers on each hand. Her quick range on the piano put me to shame. She played an extremely tricky classical piece that had one of the casting judges panting. And maybe it was just my vantage point, but it looked to me like Lin was talking on her Bluetooth while she played. I could've sworn I heard her order a pepperoni pizza.

Suddenly I didn't feel too brilliant. *This is bad,* I told myself. Allie and Bonita's auditions had been held the day before, and they'd already found out that they'd made the elite cut. Allie was listed as a member of the lead production crew. Bonita nailed her audition and earned a meaty role—starring opposite Jennifer Octavian, no less! And here I was, holding sheet music that was nothing but a prelude to pure disappointment.

"Mia Chambers," the male member of the casting panel shouted.

I thought of my mom. She had such a natural talent for performing. Give her a tough crowd and she'd tame everyone in it with her sass appeal and confidence. Why hadn't any of her genes passed down to me? I closed my eyes and tried to channel my mom's spunky spirit. *If I can't be her, I'll pretend to be her,* I thought.

"Act like you know," Bibi always told me.

"Mia Chambers!" the same casting judge shouted a few seconds later when no one from the audience stirred.

Startled, I sprang from my seat, and my wobbly legs somehow ushered me up the stage steps to the piano bench.

The auditorium felt so stuffy with judgment that it was almost suffocating. I took a few deep breaths. The first notes I softly tapped pierced the silence. Everyone waited to hear what I could do. My mother would have loved having a captive audience like this. I remembered how Mom had looked in the boardroom meeting I'd once sat in on. She had dazzled everyone with the way she carried herself. Just then, I sat up straight and proud on the bench. During the meeting, Mom also had held her long arms out like the elegant wings of an angel. So, for dramatic effect as I played, my arms gracefully lifted my hands high off the keys and floated back gently.

Once I kept on form, everything else flowed naturally, until soon, I wasn't faking it. I played with genuine tenderness and soul until each note rang with emotion. I swayed on the bench, closed my eyes with feeling for a few measures, and ended the song with a well-timed crescendo. When I walked off the stage, it hit me. For the first time in a long time, I felt like I belonged.

The next day, my name was on the list of cast musicians. I had made the cut.

CHAPTER 7

"Ready the ropes," I playfully shouted to the Rope-a-Dope squad when I saw them grouped together next to a hot dog stand. That phrase held the magic three words. It was the cue that sent jumpers into action, so when they heard it, the Rope-a-Dopers looked up like trained soldiers hearing the call of duty. That made me smile.

I didn't like being away from double Dutch or being left out of something I loved so much. So I attended the first community gig the squad had.

It was a sunny Saturday afternoon at East Orange's annual street fair, the Community Appreciation Day. A live jazz band was performing on the makeshift platform temporarily built in front of the city hall building. On the plaza below, kids were running around with cotton candy. Elders sat on lawn chairs, and a group of men and women crowded around a dominoes game going down on a folding card table. When I showed up, the Rope-a-Dope girls, dressed in coordinating baby blue T-shirts, looked excited to see me, but a bit surprised.

"Whatchu doing here, Mia?" Kendra asked when she saw me. "Don't you have equestrian practice or something?"

Sometimes I wondered how Kendra knew so much about the elite lifestyle. Maybe she was an undercover "trustafarian" or something. I ignored her.

"Hey, M-I-A," Stacie called out. I was beginning to despise that greeting. Especially because *she* was the one who was missing in action. Stacie hadn't been returning my calls or texts for the past week.

Stacie and all the jumpers—except Kendra—threw their arms around me, offering me one warm hug after another.

"It's been a while, girl," said one.

"Great to see you, ma," another jumper greeted me.

"Come on, y'all, we're next." Kendra interrupted the reunion. "The jazz band is almost finished."

Stacie looked apologetic.

"That's okay—go, go, go!" I encouraged. "I'll be down here cheering y'all on."

Because practices were held too early for me to attend, my role was reduced to being the team's hype man. But no matter how small the role, I was determined to take it on.

At least there was one rehearsal where I was expected and would be welcomed. The first mini-orchestra rehearsal for the winter musical was coming up. And I couldn't wait for that.

There were so many activities happening after school these days that the school building stayed populated long after the last bell. I had never noticed this before, because my usual after-school plan was to dash for the 2:44 bus. I used to be eager to get home at a decent time so that I could catch Stacie and the double-Dutch squad. But today was the first day of our mini-orchestra rehearsals, so I planned to stick around, too.

On my way to the music room in the annex building, I stopped at my locker to drop off my heavy book bag.

While I was there, I checked my hair in my mirror magnet. Over the weekend, I had gotten it cut into a layered pixie. Playful wisps of hair hung near my eyebrows. Toward the back of my head, the stylist had applied subtle flips to the ends. This hairstyle made my almond-shaped eyes stand out even more. My chin seemed a little pointier, too. I smiled to make sure nothing was in my teeth, which caused my dimples to deepen. Standing under the sun at the weekend's street festival had given my dark brown skin a nice glow. It was the perfect look for my new image as campus pianist.

The jangling keys Mr. Rick the custodian carried always announced his arrival.

"Hi, Mr. Rick," I greeted him as he made his way down the hallway carrying a heavy toolbox. His tired eyes twinkled when he saw me.

"How you settling in, little lady?" he asked, genuinely interested.

"Just fine," I lied.

"Now, I wanna see your name on that honor roll at least once this year, you hear me?" He reached the utility room at the end of the locker area.

"Yes, sir. I'll try my best."

"That's the spirit. Keep it up," he said before closing the door behind him.

Now I had to add Mr. Rick to the list of folks who'd be disappointed when I got my report card. Hopefully my piano performance would balance all that out.

"Excuse me." The male voice was coming from behind me.

I turned around to face the person.

"Is this the annex?" a teenage guy holding a black leather guitar case asked me. "I'm looking for the music room."

"No, it's on the other side of the building," I told him, trying to hide my surprise that there was a boy—and an African-American boy, at that!—wandering our halls. *Man, was this what I've been missing as I race to the bus stop each afternoon?* "I'm on my way there right now—I can show you."

"Oh great—thanks," he said, checking me out for the first time. His eyes glided over the features of my face as if he was suddenly aware that I was a girl his age. "This building is like a maze." He tried to make small talk as we headed for the staircase.

"Oh, believe me, I know," I said, nervously rolling my loose sheet music into a tube. "Are you from Mount Yeager?"

"Yeah. My name's Lucas." He held out his hand as we reached the first landing. "Lucas Osei."

I extended my hand, secretly hoping my palm wasn't too sweaty. He shook my hand softly.

"I'm Mia Chambers."

"Thanks for the escort, Mia." He smiled with appreciation. I could tell Lucas prided himself on being a clean-cut guy with good manners to match. His low-cut hair seemed freshly shorn. He probably had to shave it often to keep his hairline as tight as it looked today. Meeting Mount Yeager's strict grooming policy was obviously not a problem for Lucas. His oxford shirt was still tucked neatly into his belted pants. The only thing he'd ditched was his tie.

"Oh, I'm just paying it forward. On my first day here, I couldn't find the annex either and someone helped me."

"What a coincidence." He liked my story. "Did you ever run into this escort again?"

"She's now one of my closest friends here," I told him.

"Really?" he teased. "I wonder what that means for me and you."

We arrived at the music room just in time. Another minute with Lucas and he would've read the crush-orrific realization on my face. I was used to admiring crushes from a distance—like the cutie on that United Negro College Fund commercial, or that smooth-looking forward on City High's varsity basketball team. But this was just too close for comfort.

Lucas held the music-room door open for me and I walked in and pulled a seat in front of one of the vacant keyboards. Fortunately, the string section was on the other side of the room.

"Thanks again, Mia." Lucas smiled at me one last time before making his way over there.

Lin, the prodigy piano player, walked in and chose a keyboard a second later. We smiled at each other, both grateful to have made the short list.

"Your audition was amazing," I said.

"Yours too," she said admiringly.

With all the musicians warming up and chatting with each other, the music room was a cacophony of sounds.

"Can I get everyone to settle down?" an adult male voice rose above the noise. The one male member of the audition's panel of judges walked to the front of the room, arms raised like a traffic cop at a busy intersection.

"I'm Mr. Stewart, and I will be your musical director for this grand production." He looked around the room. "I know some of you from the music classes I teach over at the Mount. I am glad to get to meet the rest of you during this rehearsal period."

Mr. Stewart wore one of those suede jackets with the patched elbows. From the front, he appeared to have a full head of dark hair. But when Mr. Stewart's elbow patches faced the class, so did the round patch of skin at the crown of his head.

"Contrary to popular belief, there isn't much time to perfect our sound as a unit," he continued as he adjusted the pole on the music stand and lowered it to meet his vertically challenged stature. "But I plan to make the most of every minute we have together."

I don't know why, but Mr. Stewart's last words made me steal a peek at Lucas. To my surprise, he was looking straight back at me.

CHAPTER 8

"Ba-da-da-da," Mr. Stewart waved his conductor's stick like Harry Potter would his wand. But instead of the young wizard's jumble of unintelligible words, Mr. Stewart uttered Italian musical directives. "Adagio," he'd call out when our timing was too fast. "Staccato," he'd direct us when we were holding notes too long. Under his guidance, the mini-orchestra was sounding better and better.

After rehearsal, I grabbed the pile of music books under my seat and headed for the door. I had to meet Allie and Bonita downstairs in the auditorium where they were rehearsing. Because practice was over so late tonight, Bonita and I were going to sleep over at Allie's home, which was nearby.

"You need help with that?" Lucas caught up to me and asked.

We had been exchanging glances for the past few rehearsals but hadn't spoken since the day we'd met two weeks ago. Mr. Stewart thought it was important to keep the different music sections separate until everyone was ready to play together.

"Um…" I was caught off guard. "I'm not carrying these far—just to the auditorium." I realized I hadn't really answered his question.

"Not a problem." Lucas wrapped his guitar strap around his back and then took the slippery music books from me. "I can do that for you."

"Thanks," I said. I waved goodbye to Lin before Lucas followed me into the hallway.

"What's with all these music books?" he asked.

"I volunteered to play a few extra numbers," I said, feeling a bit shy. When I'd volunteered a week ago, Mr. Stewart had asked me if I was sure I could handle the extra assignments. It was important that I prove to myself, to him, and to everyone else that I could handle it.

"I never get a chance to speak to you," he said when we were out of Mr. Stewart's earshot.

I looked down at my black ballet flats, not knowing what to do with my hands.

"How've you been?" he asked.

"Okay," I finally said. "And you?"

"The same," he said cautiously. "But to be honest, I'm wondering how I'm gonna manage all these rehearsals, plus the mounting schoolwork I have."

I appreciated his honesty.

"Me, too," I confessed.

"I mean, I love this and all, but my parents ain't tryin'

to hear me slipping behind in any class. Not with all the tuition money they're shelling out."

Lucas's parents sounded a lot like mine.

"I know exactly what you mean." I looked him in the eyes for the first time since we'd stepped out of the music room.

"And what my parents mean by slippin' is getting anything lower than a B or B-plus." He nodded.

"By any chance do your parents know the Chambers family from East Orange, 'cause, um—I think they must've gotten trained at the same parenting school," I said.

He chuckled.

"They probably all aced Guilt 101 together." I was on a roll.

"You know, Mia, I wouldn't figure you'd be here crackin' jokes," Lucas admitted. "I mean, I see how tense you seem during rehearsals, and—"

"I've been dealing with new-transfer-student issues." I felt comfortable explaining to him.

"Ah." Lucas gave a knowing look. "The ol' fish-out-of-water feeling. I still struggle with that off and on, and I was born and raised in the next town."

"Well, East Orange feels like a long way from here," I told him.

"Well, the West African nation where my parents come from is even farther away than that!" he said, causing me to smile.

Lucas made it so easy to talk to him. By the time we got to the auditorium, I was wishing we'd walked slower to get there.

"Where can I put these down for you?" he asked me once we'd walked through the double doors. I looked at the sea of movie-theater-style fold-up seats.

"Mia!" I heard Allie's loud whisper before I spotted her waving arms. "Over here!" She was a few rows back from the stage, watching Bonita rehearse.

"There's my friend Allie," I told Lucas. "I'll go sit with her."

He followed me down the aisle to where Allie was seated with another girl.

"Allie, this is Lucas." I did the introductions.

"Hey, Lucas." Allie waved. "Guys, this is Clara Lopez, fellow stage artist extraordinaire."

"How ya doin'?," Lucas and I said at the same time.

"Hello." Clara waved. "Join us—it's a great show."

"Actually, Lucas has to—"

"Chill for a minute, Lucas," Allie said. The fold-up seat next to Allie looked like a pair of lips sloppily dining on a pile of jackets. Allie grabbed the jackets to make room. "Enjoy the free show."

He was happy to grab the seat next to mine. I was happy he was sticking around for a while. I sat between Allie and Lucas. On one side, she nudged me with her elbow as if to say, "Go, girl."

"You sure you don't mind if I hang out with you guys?" Lucas wanted to make sure his change of plans was okay with me.

"Not at all." I tried to sound nonchalant. "This is cool."

"Sshh," Allie threw at us. "Here comes Bonita again."

Bonita walked onto the stage to perform her scene. I

could immediately tell she was in character. Her usual sweet expression was replaced with a stern, stony face.

"What ever happened to the idea that people make the world go round?" she shouted in frustration as she stormed toward the center of the stage. "Money seems like the only force at work in this town."

"I'm sorry you feel that way, Ms. Lawrence, but we can't change our policy," Jennifer Octavian said vindictively from her seat behind a large desk planted stage left. Jennifer was in character, too, but her face looked the same as always.

"You may think this ends here." Bonita walked closer to the desk and looked straight into Jennifer's eyes. "But I know we'll cross paths again—sooner than you think."

We sat mesmerized by Bonita's performance. Her stage presence was charged with energy. Her character became three-dimensional to the point that I forgot that Ms. Lawrence was really Bonita.

"And…scene," the director in the front row called out. "Nice job, ladies."

The few of us watching in the audience all began applauding. Someone whistled and yelped, "Bonita—wooo!"

Jennifer caught on that everyone was cheering Bonita's performance rather than her own and she stormed off the stage.

"Keep that up and you guys are gonna have that girl hate me." Bonita looked a bit worried by Jennifer's temper tantrum when she came to join us.

"Never mind her, you deserved that ovation." I gave her a hug. "You were great!"

"Let's go celebrate with my mom's famous homemade milk shakes," Allie said.

When we all walked outside, Lucas's ride was waiting for him.

"There's my brother," he told me. "Nice hanging with you and your friends. We should do this again. Can I call you?"

I tried my hardest not to make eye contact with Bonita, Clara, and Allie as Lucas and I programmed each other's numbers into our cell phones. His back was to them, so they were doing all sorts of crazy gesturing to try to grab my attention.

"Bye, Lucas," they chimed in chorus as he went to meet his ride.

"Oooo!" they teased, giggling. "Tell us everything! Spill it!" Bonita urged.

I paused, looking at her. "Would I be telling this to Bonita or Ms. Lawrence?"

We all laughed. Then I filled them in on how Lucas and I had met.

"Mmm." Allie's imagination started running wild. "Maybe he'll strum a romantic tune for you outside your window one day."

"No, not unless he's taking requests," Clara joked along before heading home.

While Bonita and Allie chatted, I watched a woman with fiery red-orange hair get out of a sedan and wave her arms in the air. That gesture looked familiar.

"Allie, is that your mom?" I asked.

"Yup, there she is," Allie perked up. "Let's go, ladies."

* * *

"In this moonlight, your house looks like it's purple," I said when Allie's mother pulled her hybrid car into the long driveway.

"The house is purple," Allie said.

"Seriously, Mrs. Snierson?" Bonita asked.

"Call me Lake," Allie's mom responded. "Yes, it is of an eggplant hue. And let me tell ya, the neighbors love me for it."

I could easily see where Allie got her carefree, carpe diem spirit.

"Oh, my mom's a regular rabble rouser in this town," Allie said.

"Honey, if you say it like that, you'll make the girls think I'm a troublemaker," Lake corrected her. "Let's just say I try to keep the folks around here grounded."

The interior of the Snierson home matched the exterior. There were framed paintings Allie had created in practically her infancy. It seemed like her mom had accepted the person Allie was from the start.

That's amazing, I thought. Instead of forcing people to act a certain way, like my mom did, Lake encouraged Allie's self-expression, no matter what part of herself she wanted to express.

"Make yourselves at home, ladies." Lake dropped her hobo purse on the kitchen island. "I'll be back in a few to whip up those milk shakes."

"Did I say I was just staying here for one night?" I teased Allie. "I meant to tell you I'll be here for the rest of the week."

"Me too, gurl," Bonita chimed in.

The three of us bust out in giggles and headed up to Allie's room to change out of our uniforms.

The next day at school, the opening-night date for the winter musical was finally posted on the board outside the auditorium.

"December fourth has a good-luck ring to it," I told Bonita and Allie.

"It's as good a date as any," Allie said. "We'll be ready."

I was still daydreaming about having a successful opening night when I walked into Ms. Veltz's humanities class. After the bell rang, Ms. V handed back our tests without saying a word. My heart sank when I saw my grade written and circled in cruel red ink: 65. This grade would send my already-low average in this class plummeting. I felt like I was on the verge of panicking.

Ms. V had laryngitis, so she spent half the class writing assignments on the board and the other half showing a history documentary on TV. She wore a printed silk scarf around her neck, as if to protect her damaged voice box. Today was no day to wait after class to talk to her about a solution for me.

How do I fix this? I asked myself over and over.

As if hearing my thoughts, Ms. V handed out a detailed assignment for an oral presentation. "Worth forty percent of your marking period grade" was written in bold letters along the top of the page. I read the paper, hoping it was the key to digging myself out of the hole I was chin-deep in. The sheet read that the class was assigned a critical oral presentation about people who shared philosophies with literary figures we had studied. This was Ms. V's way of allowing us to introduce our personal favorites to the class. If this didn't boost my standings before the marking period ended, nothing else could.

On my bus ride home, my phone's text message signal interrupted my thoughts.

"Call me as SOON as U get home," Stacie's message read. *Oh, now she wants to catch up,* I thought. Not the best timing. Still, I was curious to hear what she had to say, so I dialed her number as soon as I got to my bedroom.

"I got the admissions letter!" Stacie answered the phone shouting. She was so wound up she sounded out of breath.

"You got an early admissions letter to college?" I was confused.

"No, no, no!" She took a deep breath to slow herself down. "We, Rope-a-Dope double-Dutch squad of East Orange, New Jersey, are invited to compete for a spot in the state championships!"

I jumped up and down so hard, my cell phone's earpiece popped out. Good thing Bibi wasn't home or else my scream would've startled her into a heart attack. I plugged the earpiece back in.

"Stacie? Are you there?"

"Yes, I'm here." She was still panting.

This was the moment we'd dreamed of when we'd started up the squad. I couldn't believe that everything had paid off.

"We did it!" My voice cracked. I felt emotional. Just when I thought the day had been built for bad news, this turn of events was spectacular enough to melt my academic worries away.

"We have a lot of time to choreograph a kick-ass routine, but we should start rehearsing this weekend." I could see Stacie scribbling in her Ideas notebook as she spoke. Suddenly the background noise on her end quieted down and Stacie's voice sobered up. "I know we haven't been hanging out like usual, but for this, gurl, let me be the first to say we need you. So for you, we'll hold one weekend practice a week."

I was so touched that I couldn't think of what to say. After a long shutout, I finally felt like I was being invited back into the fold.

"I'll be there," I said. "What day is the competition going down?"

I heard Stacie flipping through the pages of the admissions package mailed to her.

"Oh, it's right here," she announced proudly. "It's all going down on the evening of December fourth!"

Stacie's words rang in my ear long after I'd hung up with her. I felt numb. Of all the dates on the calendar, the night of the competition of our double-Dutch dreams was the same night as the winter musical.

CHAPTER 9

stress robbed me of any real rest that night. After tossing and turning for hours, I gave up on getting sleep around three a.m. After that, I waited on the sun to rise.

That had always been the case with me. The last time I'd had insomnia, I was worried that Bibi would be moving out to live with my uncle Lenny. He had been complaining that it was unfair for my mom to keep Bibi to herself. Uncle Lenny thought it was time Bibi made a change and flew down to North Carolina to live with him. The thought of living without Bibi was so distressing to me that I couldn't sleep for days. Good thing Uncle Lenny's wife was against the whole idea. Once that crisis was over, I hibernated for hours on end, happy to be back to my old self.

But that night, for what felt like forever, I lay on my back staring at the ceiling. Even though I lay awake for hours, I didn't get out of bed until six a.m. At that point I showered, dressed, and made my way down to the kitchen. I ran into my dad at the bottom of the stairs.

"Hey, sweetie." He was obviously happy to see me.

"Good morning, Dad." I avoided eye contact as I walked by.

"Hold on there," he said. "It's still early—no need to rush off. Besides, I was thinking I could drive you to school this morning. How would you like that?"

That's right—today is Friday, I thought. My dad's work schedule was more flexible on Friday mornings. Plus, since my mom was out of town on business for a few days, he didn't have to drive her to the train station.

"It's okay, Dad," I said, using my eyes to trace the letters on his red Rutgers T-shirt. "I'm fine with the bus."

"Now I know something is wrong, because my little girl would love to spend extra time in the morning with her daddy," he teased. "What's going on, Mia?"

I had to tell him something, otherwise he would get super worried. But I couldn't tell him the whole story or he'd be so disappointed in me. I couldn't bear that. Dad was always so proud of my smarts and he enjoyed matching wits with me. "She's my little genius," I'd overhear him telling his friends. What would he think if he knew I was struggling in school?

"You know you can tell me anything," he said, reading the cautious expression on my face. "Anything that's troubling you, we can solve it together."

"I've just been having a tough time fitting in at school," I told him.

"Do you mean socially?" he asked. I should've known not to be vague with a guy like my dad. He thrived on details. "I thought you made good friends at the academy. Did something go wrong at your sleepover?"

"No, no." I didn't want to mislead him. I sat on a carpeted step. "Everything with Bonita and Allie is great. I've just been feeling overwhelmed academically. The workload is just entirely different from City High."

He sat next to me.

"I know it's tough, sweetie," he said softly. "And I know that you'd rather be with your friends at City High. You're a strong person for making that transition so gracefully. But we wanted to make sure that you continue to be challenged so you can reach your brilliant potential. If things get to be too much for you to handle, you know you should never be afraid to come to me."

"I know, Dad." I tried to give him a smile.

When my dad hugged me, I closed my eyes and let my head rest on his shoulder. He always had a special way of bringing me comfort.

Dad respected my wishes and just drove me to the bus stop instead. I didn't have the energy to keep up the everything's peachy façade for the car ride to school. He understood when I told him that I like to get reading done on the bus. Truthfully, it was my last-minute opportunity to play catch-up with my schoolwork.

Once I got on the bus, my iPod tuned out the chatty passengers and I started skimming through my books. Strangely, Bonita wasn't on the bus this morning like she usually was, so I had time to study. I reviewed the authors and scholars we'd been covering in humanities and wondered which historic figure I should focus my oral presentation on. *What can I possibly teach that class that they don't know?* My classmates were all so bookish and well read. I couldn't believe how many times something or someone they mentioned in class sent me running to Wikipedia. The thought alone had me feeling like things were hopeless.

I felt my cell phone vibrating in my pocket. Someone had just sent me a text message. I flipped open my cell and read: Hv a gr8 day. C U @ rehearsal 2nite. Lucas.

In spite of my sulky mood, I smiled. His text felt like a little reminder from above that no matter how tough life got, things were never hopeless. I texted back: Thnx. U 2.

A few hours later, I was battling my demons all over again. My math teacher pulled me aside at the end of the class to issue a personal warning: "I don't know how things worked over at City High," she said with a piercing look. "But if you don't get your grades up, I'm going to have to pull you from the winter musical."

By the time I got to my humanities class, I slumped in my seat, feeling defeated until Ms. Veltz asked the class a question that stumped everyone else except me.

"In 1964, who became the youngest person to win the Nobel Peace Prize?" she asked.

Mine was the sole hand raised.

"Martin Luther King, Jr.," I said when she called on me.

My answer was brief, but I was left with a hunger to talk longer about Dr. King. There was obviously so much that the class should learn about the great man once referred to as the "moral leader of our nation." The notable figures in history that Ms. Veltz covered in this class were fascinating and inspiring, but one thing that they were not was diverse. That was when it struck me—I would base my oral presentation on an African-American.

Suddenly I felt excited and eager to get started on my project. I flipped through my notebook for a blank page, then started scribbling down ideas, Stacie style.

I hightailed it to the music room as soon as the last bell rang. I didn't even stop by my locker because I wanted to use the twenty minutes before rehearsal started to practice my extra numbers. Mr. Stewart wanted to know that I was up to that challenge. Just in case I wasn't, Lin would be my musical understudy. She was learning the same three numbers.

The music room was empty. I took my place at the keyboard and began by playing the pieces. I had enough time to play each one twice, which helped me to smooth out the kinks in my performance. With a few extra minutes left to kill, I started playing around on the keyboard. I began to play my grandma's favorite, "Clair de Lune."

"That sounds nice." Lucas was standing in the doorway watching me play.

I lifted my hands from the keyboard.

"Where did you come from?" I asked playfully.

"No, don't stop playing," he said, and walked over with his guitar. He took a seat on a nearby bench and began strumming along. His acoustic sounds harmonized perfectly with my piano notes. As I played measure after measure,

Lucas kept up his perfect accompaniment. It was like we'd been rehearsing together for years. When we'd played our last note, Lucas and I held each other's gaze for a few moments. I felt a definite connection between us. It was a nice feeling.

In the next moment, Lucas leaned toward me and—to my surprise—softly kissed the corner of my lips. He pulled back a little as if to make sure I was okay with his move. I stared back into his eyes until he leaned in once more. This time, he kissed me fully on the lips. When he pulled away again, I started babbling to hide my surprise.

"You know 'Clair de Lune'?" I asked.

"Of course," he said. "I like classical music."

"Me, too," I confessed for the first time to anyone other than my family and piano teachers. "That piece has always been my jam."

"Ah, early birds," Mr. Stewart walked in saying. "I like to see that dedication."

A group of musicians followed him in. Lucas stood up and smiled a knowing smile at me.

"I'll see you after rehearsal," he said before joining the musicians in the string section.

I was still buzzing a half hour after rehearsal. Lucas and I were sitting on the floor in front of my locker chatting nonstop.

"I never realized double Dutch could be such an intense sport." He looked amazed.

"You have no idea," I explained. "Those competitions are so off the hook you'd be blown away."

"Well, let me know what you decide to do," he said, shaking his head. "I know it's gotta be a tough thing choosing between the musical and the double-Dutch tournament."

I took a deep breath, feeling nervous at the mere thought of that night.

"There you are, Mia." Allie rushed down the hallway to me. "I've been looking all over for you."

"What's wrong?" I stood up to meet her—I knew something was wrong because Allie never rushed anywhere.

"You didn't hear about Bonita?" She looked flustered.

"No—what about her?" I asked, concerned. "I noticed she wasn't on the bus today."

"That's because she stayed home today." Allie was even speaking faster than usual. "Jennifer Octavian confronted Bonita yesterday, saying that she knows Bonita is here on scholarship because she has a parent on staff."

Allie paused to take a breath. Unless Bonita had been adopted by a white family, I couldn't think of who she could be related to at the academy.

"Bonita is Mr. Rick's daughter," Allie continued. "The news is being spread through the cast and crew. I'm sure by tomorrow everyone else will be talking about it."

My heart sank. How could Jennifer be so vicious?

"Bonita must feel horrible right now," I said almost to myself. "We've got to go see her. She needs our support right now."

"I tried calling her a few times already, but she's not picking up," said Allie.

"She's gotta come back here and hold her head up high." Lucas looked as bothered by this as we were.

"At least it's Friday," I tried to reason. "Bonita can regroup this weekend, and hopefully she'll come back Monday feeling strong enough to face this."

"Let's hope you're right," said Allie.

I was the first to arrive at the dance room we'd reserved at the local community center. Stacie and the rest of the Rope-a-Dope crew were meeting me there for our first tournament rehearsal session.

I was facing the mirrored walls when I caught the reflection of the newest Rope-a-Dope member walking in. I turned around to greet her.

"Hey—Yolanda, is it?" I wasn't sure if I'd remembered her name right. "I met you at the street festival."

"Mia, I know." She smiled and dropped her tote bag. "So Stacie says you'll be co-choreographing the routines?"

"Yup." I wondered why Yolanda looked doubtful.

"Oh. 'Cause you seem so-I don't know, kinda…"

"White?" Kendra's obnoxious voice entered the room a full few seconds before she did.

"Kendra, your jokes never get new, do they?" I was too annoyed to hold back.

"Who says I'm joking?" In absence of her laugh-track crew, she started cracking up by herself.

Yolanda looked uncomfortable, but not for long.

"Oh, you got the new Lances, I see," Kendra told her with admiration.

"Yeah, this set me back a few chips, but I had to rock it."

I obviously wasn't up on the latest gear, because I had no idea what Lances were.

"Go 'head." Yolanda offered her colorful hooded jacket to Kendra. "Try it on."

"That's lookin' tight," Kendra said, wearing the jacket and checking her look in the mirror. "Too right." She struck a pose.

For a second I didn't know if "too right" was the latest phrase or if Kendra was just making things up as she went along to make me feel out of touch. *I'm overthinking everything,* I thought. I told myself to chill and go with the flow. There was no way I was going to let Kendra make me feel like a stranger in my own community.

Stacie walked in with three other jumpers, and I was glad for the distraction.

"Oooh!" she squealed when she saw me. "You got your hair cut!" Stacie gave me a hug and then turned me around so she could check it out. "You look different," she commented.

I didn't know if that was a compliment or not. I got the impression she meant that I looked suburban. *Just shake it off,* I told myself.

"Let's get straight to business, people," Stacie announced. "What song do you think we should perform to?"

"'No Need' by Jah-Nice," Kendra called out.

Most of the girls chimed in with their agreement. Stacie

turned to me when I didn't react. "What do you think of performing to that?" she asked.

"I—I don't know if I've heard that one," I admitted reluctantly.

"What?" Kendra exaggerated her disbelief. "You sure she won't have us doing the running man or some old-ass move if she choreographs this? She ain't even up on nothin' new. Remember, this is double Dutch, not ballet—so no classical music selections and pirouettes, please."

I wondered what they would think if they knew that I and the boy I was dating liked listening to classical music now and then. Suddenly, I wasn't as eager to tell Stacie about Lucas anymore.

"Actually," I heard myself say in a confident voice, "I was thinking that we should perform to True MC's 'True Life Story' to represent East Orange."

Everyone thought this was a perfect idea—everyone, that is, except Kendra, who for once didn't offer her opinion.

At the end of our rehearsal, I left the center convinced that if I was to gain back any respect I'd lost, I had to come up with the best routine those girls had ever seen.

CHAPTER 10

I started off my Monday morning by having to run to catch the bus. My thighs felt sore as I dodged traffic on the main avenue to cut off the bus. Maybe I'd pulled a muscle the day before when I worked on choreography alone in the basement for four straight hours.

When I stepped on the bus, I spotted Bonita blankly staring out the window, looking at nothing in particular. She got startled when I sat in the empty seat next to her.

"Hey, gurl," I said gently. "Are you all right? Allie and I were so worried about you."

She looked at me with bloodshot eyes. I could tell she'd been crying. I put my hand on hers.

"I was so devastated that I couldn't bring myself to come to school Friday." She sniffed. "And I hardly ever miss school unless I'm really really sick."

I could understand the pressure Bonita felt to measure up.

"It's not that I'm ashamed of my dad. I just never wanted

people to box me into some 'underprivileged' category and treat me differently because of it."

"Bonita." I chose my words carefully, not wanting to say the wrong thing while she was feeling so vulnerable. "You can't control what people decide to think of you. The only thing you can focus on is how you feel about yourself. And from where I'm sitting, you are a sensational person who's driven, intelligent, sweet, and very talented. How can trifling things like gossip and small talk hold you down when those amazing qualities have you soaring so high?"

"Wow." Bonita exhaled slowly, then smiled. "Did you just make that up or have you been reading *Chicken Soup for the Teenage Soul?*"

"You think *you're* shocked," I joked along. "I'm over here thinking, Why can't I follow my own damn advice?"

We both starting cracking up. At that moment, the laughter felt like the best medicine our souls could ask for.

I realized why I loved being in my piano teacher Nadine's company so much. For one thing, she made no apologies for her quirky taste in clothes and furniture. And to me, she was like a guardian to pianos. Having worked at the prestigious Steinway & Sons for some time, she knew everything there was to know about pianos. She even seemed to treat pianos like individuals. I enjoyed hearing her draw links between pianos and people.

"Any piano that's played at length over a long period of time begins to lose its unique pitch and needs to be tuned," she told me. Nadine could see how burned out I was becoming. I was working hard to keep going. Besides, my talk with Bonita had hit home.

Even though it felt like my world was crumbling down, I couldn't afford to break down with it. I had my grades to think of. Doing well in this new school was just too important to me. I was spending too much energy trying to prove myself to everyone. Acing my academics was my way of proving something to myself.

It was time to stop playing everyone's song but my own.

I set out to give myself some much-needed fine tuning.

"Mia, I don't know how you came up with those moves so fast, but we all love them," Stacie was talking so loud that I had to hold the receiver a few inches from my head. "Even Kendra let it slip that she thought the choreography was tight."

"Thanks," I said sheepishly. I didn't think Stacie would be so complimentary when she heard what I had to tell her. "Stace, I have some bad news," I started.

"Oh, it can't be that bad, gurl." Stacie hadn't stopped smiling since she got the tournament admissions letter.

I swallowed. "Well, remember the winter musical I told you about?"

"Yeah."

"The opening night is at the same time as the tournament."

There was silence on her end. And then she snarled, "So, whatchu sayin', Mia?"

"I'm locked into playing the piano, and can't back out

this late in the game," I said. "But that's one reason I worked so hard to give the squad a tight routine and—"

"Kendra was right about you," Stacie's voice sounded constricted and angry.

Before I could ask what she meant by that, Stacie hung up on me.

Instead of calling her back, I set out to do the next unpleasant thing on my list. I walked out of my room and down to the den, where my mom was reading a magazine. When she watched me walk in like a zombie and then plop down next to her in a heap, she knew something was up.

"I know I haven't been the greatest daughter to you recently," I started before she could ask me what was wrong. "I was angry that you expected me to just find my place at a new school when it took me so long to feel like I belonged in my old school. I'm not as socially graceful and likable as you, Mom. What comes easy for you is a struggle for me," I said.

"Mia, honey." She put her arms lovingly around me. "I think you're mistaken. Look at how quickly you made friends with Allie and Bonita. Beyond that, anyone who'd rather shun you than get to know you isn't important anyway. And without you, Stacie couldn't have gotten Rope-a-Dope as far. I watch you get up on stage and perform with the other jumpers and you shine. Now, you achieve these things in your own unique way, but no one—not even me—can take away from the fact that you do achieve them."

Tears rolled down the sides of my face. For the first time in a long time, I could see that my mother was proud of me, just the way I was.

"I need help, Mom." I broke down. "I've been trying so hard to fit in that I messed up—big time."

She listened without judgment as I told her about the extra musical numbers, the tournament conflict, and my advanced algebra and humanities classes. For once, I was glad to have a mother who thrived on being a problem solver. We put our heads together and decided that I should start intense tutoring sessions with my dad right away. It was also clear that I had to scale back my musical numbers in the show. The sooner I could tackle the problem, the better.

Of course, this meant I was giving up some of my freedom. My mom said she'd be monitoring my assignments a lot more closely, because I obviously needed help keeping my academic schedule balanced until the musical was over. It was a small price to pay to get my life back on track.

I was worried that my dad would be disappointed in me. Instead, he was proactive and practical. The practice math quizzes he began giving me almost daily improved my comprehension of the subject. My teacher noticed the difference within just a week and even commented on it. My tutoring also did wonders for my confidence during class. Instead of worrying about what my classmates thought, I began to ask more questions without wondering if the answer was obvious to everyone else.

Even Lucas chipped in to help me catch up. We'd meet up at the bookstore café, and he'd listen to how my oral presentation was shaping up. Lucas also helped me come up with the best way to talk to the show's musical director.

Mr. Stewart had started requesting that musicians with extra pieces report to more rehearsals than the rest of the mini-orchestra members. There was no way I could fit in extra rehearsal time.

"How did he take it?" Lucas was waiting for me in the hallway outside the music room after I had my chat with Mr. Stewart.

"Not as bad as I thought he would." I was relieved.

"So you won't have to perform that night with a bag over your head?" Lucas took my hand and we began heading out of the building.

"No, corny." I nudged him in the rib. "He said that I could be the understudy to Lin, who will be taking the pieces on. Thank goodness she was happy to do it."

"That's great." Lucas was happy for me.

"No, I think you're great." I stopped walking and faced Lucas. "Thanks for being so supportive throughout everything. I really appreciate everything you've done."

He wrapped me up in a bear hug.

Suddenly I felt horrible about being ashamed to tell Stacie about Lucas. Not that Stacie would care. It had been two weeks since she'd hung up on me and I hadn't heard from her. I'd sent her a lengthy e-mail apologizing, but I guess she was still too angry to talk to me.

"That's enough, lovebirds," a paint-covered Allie said as she sauntered toward us with Bonita. Lucas and I shyly stepped away from each other.

"You're supposed to paint the set, not your clothes," I told Allie.

"Whatchu talking about?" Bonita looked Allie up and down. "She bought those like that."

It was great to see Bonita slowly getting back to her old self. She had to endure whispers in the hallways and sympathetic stares for about a week, but just like yesterday's paper, the news lost its novelty over time, and people moved on. It was finally looking like she and I were taking on our challenges in ways we never thought we could.

My last order of academic business was humanities class.

Bibi was an attentive audience when I practiced my humanities speech in front of her. If anyone would know whether the presentation worked or not, it was Bibi, because she actually remembered marching with Dr. King as a young girl.

Ms. Veltz said we could shape our presentation in any way we wanted to. I chose to pretend that I was a speaker at a civil rights organizers' meeting. The humanities class would become the civil rights leaders and planners. I figured we all took for granted the fruits of past labor—opportunities and freedoms we had. I wanted to transport everyone to a golden time when that seed was planted.

Bibi listened as I continued to act like a speaker addressing the organizers. My speech illustrated what obstacles people of the Jim Crow South were up against. During my speech, I pointed out a young newcomer named Dr. King, who would be chosen to lead what would become a historical bus boycott.

As I spoke, I saw Bibi's eyes look in the distance, focusing on the memory. Her chin jutted out with deep, quiet pride.

The next day when Ms. Veltz summoned me to the front of the class to make my speech, my throat felt dry. When I reached the lectern and attempted to speak, my tongue was stuck to the roof of my mouth. To buy myself the extra time I needed to regain my composure, I shuffled my index cards and pretended to be preparing.

I started the speech looking down and reading my index cards, even though I had it memorized by heart.

Eventually, my nerves calmed as I made eye contact with my classmates. I realized that they were into my speech. They looked impressed. Inspired, even. That fueled me even more. I began dramatizing my words with gestures and facial expressions that conveyed anguish and hope. At the end of my lecture, the class was silent even after I sat down in my desk. Then Mrs. Veltz broke through the quiet and said, "Now, that's what I consider an A-plus presentation."

With that, I had officially made it out of that humanities hole.

Either I'd started understanding Greek or I finally realized my teachers had been speaking English all along. Whatever the case, my smarts were back. And with them my confidence. I was on top of my academic game again. It felt good to see the results of my late-night and early-morning study sessions. Don't get me wrong—it was hard work. But that was what it took to get back on track. I found myself looking ahead to the future and wanting to prepare for it.

I wanted to be just as qualified as everyone around me.

Sure, my classmates lived in bigger, fancier houses and they shopped at the same supermarkets as our teachers. But my dedication to my academics leveled the playing field. And each time I aced an exam or a *pawp* quiz, I felt that it was a score for me and for urban kids like me.

CHAPTER 11

on the opening night of the musical, Bibi, my parents, and my piano teacher, Nadine, all sat in the sold-out school theater waiting for the performance to start.

"It's here," a bow-tie clad Mr. Stewart said, standing in front of all of us musicians assembled in the music room. "The night we've been preparing for. And I can say with all confidence that that audience is going to experience the most polished, talented junior orchestra they have ever heard."

Everyone erupted in applause and woop-wooping calls. Lucas and I hooked fingers for a soul-brotha handshake that ended with two loud snaps. He looked extra smart tonight in the slim black tie and white shirt all the male musicians wore. I had on a knee-length black skirt and white blouse like all the other female musicians. A shiny silver-studded barrette held my bangs back to one side.

"Let's go take our places," Mr. Stewart said, and led us out of the room to the theater.

We lined up right outside the double doors that led to the front of the theater.

"We'd like to present to you—" I heard the muffled words of a female MC announce to the audience "—our fabulous mini-orchestra led by musical director Mr. Dennis Stewart."

When the double doors opened, the loud applause was unleashed into the hallway where we stood. Butterflies tickled my stomach as I followed the line of musicians and marched into the buzzing theater. Once I was seated at the piano, I peeked into the audience to see if I could find my family. The tap-tap of Mr. Stewart's baton snapped my attention back to the piano.

He lifted both arms in the air and froze in that position for a few beats. The lights dimmed and the crowd quieted down. When every musician was at attention, he gave us that now-familiar cue and the string section played a long, slow note. I held my hands over the piano keys. When Mr. Stewart nodded sharply in my direction, I pressed down on my first few notes. At the next flick of his baton the brass section joined in. With that, the curtains pulled back to reveal the setting of a family living room, where Bonita was seen sitting legs crossed, reading the paper. The show had begun.

It was an amazing night, made greater by Bonita's outstanding performance. She was hands down the audience favorite. The applause was deafening every time she sang. The crowd cracked up every time she nailed a punch line. Even Jennifer's sidekicks sitting in the front row were cheering for Bonita! Unfortunately for Jennifer, Bonita was the night's shining star. And oddly enough, thanks to Jennifer, students in the audience congratulated a proud Mr. Rick. He sat beaming as he watched his daughter from the front row. Her performance inspired me to give my double-Dutch dream a shot.

It was tough keeping my mind from wandering. I couldn't stop thinking about what the Rope-a-Dope team must be experiencing.

By intermission, I felt relieved that my job as pianist was almost done. I just had the third act left to play. The orchestra was having a great night, and I was happy I'd made it this far without messing up once. Scaling back my numbers meant that Lin would be playing all the pieces in the final act. Lucas was packing up his guitar when I walked over to him. He didn't have to play in the whole second act.

"This is gonna sound crazy," I told him. "But after the third act, I may still have time to make it to the Performing Arts Center in Newark, where the double-Dutch tournament is going down."

"How are you gonna manage that?"

I didn't have a clue.

"Hey—my brother's here tonight. Maybe he could drive us down."

"You think he'd do that for us?" I asked.

"He might if we promise to introduce him to Bonita." Lucas had a twinkle in his eye. He might have been the kid brother by one year, but Lucas knew how to push his older brother's buttons.

"Honey, you are doing so great," I heard my mother's voice. She had come over to pay her compliments to the pianist, the same way she had to Nadine on Broadway. I felt touched by that.

"Hi, Mom." I beamed.

"Hello, Mrs. Chambers." Lucas looked charming as he reached out to shake her hand.

"Beautiful performance," she said, genuinely approving. "We're all enjoying it so much. And that Miss Bonita is just stealing the show!"

"Thanks," I said, smiling. "Mom?"

My mom looked at me sideways. "Whatchu got cookin' up in that brain of yours, Mia?"

"Uh—I was just thinking about making my way down to the arts center after the third act. Lucas is gonna get his brother to drive us. His brother is a senior at Mount Yeager and has had his license for over a year."

"Your dad and I figured you were gonna pull something like this." She sounded upset. But when she saw how anxious I looked, her face softened. "Okay, Mia," she said with a nod. "In the past few months, you've worked harder than I've ever seen. You've earned an opportunity to go to the tournament."

"Oh, thank you, Mom!"

"Mm-hmm," she said, laying on the sass. "We'll pick you up from there when the tournament's over."

During the third act, Lucas set out to find his brother. He asked me to meet him outside the front doors as soon as the act was over. When I stepped through the doors, he was waiting for me with his brother Kofi and Allie. With no time to waste, we rushed to the crowded parking lot. My heart was pumping with anticipation. I figured we had enough time to make the second round of the three-round competition. But when we got to Kofi's car, it was blocked in by another car.

"Oh no!" I was crushed.

I thought this was a sign. *Maybe I should just give up my old life and forget my old friends,* I thought. *They think I'm a sellout anyway. I mean, it's not possible to be both urban and suburban at the same time. I should just choose a side and move on. Besides, my old friends could never accept me anymore.*

"I'm sorry, Mia." Allie put her arm around me to try to console me. Lucas and Kofi stared at me sympathetically.

"I can go in and have them make an announcement," Lucas offered.

"It's no use," I said. "They're not gonna interrupt the final act."

In my anguish, I leaned on the minivan that was blocking Kofi's car and set its alarm off.

"Great," I said. "More drama."

A minute later, know-it-all Emma Bishop arrived on the scene with her older sister to shut the alarm off.

"Hey, Mia," she said. "Are we blocking you in?"

Ever since my oral presentation, Emma had started talking to me more.

"Yes." Allie sounded hopeful. "Maybe we can still make the double-Dutch tournament!"

"Cool! You guys going to the double-Dutch tournament at the arts center?" Emma asked surprisingly. *How in the world did she know about that?* I wondered. "Our older sister books talent there," she explained.

"Well, Mia is supposed to be competing with her squad, but had to miss most of it because of her commitment here," Allie explained.

Another girl I recognized from humanities class joined Emma and her sister and they all started buzzing about my situation.

"We'll be out of your way right away." Emma's sister got behind the wheel. They not only moved the van, but after hearing about our mission, they decided to follow us to the competition!

Emma turned out to be the most unexpected lifesaver ever. On our drive to Newark, Emma called her older sister, who granted a few of us access to the backstage area. As I led Allie and Lucas to meet my Rope-a-Dope teammates, it felt strange to have both my worlds collide.

The sparkly red outfits the squad was wearing was easy to find in a crowd.

"Stacie!" I called out when I saw her.

"You came!" Stacie got excited despite herself. She forgot she wasn't talking to me for that split second she saw me. Then it was back to her grudge match.

"You missed the whole competition," she said.

For a moment, things were very tense. The team was upset that I hadn't jumped with them. When I realized that I wouldn't get to jump, I had to fight back my tears. Stacie noticed how hurt I was. She hadn't expected me to show up at the competition, but she was glad I did.

"I'm sorry I was so harsh with you," she admitted, and reached out to hug me. "I was so wrapped up in my own life that I didn't realize you were having a tough time."

"No, I was trying to be superwoman, so I made everyone empty promises."

"Oh, look at how pitiful we are, gurl," she said, laughing at our blubbering.

"Hey." I remembered that I wasn't alone. "I want you to meet my good friend Allie and my boyfriend, Lucas."

"Boyfriend?" Stacie squealed as she greeted them both with a hug. Throughout all the hugging going on Kendra didn't budge.

"They're about to announce the winners!" Yolanda interrupted us.

We all quieted down and the squad held hands.

"In third place, out of Englewood, NJ—the Jumpin' Janes."

The crowd roared with applause. The squad next to us started jumping up and down, and then they ran onto the stage to pick up their trophy. When they returned backstage, they looked drunk with happiness.

"Ladies and gentlemen, we have a tie for first place," the announcer said. "The following two teams will have to perform a tiebreaking routine—and they are Nonstop Steppers from Camden and East Orange's Rope-a-Dope."

Reflexively, Kendra jumped up and hugged me. She had

the widest smile I'd ever seen on her face. Suddenly I understood her. She had dreams she was afraid wouldn't come true, just like me. Only she masked her fears by acting like she didn't care about anything or anyone. Tonight, she showed how much she did deeply care.

"For a sometimes out-of-touch girl, you can choreograph your butt off," she said, smiling.

"Now, that's a joke that won't get old," I told her.

Stacie and I had a routine choreographed specifically in case of a tiebreaker.

Stacie reached into her large gym bag and handed me a red sparkly uniform. I was glad she'd thought to bring it.

"Do you have the tiebreaker music?" she asked me.

I bit my bottom lip. I hadn't thought to bring it. I'd thought I'd miss the entire competition. I tried not to panic.

"The music is right here," Lucas said holding up his guitar.

Stacie and I looked at him, wondering if he was sure he knew what he was doing.

"Don't go out there playing us some ol' wack, bleeding-heart ballad, Romeo," Kendra told him.

"Don't worry—just worry about doing your thing." Lucas handled Kendra's snide remarks well.

As we prepared to hit the stage a few minutes later, Lucas sat on a stool on stage with a mic pointed at his guitar. He nodded at me before I shouted, "Ready the ropes!"

I could see Allie beaming offstage as Lucas began strumming on his guitar like he was on *MTV Unplugged*. The Wyclef-esque rhythm that he worked up had the audience clapping to the beat he tapped on the body of the guitar between chords. I joined the Rope-a-Dope jumpers and we skillfully jumped, flipped, and danced gingerly within the two mismatched yet perfectly in-sync egg-beating ropes.

When our routine ended, we all hurried offstage feeling like we were walking on air. It didn't matter if we won. Nothing could bring us down from our high. It felt so amazing to perform at this level. It was a dream come true.

Everyone patted Lucas on the back, complimenting him on his incredible skills.

"Yo, nobody tonight performed to a live musician," Stacie boasted. "We had that down on lock."

I gave Lucas a hug.

"You were kicking butt out there." Allie was enjoying being there.

A few minutes later, the MC got back on the microphone.

"The judges have made their decision," he announced. "Our second-place team is the Nonstop Steppers, and in first place—"

We were screaming so loud we couldn't make out anything else the announcer said.

"We did it!" I said to Stacie.

"We did it, gurl," she said.

When we went onstage to receive our award, I saw the crowd of St. Claire girls leap out of their seats cheering. I couldn't believe the support they had for us.

I stood onstage with my chin pointed out, just like Bibi's when she was filled with a strong sense of pride and triumph.

Later in the arts center parking lot, we all hung out together while waiting for my parents and Stacie's brother to pick us up. Everyone talked at the same time. Allie and Stacie were chatting like reality-show judges about the good and bad performance colors other jumpers had on. Emma was asking me a million questions about the fundamentals of double Dutch. And Kendra was challenging Lucas to play the acoustic versions of different hip-hop song hooks.

"Aw yeah!" she shouted when Lucas nailed another tune. "Uh-uh-uh." Kendra warmed up to rap along with the chords he played.

For once, I felt like everyone was focusing on what we had in common, instead of on our differences.

All this time, I'd been wearing myself out with a double act just so I could be accepted in both my former and new life. It felt great to realize that both worlds could merge and even work together, just like two double-Dutch ropes.

THE SUMMER
SHE LEARNED TO DANCE

Karen Valentin

ACKNOWLEDGMENT

Osie and Erez Parag
Thank you for helping me brainstorm
over burritos and refried beans! Your thoughts and
imagination sparked the theme for this story.

Yisel Alonzo and Adelina Molina
Both of you painted such passionate and vivid images of
your beautiful Dominican culture. The stories you told were
invaluable and very much appreciated.

Kimberly Barnes
Thank you so much for sharing your experiences.
It helped me more than you know.

Adrienne Ingrum
Thank you once again for giving my stories a place to live.

CHAPTER 1

Giselle stopped chewing her roast beef and stared at her father in disbelief. She'd been torturing herself all day wondering what surprise he had for her over dinner, but she'd never expected this.

"Can't you just tell me now?" she had begged him that morning, but he was being stubborn.

"You'll find out tonight," he'd insisted.

She knew this could either be really good or disastrous. The best-case scenario would be the new Louis Vuitton bag she'd been bugging him about for days. Her best friend, Dahlia, already had it, and Alyce was going to get it in Paris on her family vacation. The worse-case scenario would be "Guess what, honey, Katie and I are engaged. Surprise!" Just thinking about it made her nauseous. She wasn't ready for her father to get married and have perfect little white children with Katie. But the surprise wasn't the dreaded engagement announcement or a thousand dollar bag. The surprise was Juanita Maria Delacruz Martinez—Giselle's cousin from the Dominican Republic.

"She's coming here?" Giselle asked with the dry glob of food still in her mouth, something she'd been raised to never do. "Since when did…I didn't even know that you were… Wow…I'm completely confused."

Giselle had every right to be puzzled. The last time she'd seen anyone on that side of the family was at her mother's funeral eight years ago. Her father, Brian, was so distraught over the death of his wife that he closed himself off to everyone, including her mother's family in the Caribbean.

Brian took Katie's hand. Katie was smiling as if she were watching one of those feel-good movies on Lifetime.

"Katie and I spoke about it, and she helped me realize it's time for you to reconnect with your family," he said slowly.

Giselle didn't know what to say. She didn't even know how to feel. Was she supposed to throw her arms around her father and thank him for finally acknowledging her mother and the other side of who Giselle was? For years she'd tried to talk with him about her mom. She'd try to ask questions and talk about her own vague memories, but he'd always come up with some excuse to walk away or change the subject.

"We think it's important for you to know them," Katie said, that stupid smile beaming on her face. "After all, that is your family."

The smile was making her furious. Giselle didn't want to owe this woman anything, especially gratitude. *Maybe she wants me to get to know them so she can have some-*

where to ship me off to when she marries my dad, she thought.

"When is she coming?" she asked, trying to sound as casual and uninterested as possible.

"Well," Brian said, "once this deal closes I'll have some more time on my hands, so I was thinking about mid-July. What do you think?"

Giselle smirked. Since when did her father have time on his hands?

"How long?" she asked, scraping up the last bit of food on her plate.

"A few weeks, maybe longer," Brian said. He looked at his daughter and tried to read the emotion on her face. He was always terrible at that. "So tell me what you think," he said again. "You don't look very excited." Giselle took a long guzzle of her iced tea before she graced him with an answer.

"I don't even know her," she said. "How can I be excited about someone I don't even know?"

"If she's anything like your mother, you're going to love her," was what he really wanted to say, but Katie was caressing his hand and he didn't dare. Brian had spoken with Juanita over the phone, and her personality and thick accent definitely reminded him of his late wife, Jackie. Brian took a sip of his coffee and shrugged. "I'm sure the two of you will get along just fine."

Giselle went up to her room after dinner and pulled out her mother's old photo album with the faded purple flowers on the front. She nearly emptied her closet looking for it, throwing cheerleading pom-poms, leather purses, old designer coats, and school books on the floor until she found it. It had been a while since she'd looked through these pictures of her family in San Pedro.

The oldest pictures were frayed black-and-white portraits of her grandparents and a few of her mother as a baby. The rest were vibrant, colorful photos of family in the Dominican Republic—snapshots taken during the three short visits to the island with her mother. Jackie had brought Giselle to meet the family when she was seven months old, again when she was three years old, and for the last time when she was five. Giselle remembered her time there like scattered snapshots—chasing chickens in her favorite yellow dress, eating a delicious sloppy mango on her grandfather's hammock, watching her mother dance barefoot on the porch.

Giselle could see her face in her mother's dark complexion, golden brown eyes, and thick curly black hair, although her own hair had not been black or curly for years. Giselle had her wild, tight curls tamed at least twice a week at the beauty salon. Her hair was always sleek and smooth, and her natural black color was dyed a light auburn with streaks of blond.

Giselle looked at the faces of her Dominican family, these strangers she barely remembered. The album was the only collection of photos she had where she actually looked like everyone else. Growing up in Manhasset, Long Island, with her extremely Caucasian-American father, his family, and her own white friends, Giselle had always stood out from the crowd. In every photo album and family portrait hanging on the wall, she was the only one with rich, dark, mocha skin.

Giselle found a few pictures of her cousin Juanita and tried to remember the little girl with the laughing smile, but just like her other memories of that time, the images were vague. The one thing she remembered clearly was that Juanita spoke no English at all. Juanita would run up to her bubbling over with excitement and talking in Spanish as if Giselle understood every word. *I hope she speaks English now,* Giselle thought as she closed the album and got ready for bed. She spent the rest of the night unable to sleep, wondering about her cousin and what it would feel like to see her again.

"Wow," Dahlia said, dipping her fries in a puddle of thick ketchup, "I didn't even know you had other cousins!"

Giselle tried to signal the waiter so she could order another Coke. No success. She hated this diner. The food was blah and the service was slow, but it was Dahlia and Alyce's favorite. They thought the waiters were ridiculously hot.

"Yeah, I have a few cousins over there. I don't really know them, though."

Giselle cleared her dry throat. She needed something to drink. "Uhh, what is this guy's problem! I know he sees me waving my hand!"

Alyce flipped her long blond hair and turned around to face the waiter. All she had to do was smile and flutter her fingers to get his attention. He walked over as if he were a model on a catwalk for Calvin Klein. "How can I help you?" he said leaning into Alyce, who was staring back with a flirty smile.

"I would like another Coke," Giselle said, trying not to sound as annoyed as she really was.

"No problem," he said, still staring at Alyce, "I'll get right on that."

Giselle was used to Alyce's getting all the attention, but it still made her stomach twist—especially with guys that gorgeous. No one ever looked at her the way they looked at Alyce, or at most of her friends, for that matter. Regardless of the hours Giselle spent getting ready in front of the mirror, she never seemed to be anyone's type.

When Giselle finally got her drink, Alyce lifted her pink lemonade in the air. "Let's toast!" The girls lifted their glasses. "Here's to one more day of school and an amazing summer." Alyce was going to Paris, and Dahlia couldn't wait to train her new horse, Hershey, at equestrian camp; but Giselle was stuck playing host and tour guide to a cousin she barely knew. For years she would have been more than eager to spend time with her mother's side of the family, but right now she didn't know what to feel.

"Here's to a great summer," she said, hoping their toast would come true.

CHAPTER 2

Giselle looked through her closet in a rampage. She had nothing to wear. Her wardrobe was a top-notch designer collection, but nothing seemed to fit right. "These stupid hips," she hissed under her breath, looking in the mirror at her fifth outfit of the morning. Her hair was beginning to frizz up from all the humidity and she still hadn't put on her makeup. Giselle plugged in her flat iron, whipped off her three-hundred-dollar jeans and pink Lacoste shirt, and bolted back into her walk-in closet in tears. Today was the last day of school and perhaps the last time she'd see Alex until the fall.

Of all the boys on the high school football team, Alex Nixon was the only one who paid the least bit of attention to her. Giselle was too shy to initiate conversations with most boys, but the football players were especially intimidating. Alex had come to the school in the middle of the year from Atlanta. He was easy to talk to and had the most adorable southern accent. Alex wasn't the hottest guy in school, but he was far from ugly. He was tall with shaggy brown hair that framed the most amazing emerald-green eyes. It amazed Giselle how quickly Alex made friends. Even though he was the new kid in school, everyone liked him. He was funny and friendly, and just like the rest of them, he was rich. He fit in perfectly. She admired how he felt so comfortable around new people, because despite her friendships and the wealth of her father, Giselle had always felt like a bit of an outsider.

The first day she spoke with him was in science lab. She was partnered with him to dissect a frog. Giselle was grossed out, but he made her laugh throughout the whole thing and did all the nasty work so she wouldn't have to touch the dead, slimy amphibian.

Alex thought it was incredibly typical that Giselle didn't want to touch the frog. Girls here were nothing like the girls he knew in Atlanta. They were too delicate for his taste, too worried about looking cool to let go and just be adventurous or silly like him.

The one thing he noticed about Giselle, however, that stood out from the rest was her obvious insecurity. The other girls strutted around with a confidence she lacked. He could sense it from her body language alone. Alex sympathized with Giselle, because his sister struggled with the same thing, especially since their move to Long Island. She was a pretty girl but just didn't seem to recognize it. He knew what a turnoff that was for guys. Even he would only date a girl who knew and liked herself. But Alex did his best to make his sister feel good about herself and did the same for his new friend.

"Hey, Giselle, that shirt looks really nice on you," he might say to boost her ego. "It brings out the gold in your eyes." Giselle melted with each compliment and hoped it meant what she so desperately wanted it to mean—that Alex Nixon would soon be her first boyfriend.

The last class of the year was now over, and the hallway flooded with excited teenagers ready for summer break. Giselle hadn't seen Alex all day and wondered if he was even there. Dahlia ran up behind her and snapped her out of her daze.

"Josh Bullard is having a party this Saturday!" she said. "Must go shopping ASAP." Giselle wasn't a big fan of this kid. He was rude and stuck on himself, and worst of all, he pretty much ignored her most of the time. She could think of a lot better things to do than go to this party. But if her friends were going, she'd most likely go along anyway. The only thing she was looking forward to in Dahlia's little declaration was the shopping. Giselle was always ready to shop.

"Definitely," she responded, already regretting the outfit she had finally settled on that morning. "I have absolutely no clothes!"

"Paris, here I come!" Alyce said, sneaking up on both of them. The three girls emptied their lockers and headed out the door.

"Ohmigod." Dahlia said as they all looked at the commotion in front of the school. Alex was standing by a white stretch Hummer blasting hip-hop music. He was handing out invitations to his exclusive fifteenth birthday party and everyone was crowding around him hoping he was holding one for them. His friend Philip Bisbee, one of the funniest kids in school, was sitting on top of the limo with a loudspeaker, calling out the guest list and cracking jokes.

Giselle was afraid to get too happy. What if she wasn't invited? She wasn't ready to give up her little fantasy that Alex liked her as much as she liked him.

"Let's go get ours," Alyce said with her usual confidence. "I hope it's not when I'm in France."

Giselle felt her stomach turn as they walked to the Hummer.

"Bailey Green," Philip said to the freshman walking over to Alex. Bailey looked up, surprised but happy that his name had been called. "You are not invited, so sorry, but thank you so much for coming, do try again next year."

"Hey," Alex shouted up to Philip. "Stop being vicious!"

"Aw, come on," he responded, shouting into the loudspeaker as if Alex were a mile away. "Let a guy have some fun." Philip noticed Alyce making her way through the crowd. "Okay, people, let's go, make a path. Come on, clear a path for the lovely Miss Alyce."

Alex shook his head with a laugh at Philip, then flipped through the invites in the front of the box. "Alyce," he said, extending the invitation to her as she stepped up. Dahlia and Giselle stood on either side. Giselle couldn't tell if she could actually hear her heartbeat or if it was just the bass of the music blasting from the Hummer.

Alex shuffled again and handed one to Dahlia and then just looked at Giselle.

"Hey, Gigi," he said, acting as if he were surprised to see her. "Uh…how's it going?"

Giselle froze. She wanted to just crawl away. He wasn't flipping through the box to get an invite for her.

"Good," she said, trying not to sound like she wanted to cry. "I'm doing great." Giselle was just waiting for Philip to say something stupid on the loudspeaker about her not being invited.

"Oh!" Alex said with a big smile. "I almost forgot!" He flipped through the envelopes a few times and handed her an invitation. Her whole body relaxed. "Thanks."

She looked at her invite. "Giselle" it said in bold calligraphy.

"I hope you can make it."

"Well," she said, trying to act nonchalant, hoping to redeem herself for any pathetic look she might have displayed when she thought she was being snubbed. "I'll definitely try." When Giselle opened her invitation, she realized she wasn't just any guest. She, Dahlia, and Alyce were all on the VIP list. Giselle daydreamed about the party for the rest of the day. In her daydream she and Alex were dating, of course, and she was as skinny and beautiful as Alyce. *That's it,* she thought. *I'm going on a diet tomorrow!*

"Look at these hips!" Giselle grunted. "I swear, I don't know where they're coming from."

Dahlia left the dressing room to find her friend the same jeans in a bigger size.

"What do you think of this shirt?" Giselle asked Alyce, who was busy admiring the dress she was trying on. "I don't know if it's me."

The truth was Giselle didn't really know what it meant to choose clothes that expressed her own style. As much as she would have liked to think she did, Giselle didn't know who she was. She was simply a replica of her friends.

"Are you kidding me, that shirt is gorgeous. You have to get it."

Giselle shrugged. "Yeah, I guess."

Dahlia came back and tossed the bigger jeans on the bench inside Giselle's dressing room. "Let's see how those look." Giselle was mortified.

Half an hour later, the girls walked to the register to pay for their clothes. Giselle had her outfit for Josh's party, but she wanted to lose at least ten pounds before she went shopping for Alex's party next month.

"Oh my, my, my—Giselle dear," Nana said with her well-manicured hand cupping her nipped and tucked face, "I see you've been busy at McDonalds since we've last seen each other."

I hate you, Giselle thought, looking into her grandmother's eyes.

"Yeah, I'm on a diet," she responded, pulling her shirt over her hips.

"That's a good girl," Nana continued. "We don't want it to get out of hand and end up having to go through liposuction, or even worse, a gastric bypass."

"Mom," Giselle's aunt Linda said sharply, "Giselle looks fine. I think her hips are sexy."

Aunt Linda patted Giselle on the shoulder with a smile. "Honey, you look fantastic."

Giselle could always count on a snide comment from her grandmother, like "Darling, you really ought to find a lipstick that better suits your skin tone. Pink just isn't your shade."

And although Aunt Linda was always quick with a positive comeback, Nana's words always did a better job at sticking in her mind.

"I'm on a diet." Giselle repeated, more for herself than for anyone else in the room.

It was Uncle Richard and Aunt Linda's sixteenth wedding anniversary. Giselle, Brian, and Katie had driven up to their home in Cape Cod for the weekend to celebrate. Other than seeing Aunt Susan and Aunt Linda, Giselle dreaded family get-togethers. Thank God, visits were few and rare. Everyone was busy with their own lives and lived at least a good three hours away from one another.

"How's the happy couple?" Nana asked as Katie straightened out Brian's tie.

Nana had liked Katie from the start. In her mind Katie was a much better fit for her son than Giselle's mother had been. Her death was such a pity, of course, but she never did see what Brian saw in that simple girl.

"Shall we move into the dinning room?" Aunt Linda asked, clasping her hands, "Marisol has prepared a remarkable meal." With the exception of her father, Giselle's family hired staffs of cooks, drivers, nannies, and housekeepers who were for the most part black or Hispanic. Giselle always felt funny being served and chauffered by people who looked more like her than her own family.

Giselle sat next to her cousin Sadie, Aunt Susan's anorexic daughter. No one admitted it, of course, but Sadie would spend lots of time at "health spas" and come back with ten more pounds on her lanky body.

Sitting on Giselle's other side was cousin Cassie, Aunt Linda's little angel, who could do absolutely no wrong, not even in Nana's eyes. Giselle hated being jealous of a twelve-year-old, but she was.

"A toast," Uncle Barry said, lifting his champagne glass. "To Linda and Richard."

"Linda and Richard," the family echoed at the long table.

The forks and knives clinked gently on the china plates and the conversations were soft and muffled as always. Giselle watched her family and tried to remember her family dinners in the Dominican Republic. She'd been so young, but she definitely remembered a bit more commotion at the table. With only one more week to go before Juanita came to visit, her family in the Caribbean was heavily on her mind.

CHAPTER 3

TODAY was the day. Juanita's plane would be arriving at four p.m. from the Dominican Republic into JFK airport. Giselle felt a mixture of dread and excitement. Part of her couldn't wait to meet a cousin from her mother's side of the family. Finally she'd look like one of her cousins instead of being the only one with dark skin. On the other hand, Giselle was worried that seeing Juanita might bring up sad feelings about her mother. She hadn't spoken about her mom for so long; she didn't know what feelings to expect.

Brian parked the car and walked to the terminal with his daughter in silence. The same thoughts were going through his head. For eight years he had pushed back any thoughts of his wife and any reminder of her. After she died from cancer, he sold their house in Connecticut—where they were married—and bought another in Long Island. He hired Erin, a live-in nanny, to care for his daughter and occupied himself with work to distract his mind with less painful matters. Only within the last year had he begun to heal his wounds. Katie came into his life as a friend and a loving relationship unexpectedly bloomed. She convinced him to see a therapist about his past tragedy, and little by little Brian was able to face his pain. But now, as he walked toward the terminal to pick up Juanita, he felt a little nervous about having her over. *This will be good for us,* he tried to convince himself, *especially Gigi. This will be great for Giselle.*

Brian and Giselle stood by the arrival gate among the other families waiting to greet their loved ones. Giselle looked around at the Dominican faces and then at her father's pale white skin and light blue eyes. For once, he stood out from the crowd instead of her. Giselle held up a small pink sign that read "Juanita" in bold black letters.

The passengers began to file out through the narrow corridor. "Ahhhyyyyeee!" an old woman screeched as she saw her grandchildren running toward her. The scream startled Giselle and made her drop her sign. The loud greetings multiplied as more and more families reunited. *My god,* Giselle thought. She'd never seen such a fuss over greeting relatives before.

A young girl with a thick head of black curls appeared with a large flowery backpack on her shoulders.

"*¡Prima!*" she yelled, and ran toward her cousin. Giselle didn't know that *prima* meant *cousin,* and she was too busy looking at all the commotion around her to notice Juanita charging toward her with open arms.

"Ugh!" Giselle grunted as Juanita tackled her with the tightest hug she'd ever experienced in her life.

"*Tío Brian!*" she squealed, pulling him into the hug so that it looked like a football huddle. Giselle was caught completely off guard by the exuberant hello. She wriggled her way out of the hug and took a deep breath as if she had just been pulled underwater.

"I no can believe I here!" Juanita said, allowing Brian to take the flowery bag from her shoulders.

Ohmigod, Giselle thought, *this is Juanita?*

Giselle thought Juanita looked a bit like her, but on an extremely bad day. The girl's outfit looked like it came from a Salvation Army thrift shop! She was wearing a tight, shimmery red skirt with pink circles that looked like different-sized bubbles. Her shirt was a different shade of pink and had sparkling sequins on the border of the plunging neckline. Juanita had a generous figure, and the skirt did nothing to hide her big hips and huge butt. She wore red, plastic dangling earrings, her shoes were obviously fake patent leather, and her hair was a frizzball of dark curls that bounced over her shoulders.

"How was your flight?" Brian asked, knowing it was her first time on an airplane.

"I was berry eh-scared," she said, opening her huge brown eyes even wider. Juanita bent her knees and waved her arms to demonstrate the turbulence. She wrapped herself around Giselle's arm as they walked and enthusiastically spoke to her in Spanish. Giselle looked at her father, then at Juanita.

"No habla-ray Espanolo."

"Oh!" Juanita said a bit shocked. She was certain her cousin spoke at least a little Spanish.

"No-sing? No eh-Spanish, even lee-tal bit?"

"No," Giselle said, "not even a little bit."

Juanita decided at that moment that she would teach her cousin Spanish during her visit. She couldn't let someone in her family walk around not knowing Spanish. Every Dominican should speak the language, no matter where they lived.

They walked over to the baggage carousel and waited for Juanita's luggage. "Der it is!" she yelled, seeing her bright purple suitcase wobble down the conveyor belt.

"That's all you have?" Brian asked, surprised by how little she'd packed. "Hey, Gigi, you should learn how to travel like your cousin over here."

Giselle rolled her eyes.

Brian reached over and grabbed Juanita's vibrant luggage, which rested on top of the other dull black suitcases.

"I no can believe I in New Jork City!" she squealed, squeezing Giselle's arm and resting her head on her shoulder. "I berry happy I see jou again. I miss jou berry much. Ebbry-body in San Pedro miss jou berry much."

Juanita latched on to Giselle's arm the rest of the way as they walked toward the car.

What is she doing! Giselle thought. *People are going to think she's my lesbian lover!*

Juanita kept talking as they put her bags in the trunk and settled into the car. Giselle couldn't get over how loud she was talking. *Ohmigod!* she thought. *Why is this chick screaming?* Although Juanita had obvious struggles with the English language, it didn't stop her from talking up a tropical storm. She was bubbling over with questions.

"Is it berry scary jou climb dee high buildings in Manhat-tong?"

"What?" Giselle asked.

Not only did Juanita have a thick Spanish accent, she spoke ridiculously fast.

Juanita repeated her question exactly the same way.

"Is it berry scary jou climb dee high buildings in Manhat-tong?"

Silence. Brian cut into the conversation.

"Giselle, she's asking if it's scary to climb up the tall buildings in Manhattan," he said, turning his head and craning his neck from the driver's seat.

"Oh," Giselle said, "no, it's not scary…I guess."

"I will like berry much to see dee Empire eh-State Building. We go there?"

This was driving Giselle nuts.

"Can you just talk a little bit slower, please?"

Juanita laughed and apologized. "Ebbry-body in my family talk berry fast."

Are they loud, too? Giselle silently said to herself.

"Jou will be feef-ting berry soon, jes?" Juanita continued slowly. "Jou will have quinceañera party?"

"A what party?" she asked.

Giselle was completely frustrated. *Ohmigod,* she thought, *this is going to be the longest summer of my life.*

CHAPTER 4

JUANITA could hardly contain herself. She couldn't believe she was actually here in America. She'd grown up listening to her mother's stories of when she'd lived in New York City with *Tía* Jackie—Giselle's mother. The stories always sounded like so much fun, and she absolutely loved listening to the funny situations her *tía* got them into. She had been looking forward to hanging out with Giselle, who she thought would be just like her *tía* Jackie.

Juanita's mother, Milagros had always wanted to send Juanita to America to visit her niece/goddaughter Giselle. When the girls were born, just a year apart, Milagros thought they would be as close as she and her sister Jackie. After her sister died, it was difficult to get in contact with her niece. She tried to arrange visits to the Dominican Republic, but Brian refused to let her go alone and was too busy to accompany her. She tried to make trips back to America to see her niece and other cousins in Washington Heights, New York, but once she saved enough money something always came up—the money woul[...] to a more urgent cause. Milagros could hardly beli[...] phone call she'd received from Brian with his generous in-vitation to fly Juanita out to America. Although she had a hard time accepting such a splendid gift, she knew how wonderful it would be for her daughter to go to America and be reunited with her cousin Giselle.

Brian pulled into the driveway and Juanita gasped at the mansionlike house before her. It looked like the house of an American celebrity. Milagros had told her that *Tío* Brian had a lot of money, but never did she imagine someone in her family having this much wealth.

She gasped again as they walked through the front door. In her house in the Dominican Republic she could touch the ceiling if she stood on a chair. She would need a flying carpet to reach Giselle's ceiling. The living room alone was bigger than her whole house. She wondered what it would be like to live in a house like this instead of hers. Her small wooden house was home to her mother, father, two sisters, aunt and uncle, and newborn cousin.

"Hi, Juanita!" Katie squealed as she dashed out of the kitchen drying her hands with a small towel. "Welcome to America."

"Juanita, this is my girlfriend, Katie," Brian said, putting her bags on the shiny wooden floor.

"Berry nice to meet jou," Juanita said. Katie extended her hand, but Juanita quickly gave her a kiss on the cheek and a big hug instead.

Oh, aren't you sweet," Katie said, gushing at such unexpected affection. "I'm going to go back into the kitchen. I'm cooking you a nice little welcome dinner. It'll be ready soon. You must be famished."

"Famous?" Juanita asked, confused by Katie's statement.

"No, no, no, dear, famished. That just means hungry. You must be very hungry," she said nice and slow.

"Oh, hungry. Jes, I am always hungry," Juanita laughed.

Giselle and Brian gave her the whole tour—the carpeted game room with a pool table, a Ping-Pong table, and three huge arcade games; the dream kitchen, where Juanita could imagine her and her mother making their delicious meals; and the living room with no television that looked too perfect to even enter. The dinning room could hold every aunt, uncle, and cousin in San Pedro, and their den had a television with the biggest screen she'd ever seen in her life. But her favorite part of the house was the built-in pool in the backyard with a diving board and a twisty slide. For the first time that evening, Juanita was quiet. She was in complete awe and disbelief—and this was only the first floor.

The phone rang—Giselle ran to the kitchen to grab it while Brian took Juanita's bags and led her upstairs to the bedrooms. "This is your room, Juanita," Brian said, turning on the light. The room was enormous, with white and baby blue flowers on the wall and a king-sized bed in the middle covered with a cloudlike quilt. "You have your own bathroom through that door," he said. "There's plenty of closet space and there's an extra quilt in that chest. So, why don't you go ahead and settle in and let us know if there's anything you need."

"Sank jou berry much," Juanita said.

"Dinner will be ready in twenty minutes," he said, walking toward the door. "We're very happy that you've come to stay with us, Juanita."

"I berry happy, too."

Brian closed the door and the room was quiet—too quiet. Juanita walked over to the empty closet with the fancy padded hangers on the golden rod. She hadn't packed enough clothes to fill even a third of the space. It was strange to hear her own footsteps on the shiny wooden floor and the zipper of her suitcase echoing in the large room. In her house, these noises would have been drowned out by music, screaming kids, loud conversations, and laughter.

Juanita jumped on her bed and it was as soft as it looked. She snuggled under the down quilt and stretched her arms and legs across the wide bed. She could never spread out like this at home, sleeping with her two little sisters.

Giselle walked in with an armful of fresh white towels to put in Juanita's bathroom. "*Prima*," Juanita yelled, jumping out of the bed. Her cousin had explained to her that *prima* meant *cousin*, but Giselle wished she would just call her by her name.

Juanita excitedly went over to her opened suitcase and waved Giselle over to sit next to her. Giselle put down the towels and grudgingly sat.

"I have eh-some present for jou from dee family in San Pedro."

Giselle lit up. "Presents?"

The first thing Juanita pulled out of her bag was a handknit red shawl with large, colorful flowers on the ends. "Abuelita make for jou, and my moh-der make dee flowers." Juanita slipped the shawl over Giselle's head and squealed something in Spanish, obviously loving how it looked.

Giselle walked over to the mirror—she was speechless. It was the tackiest thing she had ever tried on.

"Jou can put it at night for dee cold," Juanita said, fluffing the flowers that had been squashed during the trip. Giselle was touched that her grandmother and aunt had gone to so much trouble to knit this for her, and she felt guilty for hating it. But she could never wear this in front of her friends—never in a million years!

"Oh, it's pretty," she lied. "Tell them I said thank you very much."

Juanita went back to the suitcase. She wasn't done. "Dis is for jour fah-der," she said, unveiling a gaudy painting of Dominican farmers. Giselle wondered where the heck her father would hang it. Not only was it ugly, but it didn't go with the décor of the house. "*Tío* Ruben make dee painting and sell dem in the Dominican Republic for dee *touristas*," Juanita said, holding it up with pride. "I pick dee best one for jour fah-der."

Wow, Giselle thought, trying to hide her disgust. *If that's the best, I can imagine what the rest look like!*

"Oh, okay," she said with the best fake smile she could muster. "I'm sure my father is going to love it."

Juanita pulled a lot more gifts from her purple bag. Each

one seemed to be tackier and gaudier then the one before—cheap porcelain figurines of ladies in flowery dresses, a wooden hand press for squashing plantains (some sort of banana Giselle had never even heard of), salt and pepper shakers in the shape of palm trees, maracas with the Dominican flag painted on them and lots of colorful plastic rosary beads. That purple suitcase was like a magical bag of endless gaudiness—it wouldn't stop. Giselle couldn't bear to look at one more souvenir, but the guilt of hating each gift was even worse. *That's all right,* she thought, trying to make herself feel better. *I'll make sure she goes back home with gifts for everyone that will blow their minds—real gifts.*

Brian knocked on the door to say dinner was ready. "Great," Giselle said, popping up from the floor. "Let's eat." She pulled her father into the room on her way out. "Hey, Dad, Juanita has some great little gifts for you. Why don't you go over and check it out before you come down."

CHAPTER 5

KATIE lit the candles for the last touches of her "Welcome to America" dinner. The table looked elegant and beautiful. Martha Stewart would have been proud. Katie clasped her hands with a smile, pleased with the outcome. "Bon appétit everyone," she chirped as they all sat down. Brian put the palm tree shakers in the middle of the table and Katie gasped. "Oh, honey, what in the world—?"

He interrupted just in time. "They're gifts, darling, from the Dominican Republic." Katie forcibly changed her facial expression and Giselle bit down on her lip to keep from laughing. She felt a strange kinship with her father's girlfriend as she twisted her lips into an artificial smile.

"Oh, how nice," Katie said, looking at the cheap porcelain eyesores in the middle of her perfect, elegant table. "Aren't palm trees just fun?" Giselle coughed into her napkin to cover a laugh that escaped like an unexpected sneeze.

Juanita slapped her cousin on the back a few times. "Are jou okay, *Prima?*"

"Yeah," she said, clearing her throat. "I'm great."

Brian shook his head. "Shall we eat?"

"Yes," Katie and Giselle said, reaching for the platters in front of them. They both froze abruptly, however, as they noticed Juanita with her head bowed and hands folded.

"Dear Jesus," she prayed aloud, "sank jou I here with my American family. Bless berry much dee food for eating and bless dee children who no have no-sing to eat in dis night. Amen." Juanita crossed herself and the others did the same—they had to look at her to figure out how.

"Amen," Katie said, putting her hand over her heart, genuinely touched. "Juanita, that was just lovely." She looked at Brian with her Lifetime Television smile. "Oh, honey, isn't she just lovely?"

"Yes, that was a very nice prayer, Juanita, thank you."

She had never been thanked for blessing the food before but shrugged with a smile. "Jou welcome."

Juanita was starving. She had hated the food on the airplane, and the meal on the table looked beautiful—like art. "*Buen provecho*," she said, the Spanish version of *bon appétit*.

"I hope you like it," Katie said. "I'm not quite the cook that Erin is, but I did my best."

"Erin?" Juanita asked

"Erin is Giselle's nanny," Brian said. "She's been with us for about seven years now. But at this point she's more of a housekeeper and cook, since Giselle is already a teenager."

"What means 'nanny'?" Juanita asked, crinkling the skin between her untweezed eyebrows.

Brian opened his mouth to answer, but Giselle beat him to it.

"A nanny is a woman who raises you while your father is away on business trips."

There was a brief moment of uneasy silence at the table, which was quickly filled by Katie's high-pitched voice.

"Shall we eat?"

Juanita served herself a healthy portion of chicken and reached over Giselle's plate to get the baby potatoes. Unfortunately, the food didn't taste as delicious as it looked—it was bland and tasteless. Juanita was used to rich, savory food made with lots of different spices; this food needed something. She took the palm tree salt and pepper shakers and sprinkled both over her plate. It was a little better.... Not great, but better.

"Sank jou berry much," she said loudly with her mouth full of chicken. Juanita continued to talk loudly at the table, unafraid to expose the chewed-up food in her mouth. Giselle served herself a tiny amount of food and nibbled on it slowly.

"Jou no hungry, *Prima*?" Juanita asked with her mouth full of food again.

"I'm on a diet."

"A diet!" Juanita gasped. Giselle looked perfectly fine to Juanita. "Jou no fat!"

"Thanks," Giselle said, rolling her eyes. What did Juanita know? *Look at her, she thought. She's bigger than me and she's eating like a horse.*

Giselle couldn't get over the way Juanita was eating. She was slouched over her plate, shoveling food into her mouth, and her elbows were on the table. *Nana would have an absolute fit if she saw this,* Giselle thought. She looked at Katie and her father. Did they not notice she was eating like a cavewoman?

They didn't really notice at all. Katie seemed charmed by her stories and childlike questions, and Brian loved her free-spirited nature, which reminded him so much of Jackie.

A surprising sense of comfort and happiness came over Brian in Juanita's presence. It was nice to have that spark and pizzazz back in the house. But seeing the two cousins—these complete opposites—side by side, he realized how different his daughter was from her cousin and her mother. Giselle had her mother's eyes, her shape, and her beautiful complexion, but she was reserved, just like her father. There was a silent sadness and anger in her that he knew all too well. Although he felt guilty for passing his bitterness on to his daughter, he also felt a sense of hope with Juanita sitting at the dining room table. Perhaps she could brighten up Giselle's life, just like Jackie had for him so many years ago.

Juanita kept trying to engage her cousin in conversation. So far, Giselle's answers had been short and dry. Juanita had always pictured Giselle to be just like her mother, but this was a completely different girl than she had imagined.

"When jou come to the Dominican Republic?" Juanita asked. "Ebbry-body want berry much jou come!"

"I don't know," Giselle responded, shrugging.

"Do jou remember when jou come to San Pedro, when jou have five years old?" she asked. "I remember jou cry all dee time because jou have afraid of Abuela's cow. Remember?"

Giselle shrugged again. "I don't remember that."

Giselle couldn't focus on anything but Juanita's horrendous table manners. Nana had called when they'd walked in from the airport to invite them to a dinner party. How could she bring Juanita to Nana's house? That would be absolutely humiliating. She already knew she wasn't her grandmother's favorite. The last thing Giselle needed was to introduce her cousin Juanita to Nana. It would only prove what she'd felt all along—as much as she tried, she didn't fit in.

Juanita helped Katie clear the dishes and clean up after dessert, even though Katie insisted that she just relax. As the oldest, Juanita was used to helping in the kitchen. Back home she helped cooked meals, served the men, and washed the dishes, too. It was shocking to see her cousin Giselle go to her room after diner without offering to help. Juanita could never get away with that in her house. But what really shocked her was seeing her uncle Brian clean up. The men in her family never helped in the kitchen.

After the table and dishes were nice and clean, Juanita went up to her room to unpack. The quiet room that had seemed wonderful to her in the beginning now felt lonely and almost scary. She had never spent the night alone before. Outside it started to rain and thunder, and suddenly Juanita wished she were home. On nights like this, Juanita would cuddle up with her sisters and tell them not to be afraid. As she stood there now in this big room all alone, she wished she had someone to comfort her.

Katie and Brian knocked on her door, and it made Juanita jump. They opened the door slowly to find Juanita sitting next to her suitcase with her clothes still in it.

"Okay, honey, I'm gonna get going." Katie said, walking over to her and kissing her on the forehead. "It was such a pleasure to meet you."

Brian looked at her suitcase.

"You still haven't unpacked. Is everything okay in your room?" he asked. "Is there something you need?" Juanita told him the room was beautiful but admitted it felt a little strange to sleep by herself.

"My home is berry small," Juanita said. "I eh-sleep wees my two little see-ster. I have never sleep alone."

"Don't worry," Brian said. "We'll take care of that."

CHAPTER 6

"Dad!" Giselle whispered as Juanita happily unpacked her things in Giselle's room. "Can I talk to you?" Brian and Giselle went out into the hallway.

"Are you kidding me? Why can't she sleep in her own room?"

"I told you, she's not used to sleeping alone. Just let her sleep here for a few nights until she gets used to things."

"Well, I'm not used to sharing my room with anyone, especially my bed!"

Brian didn't like her attitude.

"Juanita is our guest," he said calmly but with obvious frustration in his voice. "And more importantly, she is your cousin. Stop arguing about this, get in there, and make her feel welcome in this house."

Giselle rolled her eyes and without a word went back into her room.

"*Hola, Prima,*" Juanita said, draping a towel over Giselle's vanity mirror.

"What are you doing?"

"Abuela always cover dee mirror for dee rain and sohnder. Is bad luck if jou don't."

Juanita had already covered the mirror in Giselle's bathroom and the full-length mirror in her walk-in closet.

You have got to be kidding me! Giselle yelled in her head.

"That's great, thanks a lot, Juanita. Lord knows I don't need any more bad luck."

"*De nada,*" Juanita said, not sure how to say "you're welcome" in English.

Juanita unpacked her things and hung them up next to Giselle's designer clothes. Giselle cringed at each loud, synthetic, and thrift-shop-looking outfit Juanita put on a hanger.

"Hey, Juanita," Giselle said. "How would you like to go shopping tomorrow?" There was just no way she could allow her to walk out of the house wearing those clothes.

"Oh jes," Juanita answered. "I like berry much."

Juanita's whole family had chipped in to given her money to spend on her trip to the United States. She couldn't wait to buy an American outfit and wanted to buy souvenirs for her family with the rest of the money.

"Great, let me go tell my dad."

Juanita felt a tinge of pity as she watched her cousin leave the room. She couldn't imagine being raised by someone who wasn't even family. Juanita's house was always bustling with family, and her grandparents and aunts and uncles all lived within walking distance from their home.

What a sad, lonely life, she thought. She was happy to be here, even if Giselle wasn't the girl she had been expecting. Now she felt a purpose for her trip. She would give Giselle all the love of family she had been missing all these years.

Giselle found her father at the computer, where she knew he'd be.

"Dad, we need to take this girl shopping tomorrow," Giselle said. "I'm not even kidding; you have got to see her wardrobe. It's absolutely hideous."

Brian took off his glasses and smiled at his daughter.

"That sounds like a wonderful idea."

Giselle was about to go off on a tangent about the whole mirror business, but Brian cut her off.

"And for being such a super, concerned cousin, you can pick up that bag of yours while you're at it."

"Really?" she screamed.

"Well, I was waiting for your birthday, but...yeah, go ahead."

"Thanks, Dad."

Giselle went back to her room with a huge smile on her face. It was the first smile Juanita had seen so far.

"We're all set for shopping," Giselle said.

"*Que bueno,*" Juanita said, ready to start her cousin's Spanish lessons. "Dat mean 'berry good.' Now jou say." Juanita repeated the phrase extra slowly. Giselle was in too good a mood to protest.

"*Kay, bway-no,*" she said, twisting her mouth into funny shapes.

Juanita clapped and did a little happy hop.

"*Ay si, que bueno*. Now eh-say, '*Hola mi nombre es Giselle*.' Dat mean, 'Hello, my name is Giselle.'"

She tried, but it came out terribly. Juanita tried to fix it, but Giselle put out her hands in a "stop" gesture.

"Okay, how about 'good night.' How do you say 'good night'?"

"*Buenas noches*."

"Great...*bway-naz no-chase*," Giselle said, walking toward her bed. "I'm exhausted." Giselle looked at her bed strangely and then looked at Juanita, who was now pulling rosary beads out of her flowery bag.

"Did you put the pillows on the other side?"

Juanita explained that it was bad luck to sleep with your feet in the direction of the street. After all, she explained, that was how they buried the dead.

"Of course," Giselle said, shaking her head in disbelief. "Silly me."

Juanita handed Giselle a set of rosary beads and knelt by the bed.

"Come pray with me, *Prima*,"

"Uh, no, that's okay, Juanita. Why don't you just pray and I'll listen?"

The look Juanita gave her was enough to make Giselle take the rosary beads and kneel beside her cousin. Juanita said all her prayers in Spanish and then nudged Giselle's elbow to signal that it was her turn. Giselle tried to remember the prayers she'd learned when she was a little girl, but it had been so long.

"Uhhh…Our Father, who art in heaven, give us this, our daily bread, and lead us not into temptation, for thine, O Father…is the king and glory….Umm…Hail Mary, full of grace, the Lord is with thee…and us…us sinners…. Amen."

"Amen," Juanita said, crossing herself and kissing her fingertips.

Giselle got under the covers. "Good night, Juanita."

"*Buenas noches, Prima.*"

Giselle closed her eyes. How could she introduce this loud-talking, loud-dressing, superstitious hugging machine to her friends and family? They were going to laugh at Juanita. Giselle just knew they would, and maybe inside, they'd be laughing at her as well. Giselle did the best she could to fit in to her life. And although it wasn't a perfect fit, it was good enough.

Maybe I can change her, Giselle thought. *Maybe I can show her how to fit in and not embarrass herself.*

Giselle went to sleep, confident that she would make everything better and hopeful that she could turn Juanita into someone she could actually introduce to people.

Giselle stared at the ceiling and shook her head. *I can't believe this,* she thought as Juanita lay next to her snoring. Giselle nudged her for the twenty-somethingth time. Once again Juanita let out a single ear-popping snore, smacked her lips like a baby sucking on a bottle and then sprawled out in another position on the bed. "One, two, three, four, five," Giselle counted in the temporary silence. She already knew what would happen after "five." Bingo! Juanita was at it again, louder this time! "Unreal," Giselle spat under her breath. "She's got this thing down to a science!"

Juanita left her cousin almost no room on the bed. Giselle would push Juanita's leg over, but then her arm would shoot over near Giselle's face. *If this is what it feels like to share your bed, I'm never getting married!* she thought, trying to close her eyes tight and force herself to go to sleep.

The only person she had ever slept with was her mother, years ago. Whenever Giselle had a nightmare and started to cry, Jackie would snuggle in with her daughter and rub her head until she fell asleep again. Her mother didn't snore.

Giselle finally went to sleep in the small corner of the bed. As she drifted into her strange dream, Juanita's snoring turned into classical music, and the darkness of closed eyes became Nana's dining room. There was nothing unusual about her dream at first. It was a typical dinner with the family. The good china was set out on the table—there was no such thing as bad china at Nana's house—and the cloth napkins were rolled into the sterling silver napkin rings. Nana was at the head of the table watching her grandchildren like a hawk to make sure they didn't slouch over their plates or slurp their sparkling apple cider. "Please pass the butter, Aunt Susan," Giselle said with her shoulders back and elbows off the table. "Certainly," said Aunt Susan, passing it to her right. The conversation was minimal as always. Questions like "How are you doing in school?" were answered with "Fine, thank you. I passed my last exam with an A." Yes, Giselle's dream was extremely ordinary until the doorbell rang. *Diiiing-dooooong,* it rang, in a deep, creepy tone, as if trying to warn the family that something terrible was about to happen. "I'll get it," Giselle said, excusing herself from the table. She walked to the door, and when she opened it, there stood Juanita in a colorful, flowery polyester dress from Conway, a headdress of ripe tropical fruits on her head.

"Good evening, *Prima*!" Juanita shouted, giving Giselle her trademark bear hug. Giselle tried to scream but no sound came out. She tried to push Juanita back out the door but she had no strength. "Where's the party, *Prima*?" Juanita asked, dancing into the house. "Ay, ay, ay!"

She headed toward the dining room and everything seemed to go in slow motion. In one last attempt, Giselle grabbed her from behind, but Juanita thought she just wanted another hug. "I love jou, too, *Prima*!" she said, turning around and throwing her arms around Giselle.

As Juanita walked into the dining room, the classical music stopped with a screech. Everyone let out a uniform gasp. "*Hola,* ebree-body, I'm Giselle's coh-sing Juanita!" Nana stood up from her chair and threw down her napkin.

"Young lady!" she sniffed. "Is that polyester?" Juanita ran over to her and tackled Nana to the floor. "Hi, Grandmoh-der," she said, hugging her on the polished tiles. Giselle tried to help Nana up, but Nana pushed her away and got up herself.

"Does this belong to you?" she asked, pointing at Juanita, who was now at the table, eating with her hands. Giselle tried to speak, but she couldn't.

"I brought dessert!" Juanita shouted, pointing to the fruit on her head. Giselle's perfect, blond cousins laughed and pointed at her and Juanita, and her aunts and uncles covered their mouths with looks of disgust on their faces. Brian just sat at the table with his perfect posture, eating his food as if nothing was happening. He was oblivious as always, too busy taking care of his own needs to do anything helpful.

"I want both of you to leave," Nana said, leading them out of the house. "You obviously don't fit in to this family." Giselle got her voice back and begged her grandmother to let her stay. "Please, Nana, I do belong in this family. I'm not like her at all. I never wear synthetic fabrics and I always keep my elbows off the table. Please, Grandmother; please don't kick me out of the family!"

Giselle jumped up from her sleep and landed on the floor. Juanita let out one loud snore with a startled gasp, smacked her lips, changed her position, and went right on snoring. "There's no way I'm going to let you humiliate me," Giselle said, glaring at her sleeping cousin. She grabbed her pillow from the bed and stormed off to the guest bedroom to catch the few hours of sleep she had left.

CHAPTER 7

"HOW did you sleep, Juanita?" Brian asked her as she sat down to breakfast.

"Oh, she slept really, really great, right, Juanita?" Giselle chimed in with a big cheesy smile on her face.

"Oh jes, I sleep berry good," Juanita said.

As Giselle passed her father on the way to the fridge, she hissed in a low whisper, "Why don't you ask me how I slept?" By the look on her face, Brian already knew the answer.

"So," Brian said, trying to change the subject, "you girls are going off shopping today?"

Juanita's eyes lit up. "Is it berry big, the American shopping mall?" she asked with a mouth full of pancake. "My mohder tell me der are many stores. She say dat all de—"

"Yeah, they're really big," Giselle interrupted so her cousin would stop displaying the chewed-up breakfast in her mouth. "Hey, I have a fun idea," Giselle said, proud of her quick thinking. "Let's play etiquette class!"

"Eti-king?"

"No. Et-i—kit," Giselle said slowly, as if talking to a child.

"Ee-ti-keet," Juanita repeated even more slowly with a deep look of concentration on her face. "What means ee-ti-keet?"

"It's a class my grandmother made me and my cousins take. It teaches you the right and wrong way to eat."

"Jou go to eh-school for dis?" She shoved a forkful of scrambled eggs into her mouth to make a point. "This is berry easy," she laughed, exposing the yellow mush in her mouth.

"Not that simple," Giselle said, covering her cousin's mouth with her fingertips. "Lesson number one: never speak with your mouth full. It's gross. It's really gross."

"Easy, Gigi," Brian said, looking up from his newspaper.

"No, this will be fun," she said to both of them. "Juanita, don't you want to learn how to eat like an American?"

"I hardly think Americans can claim sole rights to good table manners," Brian pointed out. "Besides, not all Americans eat the proper way."

"Yeah, well, that's 'cause only the cool and popular ones do," Giselle shot back, giving her father a deadly look.

"I thought you hated etiquette class?" he asked, obviously not seeing the look on his daughter's face.

"Dad!" she whispered. "Not helping!"

Brian sipped the last bit of his coffee, folded his newspaper, and patted Juanita on the back. "I'll leave you two ladies to your etiquette class, then. Have fun, Juanita."

"She will!" Giselle said, shooing him away with a wave of her hand.

Giselle shot up from her chair and set the table in front of Juanita, complete with all four types of forks—dinner, salad, seafood, and dessert. She showed her how to place the large cloth napkin on her lap with the fold toward the waist. She made her practice eating her food without slouching over her plate. "You want to make sure you always keep your elbows off the table. Watch me." Giselle cut into an imaginary steak and took a bite while keeping her elbows at her side the whole time. "Now you try."

Juanita wanted so badly to laugh, but she wouldn't dare. In the short time she'd known her cousin, she'd seemed dry and passionless. This was the first time she'd seen Giselle so excited about something. She just couldn't understand why silly rules about forks, plates, and napkins could finally make her come to life.

Giselle was proud of her work so far. The next step in Juanita's transformation would be a complete makeover. Those nappy curls would have to go, and perhaps she'd suggest some blond highlights. One of the biggest disasters about her cousin, however, was her wardrobe! As far as Giselle was concerned, that was about to be taken care of.

"Girls, are you almost ready?" Brian shouted at the bottom of the stairs when Katie pulled in to the driveway.

"Crap!" Giselle said, still fiddling with the flat iron. "Hey, Juanita, can you go down and tell him I'm still doing my hair? I'll be down in like ten or fifteen." Juanita had been ready over a half an hour ago, minutes after Giselle had said they should start getting ready. All she had done was tie up her curls into a puffy ponytail, wash her face, and put on a little lip gloss. Giselle, on the other hand, had tried on three different outfits, squinted into the mirror to make sure every strand of hair was in place, and carefully put on her makeup as if she were performing surgery on herself. Juanita couldn't understand. They weren't going to a party; they were just going to the stores. She couldn't imagine anyone back home spending that much time doing their hair and makeup just to walk down the road to buy some bread.

"Yisel say in fifteen minute she will come down. She do her hair," Juanita said as she came down the stairs.

Brian let out a frustrated sigh. "That means thirty minutes."

Juanita went right over to Katie and gave her a big hug, something Katie thought was absolutely adorable. Giselle never hugged her.

"Okay, Juanita, you have to promise me to pick out whatever you like at the mall," Brian insisted. "Don't worry about the price, just have fun."

Juanita had never had the luxury of not worrying about prices. Knowing how hard her family worked for the little they had, Juanita was always conscious about how much things cost. *"Mira, que linda,"* her mother might say, commenting on a cute skirt or blouse she would have liked to buy her daughter, but Juanita would always choose the least expensive outfit, claiming to prefer the fit or color over the pricier one.

"Jes, sir, I promise," she said, unsure if that was even possible.

Giselle waltzed down the stairs in the exact amount of time Brian had predicted. Katie jingled her car keys. "So, we're ready, then?" she chirped. "I know I am. Let's go shopping."

Brian pecked Katie on the lips. "Thank you so much sweetie," he said. "Make sure Juanita feels comfortable getting whatever she wants, okay? And while you're at it, why don't you get yourself a little sparkly something to go in that new jewelry box of yours?"

"Oh really, Mr. Johnson," she purred, cuddling into his arms. "How sparkly are we talking about here?"

Giselle rolled her eyes. "I'll wait out by the car."

Giselle elected to sit in the back by herself. She really didn't feel like talking. Besides, Katie and Juanita were the talkers. Katie always drove Giselle insane with her annoying questions and dumb stories, and now Juanita was proving to be even worse! At least now they had each other to nauseate with their jabber. Maybe they'd give her a break.

Giselle wasn't exactly overjoyed about spending the whole day with these two. Picking out a new wardrobe for Juanita was more like a job than a thrill. Her only consolation—other than saving herself from the embarrassment of Juanita's current look—was the new Louis V bag just waiting for her at the store. Giselle settled into the back.

She took out her bejeweled cell phone to text her friends and ignored the two chatterboxes in the front. Ohmigod, she wrote, going 2 buy LV bag 2day!!!

CHAPTER 8

Juanita was looking forward to seeing an American mall. Her mother had visited many and had painted a picture in her mind of fancy fountains; huge, colorful carousels; high, arched glass ceilings that looked like they belonged in cathedrals; and floor upon floor of shops connected by long escalators. But Brian's daughter and girlfriend didn't shop at malls filled with stores like Old Navy or H&M. They shopped at Americana Manhasset, the Fifth Avenue of Long Island. This open air shopping center was not at all what Juanita had expected, yet she was still awed and humbled by the grandness of it all. The extravagant structures, dramatic lighting, elegant window displays, and well-suited guards at each door both enchanted and intimidated her.

"First things first," Giselle squealed when they arrived, showing that rare enthusiasm. She bolted toward the Louis Vuitton shop, leaving Katie and Juanita strolling behind. "Isn't it gorgeous!" she beamed when they finally caught up and entered the store. Juanita looked at the brown bag and shrugged. For all Giselle's fuss, it seemed a bit plain.

"Does it come in an-oh-der color, like pink or purple?" Giselle stared at Juanita with her mouth slightly open and then looked at Katie as if to say "Did you hear what this moron just asked?"

"No. It doesn't come in pink or purple." *Idiot,* she added in her mind.

"It doesn't look berry... What's so eh-special about dis?"

"It's a Louis Vuitton," Giselle said, raising her voice a bit, "that's what's special!"

"Will that be all today?" said a tall saleswoman with a silk scarf wrapped around her neck. She went behind the register, rang it up, and casually said, "That will be one thousand, two hundred and forty-nine dollars and fifty-six cents." Juanita actually gasped. Everyone turned their heads to look at her. She closed her mouth, which was open in shock. Did Giselle's father know how much this silly bag cost? Juanita thought. How many days or hours did it take him to make that much money? Did he come home tired like her father and lie on the couch with his work clothes still on? Juanita understood that Brian was rich; but the whole scene still made her feel sad for him.

Giselle slapped her dad's credit card on the counter like an ace of diamonds, and two minutes later she was on the phone with Dahlia. "I got it!" she gloated. "Yup...I just bought it right now!"

The next stop was supposed to be Barneys to pick out dresses for Nana's dinner party, but Cartier was right next door and Katie couldn't resist. She bought earrings twice the cost of Giselle's bag. In this shop of diamonds and gold, people shopped as if they were buying bubble gum at the corner store. Katie and Giselle didn't work for this money, and yet they were spending thousands without a second thought. Juanita wanted no part of it.

At Barney's, Giselle draped about ten different dresses over her arm. "Come on, Juanita," she said, "let's go try these on." Juanita reluctantly followed her into the dressing room. She was quiet for the first time since she'd arrived in New York.

"Oh my word! Oh! My! Word!" Katie gushed as Juanita stepped out of the changing booth. "That dress was made for you!" The dress was stunning. Juanita loved the way the material caressed her skin. It was soft and delicate and had no scratchy linings like the dresses she owned. She wanted to twirl around and watch the flowing fabric dance around her legs. Instead, she shrugged.

"It's not my eh-style."

Katie was stunned. Before Juanita had spoken she thought she was witnessing a real-life rags-to-riches moment. She expected Juanita to light up and spill over with excitement and gratitude.

"What do you mean? It's absolutely gorgeous."

"It's not my eh-style," Juanita repeated.

Style? Giselle shouted in her head. *You don't have any style!* She sifted through the other dresses on the silver rod, fighting the urge speak her thoughts out loud.

"Here, try this one on."

For each dress she tried on, Juanita managed to find some objection—too big, too small, too long, wrong color, too fancy, too plain. Giselle was flustered and exhausted from running around the store looking for a dress Juanita would agree to. Her frustration level was over the top. Who did this girl think she was? She should be grateful for this once-in-a-lifetime opportunity to buy a dress that didn't come from the Salvation Army! What gave her the right to be picky about it?

"No worry eh-bout it," Juanita said, refusing to try on any more dresses. "I already say to jou I have bring a dress from my home. My *tía* Arlene make it for me to go to dee American party."

"No!" Giselle begged. She could only imagine what this dress looked like. "If you don't like the clothes here we can go to another store."

The three of them went to Giorgio Armani, Dolce & Gabbana, Lacoste and Brooks Brothers. Juanita walked out of each store empty-handed. No dress, no shirts, no jeans, not even a pair of socks. She wouldn't budge. By the time they got to Ralph Lauren, Katie and Giselle had given up on her and were concentrating on shopping for themselves.

CHAPTER 9

"I'm back!" Alyce chirped over the phone. She had arrived from Paris the night before. "Ohmigod, I am sooo in love with that city! You have got to go with me the next time." Alyce told Giselle about the gorgeous cathedrals she'd visited, the trendy boutiques, the romantic bridges, and of course the Eiffel Tower. But what she hadn't done, and had missed terribly, was go to the beach. "I already called Dahlia and she's bringing the cooler. I have got to get some color on my skin. It's already July and I have *nooo* tan lines!"

Giselle hated the beach. "Cool, I can't wait," she lied. Well, only half lied. She couldn't wait to hang out with her friends and get away from Juanita for a bit. Juanita was always in her space, always talking, always hugging her! It drove her nuts.

"Hey, Dad," she said, grabbing a bunch of sodas from the fridge. "I'm going out with Alyce and Dahlia. I'll be back around seven or eight."

"What about Juanita?" he asked.

"She'll be fine." Giselle shrugged, piling cans of Coke into a plastic bag. "She's studying her English book by the pool."

"Did she say she didn't want to go?" he continued.

"Dad! I said she'll be fine. Does she really have to follow me everywhere I go?"

"You're taking her, or you don't go."

Giselle threw her hands up in the air. "Are you serious? Dad! I need some time with my friends, and I'm not ready to introduce her to anyone yet!"

"Why not? She's your cousin."

"She's weird! It's embarrassing. Look at the way she dresses. She has all these dumb superstitions, she's loud, she's too touchy-feely, just… Aaaah, come on, Dad. I don't want to take her."

At noon, Alyce's driver pulled up in front of the house. Juanita jumped into the back and bounced on the big leather seat. She couldn't wait to go to the beach. After their little shopping spree, Juanita had started to feel homesick. The ocean would make her feel better. It always did.

"I no can wait to meet jour friends," she said, giving her cousin an affectionate squeeze on her arm.

"Yeah, this is going to be fun," Giselle said in a monotone kill-me-now tone.

Alyce's Hispanic driver turned on the radio and tuned in to a Spanish station.

"I lub dis song!" Juanita shrieked, and opened her

huge brown eyes even wider. "Jou know dis singer, Juan Luis Guerra?"

"No."

"He's a berry popular Dominican singer, ebbry-body know him."

"*Ojalá que llueve café en campo,*" she sang, closing her eyes and dancing in her seat. Juanita felt good. She had been starting to wish she'd never come, but now she felt all her energy and excitement come back.

They stopped at a red light and the driver turned around. "*¿Tu eres Dominicana?*" he asked Juanita, who was still singing.

"*Seguro que sí,*" she responded with a smile. "*¿Y tu?*" she continued, hoping he'd say he was Dominican, too.

"*Ciento por ciento,*" he said, beaming with pride, then repeated it in English with a heavy Spanish accent. "Wong hundred per seng."

He looked at Giselle with a familiarity he had never shown before. "*Nunca sabia que tu eres Dominicana.*"

She looked at him with a blank stare. "What?"

Juanita translated. "He say he never know jou were Dominican."

"Oh, I am eh-sorry," he said, thinking he had misspoken. "You look like your frang, I thought you were family."

"We *are* family," the girls said at the same time—Giselle in English, Juanita in Spanish. They looked at each other with a chuckle and Juanita reached over for a little hug. "*Soy familia,*" she repeated.

Throughout the rest of the ride, Juanita and Luis spoke

in Spanish. Juanita explained why Giselle didn't speak the language and told him the whole history—starting with their mothers' coming to America years ago and ending with her own visit to Long Island now.

Giselle felt silly sitting there not saying or understanding a word, but at the same time, she kind of liked it. She hadn't heard a conversation in Spanish since she was five years old, and it made her think of her mother. Giselle curled up in her seat and just listened. A sense of calm fell over her, the same tranquility she used to feel when she was cuddled against her mother's chest.

As the car pulled up to Alyce's house, the peace Giselle was feeling quickly dissolved. She looked at Juanita's wild hair and her too-tight, brandless capris that made her butt look enormous. She should have tried harder to get her to buy something at the stores, and she wished she'd had time to flat-iron Juanita's frizz ball before they'd left the house.

"I no can believe how big deh house is!" Juanita said as they walked toward the door. It was twice as big as her cousin's.

Giselle rang the bell. *Diiiiing-dooong.* It sounded just like the bell in her dream. She took in a deep breath as Alyce opened the door.

Juanita hugged and gave a kiss on the cheek to everyone she was introduced to, even Alyce's father.

"She sure is affectionate," Alyce said, amused by her father's stiff and uncomfortable reaction to Juanita's greeting. Giselle shrugged with an apologetic smile.

"Yeah, she's a hugger."

Alyce's mother whisked Juanita off for a tour of the house in response to her comment that it was "berry, berry, beautiful." "Well, thank you so much!" she'd responded, speaking very slowly and very loudly. "Let me show you the other floors."

CHAPTER 10

The car ride to the beach was a repeat performance of her ride from the airport. Juanita was an explosion of questions, stories, and excitement. Alyce and Dahlia visibly enjoyed the spectacle and shot looks at Giselle as if to say, *"Wow, you weren't kidding!"*

"I no can't wait to swim in dee ocean." Juanita said, "My grandmoh-der say dee ocean wash away dee bad luck."

"In that case, Giselle," Alyce said with an evil smile, "you'd better dive in that water as soon as we get there."

"Yeah," Dahlia added. "Maybe then your bad luck will go away—far, far away."

Juanita laughed with the girls, oblivious to the fact that the bad luck they were referring to was her. Giselle laughed, too, but it was more of an uncomfortable chuckle. She was embarrassed by her cousin, but more than that, she was unexpectedly hurt by her friends' comments. Giselle started to regret having said such horrible things about Juanita on the phone to her friends. The three friends always backed each other up when one of them didn't like someone else.

"My luck's not so bad," she said, shrugging.

"She just doesn't want to get in the water and mess up her precious hair," Alyce said, flipping her own. She hated the fact that Giselle never went in the ocean with her and Dahlia.

Well, I don't have that silky wash-'n'-go hair like some people, Giselle snapped back in her mind. None of her friends knew how long it took or how much money it cost to keep her hair looking the way it did.

"Der she is," Juanita yelled, pointing to the ocean now in view. "It's dee American bitch!"

Alyce and Dahlia lost it. They grabbed their stomachs and laughed uncontrollably at Juanita's mispronunciation.

"Yup," Dahlia said between fits of laughter. "That's her, all right. There goes that American bitch."

"Wow," Alyce chimed in. "That is one big bitch!"

This time, Juanita understood that they were laughing at her. She looked at Giselle with big eyes and for a moment looked as if she were about to cry. To Giselle's relief, Juanita laughed instead.

"I say a bad word?" she asked, covering her mouth. "I no can say dis word dee good way."

She repeated the word slowly, but it still came out wrong.

"Eee," Giselle said, stretching the corners of her mouth. "Beeeeeach."

Once Alyce and Dahlia calmed down, they chimed in to help her say it the right way. Juanita tried over and over and then finally: "Beach." The girls threw up their arms and cheered as the car came to a stop.

The girls found a nice spot to settle in. Juanita reached into her bag and pulled out a huge towel with the Dominican flag on it and spread it out on the sand. She took off her capris and T-shirt to reveal a small canary-yellow bikini that did nothing to disguise her big hips and the little pouch of flesh on her belly. Giselle, on the other hand, kept on her tank top and threw a pair of boy shorts on to hide her extra weight.

"What is dat?" Juanita asked watching her cousin open a pop-up tent.

"Oh, this thing is the best," Giselle said. "There's plenty of room for you."

"No, dat's okay," she answered. "I love dee sun." Juanita lay down on her towel and opened her arms, welcoming the hot rays on her body. Alyce and Dahlia were lying down too—greased up, plugged in to their iPods, and absorbing the sun.

Ohmigod, Giselle thought, looking at Juanita glistening in her little bikini, *she is going to get like three shades darker in this sun!*

"Here," she said, sticking her arm out of her tent, holding the large tube of SPF50 sunscreen. "You should really put this on."

"Fifty!" Juanita gasped. "I won't get a tan with dat."

"Don't you think you're tan enough?" Giselle mumbled under her breath.

Juanita pulled an SPF4 oil from her bag, smeared it on her skin, and lay back down on the red and blue towel.

"You could get cancer if you don't protect your skin. Don't you know that?"

Giselle preached about all the ills of the sun, from skin cancer to premature aging, but Juanita just shrugged with her eyes still closed. *"Me gusta el sol,"* she repeated, vowing her love for the sun, more for herself than Giselle.

After an hour of baking, Alyce and Dahlia were peeling back the edge of their bikinis to check out their tan lines. Giselle was fast asleep in the shade. Juanita wanted to wake her up and see if she wanted to take a dip, but Dahlia and Alyce assured her that Giselle would absolutely not go in the water.

"Why she no go?" Juanita asked.

"She never goes in the water," Dahlia said. "She doesn't like to mess up her hair."

It seemed ridiculous to Juanita that something as silly as hair could prevent anyone from having fun.

Juanita led the pack and ran into the wild and beautiful foaming ocean. It wasn't as crystal clear as what she was used to in the Caribbean, but it was still wonderful.

"Come on!" she yelled as Dahlia and Alyce dipped their feet in, trying to adjust to the cool water. Juanita wrestled herself out of the ocean and joined the girls.

"No, no, no," she said, pulling them back to the sand. "We run into dee water!"

Dahlia and Alyce looked at each other with raised eyebrows.

"Uhh, I think I'll just go in slow like I always do." Dahlia said.

"No fun like dat!" Juanita protested. "We go ebbreebody...hold hand."

Alyce shrugged with a smile and grabbed Juanita's hand, Dahlia grudgingly did the same.

"*Uno, dos, tres.*" At the count of three Juanita and the girls bolted into the ocean, screaming and laughing, until they were neck deep.

Juanita was like a fish, diving into the tall waves and jumping up with a spin like a synchronized swimmer.

"Oh my God," Dahlia said to Alyce as she shook her head. "She's like a little kid."

"I know," Alyce said with a laugh. She absolutely loved her.

As the girls finally emerged from the water, Juanita spotted a group of boys sliding on the edge of the sea with waifboards.

"Ah, I do dis in my home town," she said. "My cousin have bring dee waifboard from America and he teach me."

Juanita decided to join them and take a few turns on the board.

"I go," she said to Alyce and Dahlia. "You come with me or no?"

Dahlia had no desire. She was too exhausted and hungry. Alyce was tempted, but she really wanted to tan a little longer before the sun got too weak.

"Where's Juanita?" Giselle asked as her friends came back and collapsed on their blanket. Dahlia pointed to the indistinct bodies in the distance.

"She's picking up some American men," she said with a chuckle.

"What?"

"Relax. She's just waifboarding," Alyce said. "Wow, that girl sure has a lot of energy."

Giselle could only imagine the fool Juanita had made of herself in front of Alyce and Dahlia while they were with her. She changed the subject quickly. "Do you guys want to eat?"

"Yes," they said in unison, and reached for the basket of ham and cheese sandwiches.

Juanita came back a half an hour later, breathless and dripping with salt water. She'd had a great time with the nice American boys. They were impressed at how good she was with the waifboard, especially the tall boy with the pretty green eyes. He was impressed by a few things. He liked a girl who wasn't afraid to goof around and be silly. She was very much like him; he, too, was comfortable in his own skin, unconcerned by what others thought of him. He regretted leaving without getting her number. She, on the other hand, had already forgotten his name. There were too many guys to remember each one. But Alex Nixon from Georgia couldn't get her name off his mind—Juanita Maria Delacruz Martinez.

CHAPTER 11

Juanita twirled in the mirror, then looked at Giselle. It was a bright purple satin dress with a plunging neckline and ruffles on the bottom. Juanita loved this dress. Her *tía* Arlene, a seamstress for a bridal shop in the Dominican Republic, had made it just for Juanita's trip. "You'll need something to wear if you go to a party in America," *tía* Arlene had said. Tonight was the party at Giselle's grandmother's house and Juanita couldn't wait to show it off.

The dress wasn't as bad as the flowery dress in Giselle's dream, but in her eyes it was still pretty horrific. She hoped she'd have more luck convincing Juanita to change her outfit than she'd had with suggesting to change her hair. Giselle had offered to take Juanita with her to the hair salon that afternoon to dye and straighten her hair, but her cousin had declined the invitation. Juanita liked her tight curls bouncing and dancing around her face. They matched her personality.

"Come on," Giselle had said. "Your hair will look so much better with streaks."

"I no like dat color for me."

Juanita hated the idea of dyeing her hair a color that was so obviously not her own. It was like being a really bad liar.

"Are you sure you don't want to borrow a dress from me?" Giselle asked—one last attempt to save herself from embarrassment.

"Jou no like?" Juanita asked.

"It's not something I would wear," Giselle said.

Juanita shrugged. "Dat's okay. I don't borrow it to jou. But me…I love berry much my dress."

Giselle pulled out a black dress from her closet. "What do you think of this?"

Juanita liked the fabric, but it didn't have as much personality as her dress. Besides, she was really excited to wear her own.

"I like dee dress my *tía* make."

"But I'm wearing a black dress, too. We could look alike."

"I want to look like me," Juanita shot back.

Giselle put the black dress back in the closet with a grunt. She needed a new strategy.

"Juanita," she said, sitting her down on the bed. "Everyone is going to be wearing very expensive and fancy clothes. If you show up with this handmade dress, you're going to look a little silly. I don't want anyone to laugh at you or anything or make fun of you behind your back."

Juanita started to get frustrated with Giselle. She had been a nag from the start, and everything Juanita did, said, or wore seemed to be wrong.

"My *tía* make my dress and my favorite color is *violeta*," she said with a calm but sharp tone. "I no pay big money like jou, but my *tía* make my dress with berry big love. I like my hair, I like my clo-sing, I like Juanita. I no care if dee people laugh to me."

Giselle didn't know what to say. She didn't know whether to be mad, feel ashamed, or admire her cousin for standing up for who she was. She could never do that with her friends.

"Yeah," she said, nodding, "okay."

Giselle didn't know why, but she wanted to cry. She got up, told Juanita she'd be back from the beauty salon in a few hours, and left the house, hiding the tears from her father.

"How's the water?" her stylist asked as she sprayed the nozzle on Giselle's thick hair.

"It's good," she answered quietly.

Giselle closed her eyes as the woman massaged the shampoo into her hair and scalp. This was one of her favorite parts about getting her hair done. The only other person who had ever touched her hair and rubbed her scalp was her mother. That was one of the memories she clearly remembered and missed. Giselle's stylist wrapped a thick towel around her head and led her to the chair to cut and dry.

"Uh-oh. Your roots are beginning to show," she said, looking at Giselle's natural dark color growing at the scalp, chasing her fake blond streaks.

"What?" Giselle asked. She couldn't seem to stop daydreaming about her mother and her family in DR.

"Your roots, darling," she repeated. "They're starting to come up. We should take care of that the next time you're here." Giselle nodded without a word.

When her hair was damp, it curled naturally. The only time she ever really saw her curls was when they were wet, before the stylist made them straight. She couldn't remember the last time she'd seen her curls dry. The stylist snipped away, framing her face with layers, and for a moment before it was time to dry, Giselle had an urge to go curly. But the hair dryer went on too quickly and she lost her nerve. *Not for Nana's dinner party,* she thought. *Maybe another time…maybe.*

Brian rang the bell to Nana's house as Giselle prepared herself for the worst. *Here we go,* she thought as the door opened.

"Well, hello, come inside," Nana said, gesturing with her flawlessly manicured hands.

"Mother," Brian said, tapping his cheek to hers. Katie and Giselle did the same.

"This must be your cousin," she said, looking at Juanita, then at Giselle.

"Yes, this is Juanita. Juanita, this is my grandmother Betty."

"Pleasure to meet you, young lady," she said, placing a kissless cheek on Juanita's.

Juanita had already learned to hold back on her hugs. She had encountered enough stiff bodies and surprised looks to understand that not everyone said hello as they did in her country. But she honestly thought a grandmother's greeting would be more affectionate than Nana's display.

"Jour grandmoh-der hug jou sometime?" she whispered to Giselle as they walked inside.

Giselle was still getting over the surprise that Juanita didn't try to tackle Nana. That would have been a shock to her grandmother's system. She had wanted to tell Juanita in the car not to hug her grandmother but figured she had already pushed her recommendations to the limit.

"Not really," Giselle answered. "Sometimes she gives a little half a hug." She wanted to demonstrate but Nana was right behind them.

Aunt Linda got up from the couch, where everyone was chatting and nibbling on hors d'oeuvres.

"Hi, guys," she said excitedly. Aunt Linda gave each of them a hug, including Juanita before she had even been introduced. "Juanita, it is so nice to meet you finally. I saw pictures of you when you were born and now I just can't believe it's been fifteen years!"

"Jou see baby picture of me?" Juanita asked, a bit shocked.

"Yes, of course! Your auntie was so proud when you were born. She came back from the Dominican Republic with all kinds of pictures of you."

Giselle smiled. Knowing that Aunt Linda had seen pictures of Juanita as a baby made it feel as if she was introducing an old family friend.

Aunt Susan and the rest of the family gathered around Brian, Katie, Giselle, and Juanita.

"Oh, honey, look at this hair!" Aunt Susan said after she was introduced to Juanita. "If only my hair could do tricks like that!"

Aunt Linda scrunched Juanita's curls with her hands and made an *Ohmigod* face.

"Isn't that adorable? It's very Shirley Temple chic!" She looked at her niece, with her straight hair. "Oh, Gigi, you should do this. I haven't seen curls on you since you were this big!" she said, placing her hand above her hip.

"You really think I'd look okay?" Giselle asked her aunts.

"Absolutely," they said at the same time, then laughed that the same word had come out of their mouths.

Juanita loved Giselle's aunts. She felt a little better knowing Giselle did have family who loved her besides her father and a nanny who wasn't even her own blood. It was just a shame that they lived so far away from her.

Nana came over and stood between Giselle and Juanita.

"Walita, are you enjoying your stay in the United States? I understand this is your first visit to this great country of ours," she said.

"Mom, her name is Juanita," Aunt Susan said.

"Oh," she said with a breathy laugh. "I apologize. These ethnic names are so hard for me to get straight."

Juanita answered Nana's question with the little she'd seen of America so far. She raved over the big houses and compared them with the ones in San Pedro. But, she pointed out, the houses were much more colorful in DR—beautiful colors of pink, lime, lavender, and lemon yellow—and wouldn't it be nice for Americans to do the same? She told them about the big cars and the enormous SUVs on the street and compared them with the scooters and motorcycles in her hometown. She described families of three and even four riding on one scooter. Juanita told them about the beach—she concentrated really hard on pronouncing it the right way—and compared it with the beaches she rode to on her scooter at least three times a week in DR. She described how funny it was that something like two beaches in different countries could be exactly the same but so different, too.

Nana shook her head with a smile. "You are certainly animated when you speak," she said, commenting on Juanita's wild hand gestures during her response.

"Exactly," Aunt Linda said. "Now, tell me...who does that remind you of?"

"Are you kidding?" Aunt Susan said with a laugh. "It's almost scary how much she reminds me of Jackie. I feel like I'm in a time warp."

Giselle felt her stomach drop. She thought of all the terrible things she had thought and said about her cousin. Little had she known Juanita was just like her mother. Of course she was, Giselle reasoned; her mother had come from a little town just like Juanita and had spoken very little English. She'd grown up with the same family as Juanita, and their superstitions and zeal for religion had probably been passed on to her as well. How would Giselle have treated her own mother if she had met her today for the first time? she wondered. Would she have treated this woman who was so tender and loving with harsh judgment and hateful thoughts just because she didn't fit in? The very thought made her sick to her stomach.

The family sat down at the long table. Nana had hired a French chef to cook her favorite dish—coq au vin—and had hired three servers, two of whom were Hispanic.

"*Muchas gracias,*" Juanita said to one of the servers, who looked like her, as she placed the plate in front of her.

"*De nada,*" the server responded with a smile.

"Dis feel like home, when my moh-der or *tía* serve me," Juanita said excitedly to Giselle, who was sitting next to her.

"*Gracias,*" Giselle said, repeating the words of her cousin as the server moved on to her.

"Juanita," Nana said, "that is quite an interesting dress you're wearing."

Giselle recognized the sarcasm in her grandmother's voice and cut in.

"Yes, isn't it pretty," Giselle said. "Her aunt made it for her...actually, *our* aunt made it for her. I think that's incredibly sweet, don't you?"

"Oh yes, yes," Nana responded. "Very sweet...and very shiny."

"Shiny is better than dull, that's what I always say," Giselle said, reaching for her fork. Aunt Linda gave Giselle a knowing smile. She was proud of her niece, whose subtle defense didn't give Nana a chance to critique Juanita too harshly.

Giselle noticed Juanita folding her hands and about to lower her head.

"Shall we bless the food?" Giselle quickly said, folding her hands as well. Everyone looked at her with a bit of surprise but folded their hands and bowed their heads. There was a moment of silence and Nana cleared her throat. "Giselle, dear, we're waiting."

"Oh," she said, suddenly realizing they were waiting for her to pray since she had suggested it. She instantly regretted saying a word. "Uhhh...Bless this food... O God... Thank you...for the food.... Amen."

"Amen," they echoed around the table. Juanita crossed herself and kissed her fingertips, then reached for her cloth napkin.

"Like dis, *Prima*?" she asked, placing it on her lap with the fold toward the waist. Giselle opened her eyes wide with a smile. Juanita had remembered.

"Perfect," Giselle said. "That's absolutely right."

Juanita told the family about Giselle's etiquette lesson and asked them to make sure she remembered everything.

"How wonderful," Nana said. "It's nice to know my granddaughter listens to me when I teach her how to act like a lady."

"Oh, I listen to alright," Giselle said. *Maybe I listen a bit too much,* she commented in her mind.

"Speaking of which, how's your diet coming along?" Nana asked.

Giselle paused for a second. "Oh, I'm not on it anymore," she said, surprised by the boldness she was feeling at the moment. "I've decided that I'm not really fat, Nana. I just have a big butt. You know, I'm half Hispanic. We're famous for that sort of thing."

"Giselle," Brian said quietly, shaking his head but trying

very hard to disguise how much he wanted to laugh. He had never heard her talk that way to his mother.

For the first time, Nana was speechless. She didn't know how to respond. Aunt Linda cut into the silence with questions for Juanita, who was more than happy to respond. The rest of the evening Juanita was the loudest one at the table and flailed her arms about with passion as she told her stories—but she paid careful attention not to speak with her mouth full and to keep her elbows off the table at all times.

That night as the girls said their prayers, Giselle silently thanked God for this new feeling inside her. She couldn't describe it or even understand where it had come from, but it felt like something inside her had blossomed before her eyes. That night she kept Juanita up late, asking questions about her family in the Dominican Republic. She wanted to know more about their lives and their lifestyle. She wanted to know what made them happy and sad, what interesting experiences they had, what dreams they had for the future. Giselle wanted to know more about them, because deep down, she desperately wanted to learn and understand more about herself.

CHAPTER 12

Three days later Giselle and Brian were on their way to show Juanita New York City and have dinner with her mother's cousins in Washington Heights. Katie wanted to come along but was swamped with work at the office. Giselle was happy that it would only be the three of them.

"Der she is!" Juanita shrieked, seeing the New York skyline for the first time. She stuck her head out the window and snapped about a dozen pictures. "*Ay dios mio,* I feel like I'm in dee movies!" She couldn't believe she was really in New York City! She'd heard stories from her mother and seen it on television and received postcards from family members, but seeing it with her own eyes gave her an unexpected rush of euphoria. "Dat's de Empire Eh-state Building, where King Kong climb!" she screamed. Giselle spit out an unexpected laugh but quickly covered it up with a few strong coughs. Once Brian crossed the bridge and parked the car in the garage, the tour began.

* * *

Brian and Giselle had to guide Juanita like a blind person along the city sidewalks because she couldn't stop looking up at all the tall buildings.

"How tall is that one?" she'd ask to a duet of "I don't knows." "How about that one?"

Brian promised to look up all the facts when they got back home.

"Watch out!" Giselle shrieked, pulling Juanita to the side as an obese businessman rushed passed.

"Sank jou, *Prima*," she said, giving Giselle's arm a little hug. "I ne-ber see so many person in one place before."

"I've never seen so many *people*," Giselle corrected, keeping her promise to help her cousin improve her English. Juanita repeated it the right way with a smile as they approached the south entrance of Central Park.

Juanita loved the bustle of activity in the park, the Rollerbladers and joggers, the crowded green lawn filled with people lying out in the sun, playing guitars, and tossing footballs and Frisbees.

"Jou have dis?" Juanita asked, pointing to the Rollerbladers zigzagging through a line of bright orange cones.

"No," she said. "People in Long Island don't exactly go Rollerblading from place to place. I'd look kind of funny Rollerblading in my neighborhood."

Juanita shrugged.

"I want lie down in dee grass!" she said leading them to the entrance of Sheep Meadow. Brian went to get some hot dogs and Cokes for their picnic.

"But we didn't bring a blanket," Giselle argued. "We'll get grass stains."

Juanita took off her shoes and felt the cool, soft blanket of lawn under her toes.

"I don't care," Juanita said, finding a nice spot to lie down and absorb a bit of sun as she waited for Brian to bring the food.

"Do you think we can find a spot under a tree? I didn't bring my sunblock."

Juanita reached up to grab her cousin's hands to pull her down next to her.

"I can't!" Giselle shouted, fighting Juanita's tug. "My pants will get dirty. And my face is going to get too dark."

"*¡Ay Prima, tu eres como una vieja!*"

"What?"

"An old lady, jou act like old lady," Juanita said, shaking her head. "Jou worry, worry, worry and have no fun."

"That's not true!" Giselle protested. But when she really thought about it, it was absolutely true. She'd spent her whole life worried about everything—how she looked, how she acted, what people thought of her.

"Come," Juanita said, walking to a nearby tree. She pulled a light jacket from her bag and let Giselle sit on it.

"Thanks," Giselle said, feeling embarrassed and silly that she was being such a baby.

After they ate their hot dogs under the tree, they walked to the small pond to look at the rowboats and gondolas. As they walked, Juanita heard the faint sound of merengue in the distance.

"Listen," she said, stopping in her tracks.

Brian and Giselle followed her as if she were a hound dog hot on the trail. She started to shake her hips the moment she found the small band of young musicians.

"*Vente, Prima,*" she said to Giselle as she pulled her in to dance. Giselle pulled back and stiffened her body.

"No, no, no, I don't know how."

"I teach jou."

"Yeah, like later, in my house. Not in front of all these people."

"No more worry about people. Jou dance! *Baila, Prima, baila!*"

Juanita grabbed her cousin's hands and moved her body to the rhythm.

"*Uno, dos, tres, quarto. Uno, dos, tres, quatro,*" Giselle moved her feet to Juanita's count. Other than a homeless man dancing with his shopping cart, they were the only ones dancing. Giselle looked around at the people. Some were looking at them while others just did their own thing.

"Eh-stop looking dee people. Look to me!"

Giselle looked at her cousin's smiling eyes.

"*Muy bien,* now shake dee hip." Giselle loosened up and began to really feel the music. In that moment she didn't care if she was doing it wrong or if she looked like a fool to anyone else. She was having fun, dancing in the park with her cousin.

Brian cut in and twirled his daughter around. He was shaking his hips side to side like a pro. Giselle was shocked. She'd had no idea he knew how to dance to this stuff.

"Your mother taught me," he said with a smile, reading the look of confusion on her face.

Juanita clapped her hands and jumped up and down.

"*Ay, que bueno, Tío* Brian! Berry good, berry good!"

After they danced, Brian took his daughter in his arms and hugged her tighter than he had in a long time. Giselle clung to her father with an unexpected lump in her throat that she couldn't swallow.

"I love you, Gigi," he said, still holding on to her.

Giselle tried to say something, but instead she started to cry. Brian hugged her tighter.

"I'm so sorry," he said.

Giselle cried even harder. They stayed like that for a while as people passed and curiously stared. It wasn't cool or even proper to make such a dramatic scene in public. But neither of them cared. The music continued to play and Juanita stood nearby, too confused to shake her hips.

CHAPTER 13

Giselle washed her face in the sink of the public restroom. She looked at herself in the mirror—her makeup was rinsed away and her eyes were still red. Giselle smiled at her image. She had lipstick, mascara, and blusher in her Louis Vuitton bag but decided just to wipe her face with a paper towel and spend the rest of the day with a fresh, natural look. Juanita was standing by her side with a what-just-happened look on her face.

"Are jou okay?" she asked quietly.

"I'm great," Giselle said with a smile. "I feel really good. Don't worry, nothing is wrong. My dad and I just had…a moment, that's all."

They walked over to the tree where Brian was waiting and then made their way to the horse-drawn carriages on Fifth Avenue. Juanita was used to seeing horses trotting down dirt roads in her home town or lazily eating in her grandmother's small stable. It was funny to see these beautiful animals in this big, busy city, surrounded by buildings and people in suits rushing past. They seemed out of place.

The three of them got in the carriage, Brian in the middle with the girls on either side wrapped around one of his arms.

"What's the horse's name?" Giselle asked the driver.

"Her name is whatever you want it to be while you're riding," he said, gesturing toward the horse so she could name her. "What'll it be, pretty lady?

Giselle laughed. "I don't know," she said, shrugging.

"Come on," he persisted. "Whatever word that's on your mind."

There were lots of words on Giselle's mind—*love, liberation, family, roots, joy.*

"Merengue," she finally said, doing her best to roll the *R*s as Juanita had shown her. "Her name is Merengue."

The next stop after Central Park was the Empire State Building. Before Juanita got on the elevator to the observation deck, she took a deep breath, crossed herself, and said a quick prayer.

"My moh-der and *Tía* Jackie were eh-stuck on an elebator when they first came to New Jork."

"Really?" Giselle asked, wanting to hear more. "How long were they stuck?"

Juanita pulled at her ears, which were tingling from the elevator's speed.

"Here," Giselle said, giving Juanita a stick of gum. "That'll help your ears pop."

Juanita chewed the gum and told the story of their mothers

stuck on an elevator. Giselle learned that her mother was the brave one of the two sisters. Juanita's mother had cried the whole time, while Jackie had done everything she could to make her big sister calm. She had tried to make her laugh by singing a song to the elevator gods so that it would move again.

"Were there other people in the elevator?" Giselle gasped, surprised that her mother was that silly.

"Many."

"She wasn't embarrassed?"

The little story brought a smile to Brian's face. "Your mother wasn't easily embarrassed," he said with a chuckle. "She never told me this story, but it sounds like something she would absolutely do."

The elevator doors opened and they walked out onto the terrace of the observation deck.

Juanita put her hands on her face and said something to herself in Spanish. Giselle didn't understand the words but understood exactly how her cousin felt. The two girls stood there looking at the city. Everywhere they turned, the view stretched out toward the horizon with endless possibilities. In that small moment the world seemed to open up for both of them. Juanita was a long way from dirt roads, pigpens, and cackling chickens. And although Giselle had seen this view before, she felt as if she were looking at it now with new eyes. Just like the buildings in the distance, things that had seemed so huge and important before now looked small and trifling. She was spending the day with her father, her cousin, and in a way, her mother, too. As she stood over a thousand feet in the air, she truly felt as if she were on top of the world. Juanita wrapped her arms around her cousin and for the first time Giselle didn't mind.

The three of them walked around the city; ate soft, warm pretzels from carts with colorful umbrellas; went to the Metropolitan Museum of Art; and even took a helicopter ride over the city for twenty minutes. Brian had wanted to take them to see a Broadway musical, but the invitation for dinner with Juanita's cousins was for seven o'clock.

They hailed a cab back to the parking garage and headed to the predominately Dominican neighborhood in upper Manhattan—Washington Heights.

A flood of memories came to Brian as they reached the neighborhood where his wife used to live before they were married. It had been years since the last time he was there, but it felt like only yesterday. He looked at the small details of the neighborhood as if they were old friends—the Dominican flags hanging over the streets, the Piragua man selling snow cones, the men—both young and old—playing dominoes in front of corner bodegas where he could buy sodas in flavors like coconut and pineapple.

They parked the car in another public garage and walked to the family's apartment. There was Spanish music coming from open windows and cars. The streets were bustling with people laughing, speaking Spanish, and making wild hand gestures like Juanita.

"Rosita is our moh-der's cousin from Abuelito's family.

She come ebry year to Dominican Republic," Juanita said as they approached the apartment building.

"One-twenty-six," Brian said, looking up at the number on the door. "Here it is."

"Oh my!" Giselle said at the third level of stairs with two more flights to go. "I can't believe there are no elevators in this place!"

The three of them climbed the long, narrow, and rickety stairs until they reached a door with a bad paint job. Juanita excitedly knocked on the door and when it opened there was an explosion of hugs, kisses, shouting, and laughing.

"*¡Mira, que linda te ves, mi amor!*" Rosita said, cupping Juanita's face with both hands, telling her how beautiful she looked.

"Gisellita," she said, turning to Giselle. "I can't believe how much you've grown! *Ja una mujer,*" she said, telling her she was already a woman. There were about fourteen people in the small apartment. Giselle must have spent a whole five minutes receiving hugs and kisses from people she'd never met; they all greeted her as if they'd known her all her life. Giselle was introduced to Rosita's teenage daughters, Lisa, nineteen; Marisol, seventeen; and Evie, thirteen. They were like a cross between Giselle and Juanita. Two of them had their hair straight, while the oldest wore hers in long curls. Their clothes weren't the designer outfits that Giselle had, but they looked more expensive and up to date than Juanita's wardrobe. They all spoke perfect Spanish and perfect English.

Everyone in the room seemed to talk at the same time.

They had to shout over each other and the merengue music to be heard. *No wonder Juanita screams when she talks,* Giselle thought. It definitely wasn't the neat, orderly family function Giselle was used to, where everyone took their turn to speak. The scene was both nerve-racking and fun at the same time.

The pungent scent of the food in the kitchen danced around in each room. It smelled delicious. Giselle sat down with her father on a couch with intricately designed velvet fabric covered in a layer of plastic. *Crunch,* it went as she sat down. There were plants everywhere—hanging plants, plants on long stands, plants on different wooden furnishings. Some were real and some obviously fake. There was way too much furniture for the small apartment; a large wooden entertainment center with fancy carvings on the corners, an oval glass coffee table taking up too much space in the living room, bookcases, and the large couch with matching love seats. There were little porcelain figurines with tiny colorful ribbons glued to them. They were displayed anywhere that would hold the little communities of swans, elephants, baby booties, and umbrellas. Each ribbon had gold inscriptions marking various occasions—*Marisol's quinceañera, July 7, 2005; Leslie's baby shower, January 27, 2000; Bernardo's graduation, June 21, 1998.* Over the couch was a painting just like Giselle's, of Dominican farmers working in the field. *Tío* Ruben's work apparently got around.

CHAPTER 14

Giselle was the center of attention, just as Juanita had been at Nana's. "You are so beautiful," everyone kept saying, in English and Spanish, as they fussed over her and Brian. She'd never had so many people tell her she was something that even she didn't believe she was.

"Thank you," she'd say, as if really saying "Are you serious?"

Rosita sat Brian, Giselle, and Juanita at the small table along with her husband's parents. Everyone else sat in various spots in the kitchen and living room, eating with their plates on their laps or on little folding trays. Rosita never sat down. She moved back and forth from the kitchen to the table, adding food and refilling glasses with juice and tropical soda. After a short prayer by Rosita's husband, everyone dug in. Giselle took a bite of the beef stew they called sancocho and opened her eyes wide. It was delicious. She had never tasted anything like it in her life. It had so much flavor. She found herself leaning over the dish and shoveling spoonfuls of it into her mouth.

"This is delicious," she said to Rosita.

"I'm glad you like it," she said, rubbing Giselle's shoulders. "It was your mother who taught me how to make it when she came here with your tía Milagros."

"Really?" Giselle shouted, too excited to swallow her food first.

"Oh yeah, she was quite a cook," she said.

Brian nodded with a smile as he chewed. "Yes, she was," he said. "I never thought I would taste this dish again. It tastes just the way she used to make it."

"I can teach you how to make it if you'd like," Rosita said to Giselle. Giselle never even had to scramble her eggs in the morning, let alone make a beef stew, but she beamed at the idea of making a meal passed down from her mother.

Despite the seating arrangements, everyone found a way to talk to each other, projecting their voices from the couch to the table, the table to the kitchen. They made jokes, laughed, and filled the room with an energy that was nothing like dinners at Nana's.

As they sat around eating, one of the many little kids waddled over to the light switch and turned it off with a giggle.

"*¡Se fue la lu!*" everyone shouted, and laughed as his mother switched it back on and picked him up.

"Giselle," Lisa shouted as she sat on the kitchen counter, wanting to let her in on the joke, "do you remember when the lights would go out in San Pedro?"

Giselle tried to think but nothing came to her. "No," she said. They explained how small towns like that are run by generators that often cut off electricity, leaving them in the dark for minutes at a time.

"When dis happen, ebry-body say '*se fue la lu*'!" Juanita said. "Dat mean dee light went out!"

"I love when that happens," Evie said, pouring soda for her aunt. "Everyone lights candles and tells scary stories until the lights come back on."

"Yeah, well, I wasn't loving it when it happened at my *quinceañera*," Lisa said.

"What's a *quinceañera*?" Giselle asked, remembering when Juanita had mentioned something like that the first day they'd met. Everyone seemed to stop chewing in disbelief.

"Wow, how do you not know what a quinceañera is?" Evie asked.

Giselle shrugged. "I live in Long Island, the last time I went to DR was when I was five, and I haven't really been around any Hispanics since then."

Lisa explained that a quinceañera is a Hispanic version of a sweet sixteen, except you do it when you're fifteen. "You should be planning yours," she added. The family and friends responded to Giselle's statement with all the information they could offer about the Dominican Republic— the island's history, customs, and traditions and various stories about the family.

"You should come with us the next time we go to DR," Rosita said. "Everyone would just go crazy over you! They've been waiting a long time to finally see you again."

The idea sounded fabulous. The more they spoke about the island, the more Giselle wanted to go back to the Dominican Republic. Brian nodded his approval. "That sounds good to me." Everyone got excited, even Rosita's daughters, who immediately started telling her all the places they would visit.

After dinner and a dessert of caramel custard called flan, Juanita made Giselle show the family her new merengue skills. Everyone clapped to the music, cheered her on, and took turns dancing with her. It was an amazing night. When they finally got ready to leave, Giselle understood why Juanita loved to hug so much. She squeezed each person goodbye as if she didn't want to let them go.

Brian topped off the night with an unexpected surprise. As he got the car out of the garage to head home, he decided to drive around to see if he could remember where Jackie's old apartment was. It took him a while to refamiliarize himself with the area, but soon he knew exactly where he was. He turned the corner at the small Pentecostal church and drove halfway down the block.

"Get out, girls," he said, opening his door.

They got out and looked at him, puzzled. "What is this? Why did we stop?" Giselle asked.

"Look," he said, pointing to the dilapidated red apartment building. "This is where both your mothers lived when they moved to New York City. I used to pick up Jackie here almost every day when we were dating."

The girls were silent. They just looked up and stared at the bit of history they shared. "Which one was their window?" Giselle asked.

CHAPTER 15

A few days after their New York City day trip, Giselle went in to get her hair done. She sat down in the chair as her beautician looked at the dark layer of hair growing at the scalp. "So, you want to cover up your roots today?" her stylist asked.

"Actually," Giselle said, "I'd like to go back to my roots. I want you to dye it dark brown, my natural color." She had made the decision without telling a soul. She wanted it to be a surprise. It felt good to make a decision for herself, without asking her friends what they thought first.

"I think that would look fabulous," her beautician said.

Giselle nodded. "So do I."

The stylist went to the back and mixed a solution of paste to match Giselle's natural color, then applied the goop to every strand. She let it sit for thirty minutes, then washed it thoroughly in the sink.

"Okay," she said to Giselle, about to pull the towel off her head. "Are you ready to see?"

"Oh my," Giselle said when she saw, touching her hair and leaning toward the mirror. "It looks even better than I thought it would."

"Since you're embracing your natural look, why don't we give these curls a go?" her beautician asked. She had always wanted see Giselle go curly.

"That's exactly what I was going to ask you to do," Giselle responded with a laugh.

She leaned her head back and let her beautician diffuse her hair and spray it with defrizzing gel. Soon Giselle was looking at a full head of bouncy, curly hair. She was speechless. Giselle looked exactly how she felt—different, transformed, completely new.

Katie and Juanita came back to the beauty salon to pick up Giselle. Their nails were still drying from their manicures. Juanita loved the color on her nails almost as much as the amazing massage and sugar scrub she'd had on her hands and arms. She was really starting to get used to the royal treatment. Katie opened the door carefully, trying not to nick her wet nails, and looked around for Giselle.

"Do you see her?" Katie asked Juanita as she scanned the room.

Katie went up to the reception desk. "Yes, hi. I'm looking for Giselle Johnson; she had an appointment for two o'clock? I'm a bit late to pick her up. She didn't leave, did she?"

Juanita jumped out of her chair in the waiting area and let out a scream. Katie gasped and looked at Juanita to see what was wrong only to see her staring at a girl with dark, curly—

"Oh my word! Giselle!" Katie squealed when she realized who it was. "Oh my word, look at you!"

Giselle twirled around with her head lifted high. "Do you like?"

"Ay, *Prima*. Berry, berry pretty!"

"Oh, Giselle," Katie said, touching her hair carefully. "It's so beautiful. My word, I never knew your hair had this much life! And the color is so perfect."

"I just wanted to try something different, you know?" Giselle said. "And this just felt right."

Giselle looked in the mirror one last time before they left. She not only looked beautiful, but for the first time, she felt beautiful, too.

After the beauty salon, Katie reasoned that a new look deserved a new outfit. Juanita had her heart set on seeing the typical American mall like her mother had described, so they went to one. They also figured Juanita might agree to let them buy her something if it was a little less expensive. She did. Juanita found a pink, collared short-sleeve shirt and a faded brown denim mini skirt from Abercrombie & Fitch. The skirt was shorter than anything she'd ever owned. Her mother would probably disapprove, but Katie convinced her it was absolutely adorable.

Giselle decided to find a dress for Alex's party, which was in one week. Betsey Johnson seemed to be the right store. The designer shared Giselle's last name and her designs were fun and adventurous—something Giselle was definitely feeling at the moment. She even had Juanita help her pick out some dresses.

"Oh, I love that, Gigi," Katie said as Giselle walked out in the third dress she'd tried. It was a black sleeveless dress with thin lace ruffles layered down to the edge and two inches of bright red chiffon gathered and peeking out beneath the hem. She had two more dresses to try on, but she already knew this was the one.

The day of Alex's party had finally come. As a VIP, Giselle had the right to bring a guest, and Juanita couldn't have been happier to go. That morning Giselle had two women come to the house to give her and Juanita manicures, pedicures, facials, and Swedish massages by the pool.

"Ay, *Prima*, can we do dis ebbry day?" Juanita slurred with her eyes half closed as she lay on the massage table. Her nails were flawless, she'd just had her very first facial, and the masseuse was putting her into a trance. Juanita was getting used to the good life. After their pampering by the pool, Giselle went with her father for a few hours to run errands while Katie stayed with Juanita.

"Katie," Juanita said, when Giselle and Brian finally left. "Can jou take me to dee beauty salon?" Juanita told her how she'd decided to have a new look, too. *Why not?* she reasoned. She was bold with everything else, why not her hair? Regardless of how she felt about hair dye—especially light colors—Juanita was curious to see how the streaks Giselle had suggested would look on her. If she didn't like it, she could always go back to dark hair just like Giselle. Juanita absolutely loved the drastic change in Giselle and thought she'd be daring, too. She wanted to keep it a secret and surprise her cousin.

"Oh, how exciting!" Katie said. "I think that will be so much fun." They jumped into the car and took off.

"Can I do your makeup when you're done?" Katie asked, looking intently at the road.

"Ay, *sí!* Jes, please," Juanita said. "Make me look like an American Celebrity."

"Ooh! Can I tweeze your eyebrows, too?" Katie continued.

Juanita batted her eyes like a superstar. *"Sí."*

For two hours Juanita was fussed over as if Giselle's hairdresser were creating a masterpiece. She laughed at her funny crown of tinfoil layered and folded on top of her head. It itched so badly, but she didn't dare touch it. After her hair was washed and scrubbed, Juanita kept her eyes closed as it was styled. The only way she knew it was looking fantastic was listening to Katie repeat her favorite phrase over and over—"Oh my word!"

"Okay," the beautician said, feeling as if this were a reverse déjà vu. "Are you ready to see?" Juanita looked in the mirror and gasped. She looked so different! She didn't even feel like herself, but she had to admit she looked pretty amazing. Juanita touched her hair. It was silky soft, and she could actually run her fingers through it.

"Sank jou berry much," she said, giving the beautician a big hug before she and Katie went to the reception area to pay.

Juanita took out the money from her family, which she still hadn't had a chance to use.

"Put that away," Katie demanded. "Are you kidding me? Brian would kill me if I let you pay!" It was getting easier and easier to accept their generosity. After all, she'd finally rationalized, spending money was just as natural to them as saving it was to her family back home. They just lived in different circumstances.

After the salon, Katie bought Juanita the beautiful dress from Barneys she had loved the first time she went shopping, the one that caressed her skin and had no scratchy lining. They raced home and Katie did Juanita's makeup before Giselle and Brian came home.

"Wow!" Katie said, impressed with the whole transformation. "You look incredible."

Juanita danced in front of the mirror. She twirled and looked at herself from every angle. She couldn't believe she was looking at herself.

CHAPTER 16

GISELLE'S jaw dropped. She didn't know what to say. When did this... How did she... What in the world just happened? Juanita stared at her cousin. She'd thought Giselle would have done something by now—screamed, smiled, jumped up and down...something.

"Jou no like it?" Juanita asked.

"Oh, no, of course...you look great. You look...very different." Giselle couldn't tell her how she really felt, not as excited as Juanita was, twirling about in her new dress. Juanita looked exactly like Giselle had just days earlier, the same way she'd looked for a long time.

Juanita was the one who had inspired her to be her own person, accept her own natural beauty, and stop trying to look like everyone else around her. And here she was, her inspiration, combing through her straight highlighted hair, looking like everyone Giselle had ever tried to imitate. Not only that—Juanita seemed to absolutely love it. It was as if she'd come to a realization that this look was a huge step up from her old look—Giselle's new one.

"You look great," Giselle said again. "Seriously, I can't believe you did that." Giselle excused herself quickly so she could start getting ready for the party. Suddenly she wasn't so sure about her new look. Maybe she should have waited until Alex's party was over. It was too late; there was nothing to be done now.

Alyce and Dahlia rang the bell at nine o'clock sharp as Alyce's driver waited in front of the house. Giselle had told them to come inside so she could unveil her new look. Little had she known when she'd told them that there would be two unveilings. Brian answered the door. Giselle was still upstairs working on her makeup and Juanita was at the top of the stairs, ready to make her grand entrance.

"Hi, Mr. Johnson," the girls chorused as they walked in. As if on cue, Juanita waltzed down the stairs.

"Ohmigod!" Dahlia said, looking at Juanita. "Ohmigod, you look so hot!"

"Turn around!" Alyce shouted. As Juanita did, they both went into a frenzy of loud shrieks and repetitive compliments. Juanita was flattered. No one had ever made such a fuss over how she looked. Getting that sort of attention had never been very important to her, but now that she was getting it, the feeling was actually incredible.

"Sank jou berry much," she said, fidgeting with the Tiffany bracelet Katie had lent her.

Giselle heard the commotion downstairs and rolled her

eyes. Her nerves were shot. She still wasn't ready; she wasn't feeling the new look, and she wanted to look perfect for this party. Giselle heard the girls running up the stairs. She wanted to lock her door until she was ready, but they were already nearing the room. She looked once more in the mirror, shrugged, and stood up.

"No way!" Alyce screamed with a laugh. "What in the world is going on here?" Dahlia screamed, too. "Oh my goodness, Giselle, you look so different! Wow! Like, now you *really* look Hispanic."

"I know, right?" Alyce chimed in. "I was just about to say she looks so ethnic."

"So, what is this," Dahlia asked, "you guys just decided to switch your looks?"

Giselle shrugged. "I guess so."

When the girls got in the car, the conversation switched to the party.

"I heard this party is going to be ridiculous," Alyce said with a burst of excitement. "Alex's dad rented like three Hummer stretch limos to take all the VIPs from the first party to the second one on the beach." The girls talked with an electric enthusiasm about the party, but no one was more excited or nervous than Giselle. She pulled out her compact mirror to check her makeup again. No one in the car knew that she liked Alex, not even Juanita. At that moment, with all the excitement and nerves, she wanted nothing more than to blurt it out. But she had already learned that to share your hopes meant that everyone knew about your disappointments, too. She didn't want anyone's pity. The last time she had told her friends about a crush, they'd seen him kissing Jennifer Lackley a week later.

"Aw, I'm sorry, Giselle," Alyce had said with this look of sympathy Giselle never wanted to see again. From that day on, she'd kept her infatuations to herself.

When they pulled up in front of the party, Giselle's heart was pounding and she felt a little nauseous. The girls showed their invitations to the woman checking and scratching names off a long list and then walked through the door. Juanita felt like a celebrity on the red carpet. She looked amazing, and the whole scene so far was like nothing she'd ever experienced. They squeezed through the maze of teenagers. The music was pulsing, colorful lights were spinning on the dimmed dance floor, and all around them were unbelievable acrobats performing for the crowd. There were trapeze artists swinging above them, contortionists twisting their bodies on platforms, a woman balancing a handstand atop a bald man's head, jugglers tossing glittery cones, and a woman spinning two chains with balls of fire on the ends. It was like a crazy dream. Everyone was dancing in a bit of a daze, staring at the acrobats floating about.

"I told you this party was going to be amazing!" Alyce shouted over the loud music.

Giselle looked around to see if she could find Alex, but there were too many people.

Juanita had already started dancing. She was waving her arms in the air to the beat, shaking her hips and closing her eyes. This night was like the cherry on top. She'd never thought she was going to enjoy her visit to America as much as she was. As she danced, she celebrated this moment in time that she knew she'd remember for the rest of her life.

"Ladies and gentlemen," the DJ said on the microphone. "Let's give it up for the man of the hour and wish a big Long Island happy birthday to your very own Alex Nixon!" The music played even louder as Alex made his entrance, ten feet tall on a pair of stilts. He was wearing a crazy costume with a joker's hat, and wild clown designs were painted on his face. He looked like a real performer. He was even dancing around a bit on the stilts. He reached into a velvet bag and tossed a handful of colorful Mardi Gras beads to the crowd. At the same moment a shower of confetti filled the air like a blizzard. It was spectacular. Everyone went crazy diving for the beads and cheering Alex on as he crossed the room. He walked over to the DJ and took the microphone in his hands.

"I just want to thank y'all for coming to my party," he said in his Georgia drawl. "Y'all have a good time and I'll see you in a bit!" The crowd cheered again as he made his exit.

"Hey guys, let's check out the VIP room," Giselle said, hoping Alex would go there after he changed and washed off his clown makeup.

"Ooh, yeah, let's go!" Dahlia said, volunteering to lead the girls through the dancing crowd.

They showed their VIP tags to the huge man guarding the door, then walked in like movie stars. There was a

large fountain of gooey chocolate fondue in the middle, surrounded with strawberries, banana slices, pieces of apples,
and marshmallows on sticks. There was a smaller dance
floor, and huge bedlike couches along the walls. In one
corner was one of those statue performers who stand really
still for a long time, and on the other side of the room on
a small stage was a man eating fire.

"I neber see some-sing like dis before," Juanita said to
all three girls, still in disbelief. "For my birs-day, I just eat
dee cake in my house with my family."

Alyce and Dahlia laughed. Giselle was too busy scouting
the room for Alex.

After a few minutes Juanita needed to use the bathroom.

"I'll go with you," Alyce said. "I have to go, too." Dahlia
decided to go along also, but Giselle didn't want to miss
seeing Alex. "You guys go ahead; I'll be by the fondue."
The girls made a little train, weaved in and out of the
crowd, and left the VIP room to find the ladies' room.

Alex had just cleaned his face, changed, and left the
dressing room area, which was near the bathrooms. He
saw a familiar face dancing in a three-girl conga line, but
that couldn't be the girl from the beach. Besides, this
girl's hair wasn't even the same color. He took another
look just in case and then grabbed her arm when he
realized it was her.

"Juanita?" he said, stunned to see her there.

"Oh," Juanita shouted with a smile, trying hard to remember his name. "Hi. What jou do here?" Alyce and
Dahlia looked at the scene with a bit of surprise.

"It's my party," he said. Juanita felt like an idiot. "What are you doing here?" he continued.

"I come with my coh-sing, Giselle."

"I'm so glad you're here," he said, beaming. "I would have invited you myself, but I never got your number."

"Oh, sank jou," she said, shouting over the music. "*¡Feliz compleanos!* It's a berry nice fiesta!"

"Thanks. You look so different. I almost didn't recognize you!"

She touched her hair. "Yes, I color it yellow." Alex laughed, and then, as if coming out of a daze, acknowledged Alyce and Dahlia. "Oh, hey, guys. Thanks for coming to my party."

"It's awesome," Alyce said, smiling at him and then at Juanita. "The acrobats are amazing. We're having a great time.... Happy birthday."

"Yeah, happy birthday," Dahlia chimed in.

Juanita excused herself and the girls to go to the restroom and promised him a dance when she got back.

"Okay, okay, okay..." Alyce said, completely confused, as they entered the bathroom together. "When did you meet Alex?"

"The bitch... Ay! I mean, the beeeeeeeach."

"Ooooooh," they both said in unison, understanding now that he was one of the guys waifboarding that day.

"He likes you," Dahlia said, nodding with a smile.

"Oh, absolutely," Alyce added. "It was so obvious."

Juanita was used to attention from boys. She had many admirers in her town. Normally she would have shrugged it off, but no boys in her town had money like this. Besides, it might be fun to go home with a story of an American romance with a rich gringo, just like *Tía* Jackie had.

CHAPTER 17

Alex walked into the room and Giselle swallowed the chocolate-covered strawberry in her mouth with a nervous gulp. Everyone crowded around him in an instant to wish him a happy birthday. Giselle stood there trying to convince herself to be confident. You look great, she argued silently to herself. Stop beating up on yourself and just have fun. She lifted her head and made a decision to be bold and just go up to him with all the confidence she could muster.

"Happy birthday, Alex!" she said, walking toward him with a little shake in her hips. He looked at her for a second and then realized who it was.

"Gigi?" he said with the smile she had hoped she'd see. Alex thought she looked great. He loved the hair and was just about to tell her when he noticed the glob of chocolate on the corner of her mouth.

"Go like that," he said, wiping his own mouth with the tips of his fingers.

"What?"

"Got a little chocolate there on your…"

Alex didn't have to finish his sentence. He probably did, but she didn't hear it. She touched the chocolate sauce on her mouth a second after she'd asked "what?" Giselle was mortified, and Alex could see it on her face.

"Don't even worry about that," he said, putting his arm around her neck with a carefree laugh. "That fondue is pretty good, huh?"

"Yeah," she said, feeling just a little bit better now that his arm was around her. The DJ mixed in the next hip-hop song and Alex bounced up and down to the pounding bass. Giselle lifted her arms and started dancing too. She refused to let a little chocolate ruin her time with Alex.

The girls saw Giselle dancing as they walked back into the room and quickly joined her and Alex. Juanita moved her hips like a belly dancer and twisted her hands as if she were a snake charmer. She was by far the best dancer on the floor. Alex slowly danced away from Giselle and soon was face-to-face with a smiling, dancing Juanita.

Giselle stopped dancing and watched Juanita dance with Alex. She felt her whole body go numb. Alex was focused on her cousin with an obvious attraction, and Juanita was eating it all up. Alyce looked at Giselle with a huge smile. "Juanita has an admirer!" she shouted, loving the little romance novel being played out in front of her eyes. "Isn't that cute?" Giselle tried to smile, but it came out as a smirk.

She tried to convince herself that it was just a dance. Lots of people would be dancing with Alex tonight, it didn't mean anything.

"They're just dancing," she said to Alyce. "Why does everything have to be a soap opera with you?"

She took deep breaths and continued to dance, but she couldn't help looking over at her cousin with the guy of her dreams. *Why did I do this to my hair?* she thought, feeling ugly again. Giselle slowly stopped dancing and left the room without a word. She ran outside to find a place where she could be alone. When she finally found a spot, she looked around, took two deep breaths, and then bawled out loud like a little girl. Her stomach went into spasms as tears and snot ran down her face. *Thank God I didn't tell anyone,* she said to herself as she wept. Her only consolation was that no one knew how she felt about Alex. No one would ever know about Giselle's humiliation of losing Alex to her loud, eccentric cousin.

Juanita didn't even notice her cousin was gone. She was too busy moving her body to the music. Once she got started, she could dance all night long without stopping for a moment of rest. Alex didn't have much rhythm at all—not like the boys back home, who could dance circles around him—but she loved how he didn't care. It was fun to dance with him. As she danced, she couldn't help feeling as if she were Cinderella at the ball—without the jealous stepsisters, of course, and with the freedom to dance way past midnight without a care in the world.

After Giselle washed the tears off her face and reapplied her makeup, she came back to the party.

"Where were you?" Alyce shouted over the reggae music.

"I don't feel well," she said, looking at Juanita and Alex still dancing with each other. They looked too cozy. There was no doubt about it; they were completely into each other.

"I think I'm going to call my dad to pick me up," she said, putting her hand over her forehead. "I have a killer headache."

"Are you serious?" Dahlia screeched. "Man, that totally sucks. Are you sure you don't want to run to the store, get some meds, and see if it goes away?"

"No," Giselle said. "I really need to lie down."

She went back outside and called her father. He was having dinner with Katie but told her he'd be there as soon as he could. As Giselle hung up, she saw Juanita rushing toward her.

"*Que pasa, Prima,* jou sick?" she asked, her forehead scrunched up with concern. Giselle felt her body heat up. She had to take a deep breath in order not to explode right there and then.

"I'm okay, I just have a headache."

"You go home now?" Juanita asked.

"Yes."

"You want I go with you, *Prima*?"

She looked Juanita square in the eyes. "No, that's okay. You can stay. I wouldn't want to mess up your night or anything. You look like you're having way too much fun to leave."

Juanita smiled and did a little hop. "I am! I neber see a party like dis in my life. But I go home if jou like me to, okay, *Prima*?"

"No," Giselle said, rolling her eyes. "I want to go home by myself."

"Jou want I pray for jou?"

"No!" Giselle shouted. "Leave me alone. Just leave me alone!" Juanita stepped back and looked at her cousin in shock.

Giselle fought back her tears. "Juanita, I'm fine, just go back inside and have a good time. My dad will be here any second and I'll just go home and go to sleep. Go ahead. Enjoy. Alyce will take you home tonight."

"Okay, *Prima*," Juanita said. *My goodness,* she thought. *She gets grouchier than me when I'm sick.*

As Juanita went back inside, three stretch Hummers pulled up in front of the club, waiting for the VIPs to be transported to the next party at the beach house. In all her daydreams since she had gotten the invitation, Giselle never could have imagined this night turning out the way it did.

CHAPTER 18

JUANITA never could have imagined the night turning out the way it did. She was in one of the biggest cars she'd ever seen in her life, had just left the most amazing party she'd ever experienced, and was having an incredible time with an American boy. The Hummers pulled up to an enormous house on the beach. There was a huge bonfire on the sand—it must have been eight feet tall—and there were comfy lounge chairs scattered around it. On the large wooden deck facing the ocean there were tables filled with food, and the funky, chilled-out music in the background set a perfect laid-back atmosphere.

"So," Alyce said to Juanita when Alex stepped away. "Are you going to give him a big ol' birthday kiss or what?"

Juanita blushed. "I no going to kiss him. I don't know him berry much."

"Are you kidding?" Dahlia said. "It would be perfect. Look around, it's like a movie set for a love story!"

Dahlia was right; it was the perfect setting for a kiss, and it would make a perfect ending to a perfect night and a perfect trip to America. Back home she never had this much freedom to stay out late, unaccompanied by family or family friends. She loved the amount of independence American teenagers seemed to have. When would she ever get the opportunity to enjoy a night out like this again?

When Alex came back, he and Juanita took a long walk by the water. He kicked nervously at the waves washing over his feet as they talked.

"I'm really glad you came tonight, Juanita," he said.

"Me too," she answered. When he leaned in for a kiss, she closed her eyes and let herself be kissed…like a character in a real American love story.

Juanita got in so late that she decided to sleep in the guest bedroom. She didn't want to wake up her cousin, especially if Giselle was feeling sick. The next morning she peeked in Giselle's room—she was still asleep. She couldn't wait for her to wake up so she could tell her all about her little adventure and her kiss by the ocean. Juanita went downstairs to make breakfast for everyone to ease the urge to wake her up and tell her everything.

"Good morning, Juanita," Brian said as he shuffled lazily into the kitchen. "Breakfast smells delicious."

Brian let her serve him a plate of fried eggs and bacon with buttered toast. "I'm surprised you're up," he continued. "I thought you'd be dead asleep after getting home so late." Juanita loved the way he said "home" as if she truly lived here.

"My body still wants to dance," she answered, dancing in her fuzzy socks. Brian laughed, then bit into the crispy strips of bacon on his plate.

"Hey, Juanita," he said. "Did anything happen at the party to make Giselle want to leave?"

"She had a headache," Juanita answered.

He nodded. "No, I know. That's what she said, but I just wanted to make sure. I heard her crying all night, that's why I'm asking."

Juanita tried to think, but Giselle had left the party before it had really even begun.

"Maybe she have really big pain in her head…. *La pobresita.*"

Juanita decided to take Giselle's food upstairs. If she was that sick last night, she probably should stay in bed all day. She fixed a plate and a tall glass of orange juice, put them on a tray, and carefully brought it upstairs.

When she opened the door, Giselle was already awake and sitting up in her bed.

"Good morning!" Juanita said, putting the tray on her cousin's lap.

"Thanks, but I'm not hungry,"

"*Prima*, jou should try," Juanita insisted. "It's berry, berry good."

"Very!" Giselle shouted impatiently. "It's *very* good. *Very* with a V. Stop with the berries, you sound like freakin' Strawberry Shortcake!"

Juanita didn't like her cousin's tone but brushed it off as the bad mood of a grouchy sick person.

"How jou feeling in jour head—pain?" Juanita asked, trying not to sound bothered by Giselle's last statement. She wanted her to be in a good mood so she could tell her what had happened with Alex.

"I'm fine," she said, wishing Juanita would stop being nice so she could be mad at her in peace. Giselle put the tray to the side and got out of bed to go to the bathroom. She looked in the mirror and scoffed. Her hair was sticking up and pushed dramatically to the side. She had never had this much bed-head when her hair was straight. She tied it back in a ponytail, washed her face, and brushed her teeth as slowly as possible, prolonging her seclusion. Giselle knew Juanita would be there when she got out—and she was.

"Giselle," Juanita blurted as her cousin finally came out of the bathroom, "I kiss dee boy Alex on the beach!"

Giselle felt as if she had just been punched in the stomach. She felt the insides of her body shake, and she couldn't seem to control what came out of her mouth next.

"Wow, is that what you do in your country, kiss boys you barely know?" she said in a tone that was meant to cut her cousin deep. "They have a word for that over here in America, you know—it's *slut*." Juanita knew this word and knew she wasn't even close to being that—she didn't even want to have sex until she was married. Her eyes widened and she stood up to defend herself, but no words came out of her mouth.

"You want to get a reputation like that for a stupid boy like Alex?" Giselle continued, getting louder and louder as she went on. "Besides, the only reason he even touched you was because he thought you were rich. Trust me, no guy in this neighborhood would even look at you if they knew you lived in a little shack in a third world country. You don't believe me, try going to another party looking the way you did when you first got here, with your nappy hair and cheap, tacky clothes!"

Juanita understood exactly what was going on; she'd kissed a boy Giselle liked. She knew the sound of jealousy and it was coming out of Giselle like a bad odor—but it didn't take away the sting of her cousin's words.

"Why jou no tell me jou like Alex?" she asked, with her voice shaking. "I don't kiss him if I know."

"What?" Giselle shrieked. "I don't like him! I have better taste in guys than you do. I have better taste in a lot of things, are you kidding me?" She walked over to the closet. "Look at this skirt," she said, pulling out the skirt Juanita had been wearing when they picked her up from the airport just weeks ago. "Can you not see how ugly this is? Are you freakin' blind?" Juanita grabbed the skirt from Giselle's hands and gave her a deadly look. They stared at each other silently for a few seconds and then Giselle stormed out of the room. Juanita grabbed her purple suitcase and stuffed it with all her "tacky" clothes. She ran around the room looking for her things with a desperation—she wanted to get out of that house immediately.

Brian had heard the commotion and went upstairs to the room. He saw her packing her things and demanded to know what was going on. Juanita didn't stop.

"I want to go in my coh-sing house, in Washington Heights."

"No, Juanita," he said, taking the bag away from her. "Please stop this. Just tell me what's going on."

She tried to talk but she started to cry instead.

"What is it?" he asked again. "Did you two girls get into a fight?"

Juanita tried hard to control her breathing so she could speak, but all that came out was "I want to go...please."

Brian let her finish packing and went to find Giselle to see if he could get to the bottom of this. But when he found her, she was even more hysterical and incoherent than Juanita.

Brian gave up. He called Rosita in Washington Heights and told her that he and Juanita were on their way. About an hour later Giselle heard them leave the house. She looked out the window as they drove away. They didn't even say goodbye.

CHAPTER 19

Giselle was used to a quiet house, but it had never felt as quiet and lonely as it did now. Her head was pounding from crying so much, and she had to take two Motrin to stop the pain. She wished it would take away that empty feeling in her gut, too. Giselle picked up Juanita's new outfits that were thrown on the bed. She knew her cousin had left them here on purpose. Giselle probably would have done the same thing. As she folded them, she heard her father pull into the driveway. Maybe Juanita had changed her mind and come back with him. She looked out the window, but her father was walking back to the house by himself.

Brian walked up the stairs determined to find out what had happened. Juanita had been silent for the whole ride and wouldn't answer any of his questions. Brian was not used to getting involved with his daughter's affairs—that had always been the nanny's job. But he now understood more than ever that Giselle needed him. When she had cried in his arms that day in the park, he knew he could no longer pass the responsibility of raising his daughter to someone else. He needed to be more present and active in her life, as uncomfortable and awkward as that might be.

"Can I come in?" he asked, knocking on the door.

"No."

He opened the door anyway and sat on her bed. "Why did Juanita leave?" he asked. Giselle folded her arms without saying a word.

"Giselle, you can talk to me. I'm not going anywhere until you tell me what's going on."

"I can't," she said, starting to cry. "You're going to be mad." He held her close to him and let her cry in his arms.

"It's okay if I'm a little mad. It doesn't mean I'm going to love you any less. Tell me what happened…. Why are you so upset?"

"I said horrible things," she confessed between frantic, tearful breaths. "She has every right to hate me right now."

"What did you say?"

"I didn't mean to," she said. "I called her a slut because she kissed Alex Nixon at his party." Before her father had a chance to respond, she spilled everything out. She was feeling like a dark rain cloud, ripe and ready to pour down.

"He was supposed to kiss me," she cried, "but nobody is ever going to kiss me because I'm ugly."

"Giselle—"

"It's true! No one ever looks at me that way. I always thought it was because I was too dark for the boys in my school. And when I finally meet someone who I think likes me, he goes and kisses her. What's wrong with *me?*"

"Hey," he said, making her look at him. "There's nothing wrong with you." He smiled and wiped her tears with his hands. "Are you kidding me? You're beautiful. You look just like your mother. You don't need a boy to kiss you to make that true, it already is. You're beautiful." He kissed her on the forehead. "One day—hopefully not too soon—but one day someone is going to fall in love with you the same way I fell in love with your mother. There's nothing wrong with you, Gigi, you're terrific. Just be who you are and don't worry about what other people think."

Giselle sniffled. "I don't think I know who I am."

Brian took a moment to think about what she had just said. He'd often felt the same way about himself.

"That's okay, Gigi. Maybe you don't have to know everything about yourself right now. I don't think anyone has themselves figured out one hundred percent." Brian thought a little bit more and then had an idea. "You know, Gigi, moments like these are perfect times to start figuring out the kind of person you really are. You have a choice. You could be the person who runs away from a relationship, or you could be the one who fights for it. Trust me. You'll regret it when it's gone."

Giselle looked at him with a knowing smile as she wiped away the last of her tears. He rubbed her back. "I don't mind taking another trip to Washington Heights," he said.

Giselle wanted to, but part of her was afraid.

"Oh, Dad, I don't know if she can forgive me for what

I said. She must be so mad at me right now. I really said a lot of bad things."

"That's up to her," he said, getting up. "But it's up to you to make the first step and apologize."

The trip to Washington Height was the longest ride ever. Giselle was imagining the worst. What if Juanita had told everyone what she had said and they all hated her? So many times she wanted to tell her father to forget about it and go back home. But she wanted to prove to herself who she was capable of being. She wanted to be the person who did the right thing, no matter how uncomfortable it was.

Brian parked the car, and soon they were ringing the buzzer to Rosita's home. They climbed up the stairs to the apartment, and this time Giselle didn't mind how many there were. As she stood by the door, she wished she were still climbing stairs instead. Brian knocked and they waited. She could feel her blood pulsing under her skin. Juanita opened the door as if she knew it was for her.

"You left this," Giselle said, extending the bag of clothes they had bought Juanita while in Long Island.

Rosita stepped in by the door with her warm, friendly face. "Hey, guys, come on in." She led them into the apartment. "Are you guys hungry? I was making some empanadas for my girls when they come back. I could make a few more." Brian and Rosita disappeared into the kitchen, leaving Giselle and Juanita alone in the small living room.

They both sat down on the plastic couch. *Crunch.*

"Juanita," Giselle said slowly.

"I know, *Prima*," Juanita said, touching her cousin's back. Giselle felt a weight of guilt lifted off and she hugged Juanita tighter than she ever had before.

"That was easier than I thought," Giselle said, laughing and wiping away her tears.

"We're family," Juanita said. "Mami and *Tía* Jackie fight many time, but they always keep dee love."

Rosita came out, served them their empanadas, and left them alone to talk again. They spoke about Alex, her nanny Erin, Giselle's friends, her grandmother, her insecurities, her talk with her father. She wanted to make sure Juanita understood her life, and more importantly, she wanted to make sure her cousin understood how much better her life was now that Juanita was in it.

Juanita didn't go back to Long Island to finish off her visit in the United States. Instead, Giselle stayed with her cousin in Washington Heights. Together, they slept on the pullout couch in the living room, bought gaudy New York souvenirs for the family back in the Dominican Republic, rolled their eyes at the boys who'd whistle at them in the street, learned to make Jackie's famous dish of sancocho, and danced merengue every day.

"Okay, honey, have a great day," Brian said as he switched the gear to park. Giselle hugged her father and stepped out of the car. It was her first day back at school.

Her hair was still dark but it was pin straight that day. Yesterday it was curly, and a week before it was in two hundred tiny braids. One of the many things she had learned about herself that summer was that she liked to change her hair. She was even thinking about going red, and maybe on the next visit to the salon she'd cut it all the way up to her shoulders. As she walked to class, her purple boots clicked on the floor like tap shoes. It was an unconventional color for the people in her school, but she loved her new shoes and didn't care what anyone else thought about them. That morning she'd tried on the flowery shawl that her grandmother and *Tía* Milagros had made for her. As she looked in the mirror, she came to the conclusion that she still thought it was really ugly. If she had liked it, she would have worn it, but she decided it would serve better as a comfy throw for watching movies on chilly nights.

Giselle carried herself differently, and everyone would notice the change. Even Alex no longer felt the need to give her forced compliments to boost her ego. She held her head a little higher; she walked with a confidence that she vowed no one could ever take away—not her grandmother, not her friends, not even the boys on the football team. Giselle still didn't know who she was. But she was determined that just like learning meringue in the park, she would have fun as she figured it out.